SLOW
TRAIN
TO
SUBURBIA~

SLOW TRAIN TO SUBURBIA~

CHARLES WEBB

THE CHOIR PRESS

First published in the United Kingdom in 2016 by
The Choir Press

ISBN 978-1-910864-63-0

Set in Minion 10½ pt

Disclaimers

'Sometime too hot the eye of heaven shines,
And often is his gold complexion dimm'd;
And every fair from fair sometime declines,
By chance or nature's changing course untrimm'd.'

William Shakespeare *'Sonnets'*

CHAPTER ONE ~

~ And When Did You Last See Your Father?

———— e·ɔ ————

A s dusk approached on that oppressive Thursday evening in
July 1911, George Chesshyre surveyed the endless suburban
streets of South London. A tallish, thinnish man of fifty-five, he
wore a light linen suit, far from new, and showing the signs of
wear and tear inevitable after many railway journeys to and from
the City, packed tightly with fellow 'commuters', a term George
had recently heard and thought he disapproved of as sounding
too 'American'. As a further concession to the sultry summer
weather he had, at the insistence of his wife, foregone his usual
wing collar and taken to wearing soft-collared shirts though he
secretly felt improperly dressed for the office. He had, however,
insisted on keeping his black Church's brogues which had worn in
beautifully and were 'easy' on his feet even on the interminable,
blistering flags. A straw boater topped him off and he carried a
battered leather case in his right hand. His complexion was florid,
more so from the exertions of the last hour or so, and a magnificent Elgarian moustache, adorned his upper lip. It had once been
dark, black almost, matching the colour of his hair, but had
recently begun, by degrees, to show signs of grey. His wife had
hinted that he should shave it off – moustaches were becoming
old fashioned and it was so much easier to shave now that the new
safety-razors had come in – but George was resolute and said that
he would feel improperly dressed without it. This logic puzzled
his wife and she had quickly dropped the matter, turning her
attention instead to the benefits of soft-collared shirts.

To the casual bystander, of whom there was none in the
vicinity so we have to imagine one, George gave the distinct
impression of being lost. Why should this be so we ask? In order
to answer this question we must turn the clock back a little and
retrace our hypothetical steps to the City of London. The Square
Mile, bustling by day with brokers and bankers; all but deserted

by six o'clock as the bees leave their hives and return to their dormitories in the suburbs. Over London Bridge they swarm or pack the trains at Liverpool Street and Waterloo, fanning out to quiet streets and avenues. Sleepy closes and drowsy roads. To wives and children; dinners, edible and otherwise; pleasant conversation or rows and sulks; bath times and gardens; roses and runner beans.

Of course the City of London is of great antiquity. Roman remains are sometimes unearthed during building works and excavations and more than two thousand years of history lie beneath its streets. Those curious enough to wander its environs are fascinated by the little narrow roads and alleyways. The Great Fire of 1666 laid waste much of the City and Sir Christopher Wren laid out plans to rebuild featuring wide boulevards and thoroughfares but his ideas came to nothing and the City was rebuilt largely on its medieval footprint. Should our curious wanderer venture in the vicinity of the Dutch Church hard by Austin Friars he may find himself standing outside the premises of Messrs Fysh, Fysh, Iceberg and Fysh, Stockbrokers. At five o'clock on the afternoon of Thursday 13th July, 1911, had he looked through the glass-panelled doorway to where a flight of steps led up to the offices, he would have encountered George Hector Chesshyre, senior partner, leaving for the day.

George's office on the second floor was large and impressive as befits a senior partner of a middle ranking broking house. A substantial mahogany desk stood directly in front of the west-facing window, important looking leather bound ledgers stacked neatly by the ink well. A candlestick telephone stood silently awaiting its next important call. A large, comfortable, leather upholstered chair stood importantly behind the desk. More important looking ledgers were filed neatly in glass-fronted mahogany cases that stood against the walls. The floor was covered in a Hereke Turkey carpet of important origin and great cost. Altogether it was an important looking office.

By three o'clock that afternoon George was beginning to flag. The sun had, by degrees, moved round the sky and was by now shining directly through George's window. George was hot. And

George was getting hotter. Some weeks previously the shutters had jammed and had been taken down by Jenkins, the caretaker. 'Don't you worry, Mr Chesshyre, I'll 'ave 'em back in a jiffy, good as new.' Then the blind jammed. 'Don't you worry, Mr Chesshyre, I'll 'ave it back in a jiffy, good as new.' Needless to say, neither shutters, blind nor Jenkins had been seen since.

The last straw was the window itself. A sash affair, probably of Georgian origin, and with a capricious temperament that sometimes allowed itself to be opened and closed and, at others, refused obstinately to co-operate, no matter what the weather or time of year. At three o'clock on the afternoon of Thursday July 13th 1911, the hottest time of the day on the hottest day of the year during the hottest summer that anyone could ever remember, the sash window was unbending in its decision to remain shut. George soldiered on as best he could. Fortunately the high back of his chair afforded some relief as it blocked the fiercest rays for an hour or so but by four, the sun, having moved round, and having lost none of its ferocity, was emerging from the penumbra, the eclipse having run its course. 'I see you, George Hector Chesshyre,' it seemed to say; 'I see you, and wherever you are, wherever you go, I'll find you and I'll fry you to a crisp.' Once or twice he considered putting his straw boater on but decided against it when he thought about the strange looks, and worse, such a practice might encourage, particularly among the more junior members of staff such as Warbeck and Simnel who had occasion sometimes during the course of the day to knock on his door in order to get something signed. No, it was no good. He'd have to do something about it. Take some decisive action. His desk would have to be moved. He'd bring it up at the board meeting tomorrow.

Despite the advancing hour, the heat hit him like a furnace as he came out into the street. St Mary Woolnoth had just struck the quarter as he passed down King William Street and, by now well advanced over London Bridge, it suddenly occurred to him that he had moved house *in absentia* during the day and that he no longer lived in Lower Sydenham but had to find his way to Streatham. Now, not having started out from Streatham that morning, this posed a bit of a problem. He had it in mind that the nearest station to his new house was Streatham Common; but it could have been Streatham Hill. He remembered his wife going on about it but he hadn't really been paying much attention. Well, the stations couldn't be *that* far apart and so, as there was a train calling at Streatham Common due to depart at ten to six, he thought he'd go for that. Of course there was a *difficulty.* His season ticket allowed him to travel between Sydenham and London Bridge but Streatham of any hue was out of bounds. Never mind. He'd sort it out in the morning. Emerging from the ticket office with a single to Streatham Common he was just in time to squeeze into the last compartment of the last carriage. It was already full and he was obliged to stand. There was no air and three young men were smoking pipes, the effluvium from which merged to form a noxious fug. Of course the windows wouldn't open. The leather strap on one side was missing and he couldn't reach the other, there being a large gentleman attempting to read the 'Evening Standard' blocking the way. It was, therefore, with some considerable relief that he eventually alighted at Streatham Common. He was, however, obliged to squeeze past Standard man, the platform being on the far side. During the extrication process he managed to tread on a few toes which should have caused him great satisfaction but didn't. All he could manage was an effusive but general apology to all whose metatarsals had been so cruelly abused. Safely disembarked, all he had to do now was find his new house. He was rather looking forward to an easy stroll in the early evening air which was now, although still hot and humid, at least free from the combustible emanations of Messrs. Wills, Player's and Ogden's. It was at that point he suddenly realised that he didn't have the faintest idea of his new address. They'd looked at several houses over the past few weeks and had finally decided on a very nice villa in a quiet location. He could see it in his mind's eye but couldn't remember the name of the road. He walked up and down the platform racking his brains. Three trains came and went but no address came into his head. Then it occurred to him that he might have jotted it down in his pocket diary. He scoured the last month's entries. It is often said that doctors have illegible handwriting. This may well be so but stockbrokers would probably run them a pretty close second. Again he trawled through the whole of June and the first week of July. Nothing much jumped out at him except: 'C's B'day. 19th'; He had no idea who 'C' was and anyway it was too late now. There was a cluster of scrawl on Saturday June 10th.; something that looked like 'Scunthorpe – 3; Do'n – 9'. For a moment he thought it might refer to a football result but quickly discounted this idea because he didn't have the remotest interest in football. He noticed that 'Do'n – 9' was heavily underlined. This must mean something. He racked his brains. Then he hit upon it! It was Dormin Road – Number 9. Yes, that was it! He'd remembered. What a jolly good thing he'd noted it down and how silly of him to forget! With renewed confidence he strode towards the station exit. He'd be in his new home in no time. Handing his ticket in, he enquired of the collector confidently; 'Could you please direct me to Dormin Road?' The collector eyed him suspiciously, all the time continuing to collect tickets from passengers alighting from a newly arrived train and who, presumably, knew where they lived and were going there directly.

'Never 'eard of it,' he said eventually.

'It's quite near here I believe,' said George, not in the least put off by this negative response.

'Sorry, guv. Ask the copper on the corner.' He jerked his head in a vague sort of direction towards the station entrance and went on collecting tickets.

Of course. When in difficulty, ask a policeman. George approached him hopefully. A big man with an impressive corporation and an equally impressive moustache. George found this reassuring. Presumably this policeman had, like himself, resisted the dubious advantages of the safety-razor. His helmet added to his stature although he periodically bent his legs in the way that policemen are apt to do when standing sentry, their hands invariably clasped behind their backs as if in readiness to surprise the unwary and cuff them on the slightest pretext of suspicion. 'Excuse me constable, could you please direct me to Dormin Road?' he asked. The policeman eyed George suspiciously.

Apparently it was the custom of uniformed officers of the constabulary (and those of the railway service) in those parts to suspect anyone who was not intimately familiar with the area of felonious intentions and of going equipped, with malice afore-thought. A policeman's lot is, indeed, not a happy one. Bending his legs in the aforementioned manner, thus momentarily bringing his eyes level with George's, he offered his very thought-fully considered opinion:

'Never 'eard of it.' He assumed his normal height and continued to survey the immediate scene, having, as far as he was concerned, dealt with George's enquiry to his entire and complete satisfaction.

'It's quite near here,' George added hopefully, not quite ready to give up yet.

'Not on my patch,' replied the policeman, exhaling in the sort of way that people do when dealing with enquiries they consider to be getting on the tiresome side and, in contradiction to his previous knee bends, stretching himself up to his full height and rocking once or twice on his feet whilst looking at the sky which, presumably, displayed goings on of infinitely more interest than questions from awkward civilians. 'Why d'you want to go there?' he added eventually, continuing to survey the heavens.

'I live there,' said George confidently, feeling sure that this intelligence would jog the officer's memory, at which he would offer immediate and precise directions. Instead he was faced with further interrogation.

'You live there?' More rocking, more sky surveying.

'Yes.'

'Well, you should know how to get there then shouldn't you?' A double rock and a look which conveyed complete satisfaction with the state of the sky.

'Yes, but I've only just moved there today.'

'Well, why aren't you there, then?' A small cloud had appeared and had caught the constable's interest lest it should dare to deposit unwelcome precipitation over his domain.

'Because I don't know where it is from *here*.' said George, a note of exasperation coming into his voice. At this point he was not sure who was the more confused, the constable or himself. However, help was at hand. A police sergeant was approaching, hands clasped, in the customary fashion, behind his back.

'Nah then, Penrose, what's goin' on 'ere?' Although this question was directed at constable Penrose, the superior officer, who was a good foot shorter than the former, looked at George in a sideways fashion, reminiscent of the manner in which the constable had summed him up a moment or two before. George was becoming more and more convinced that he was guilty of some, unknown to him, misdemeanour and fully expected to be spending the night in Streatham Gaol.

'Gentleman's lookin' for Dora Road, sarge.' Fully two bends of the legs and a single rock forwards and backwards were achieved during the time it took for him to relay this information to the sergeant who, on being apprised of this intelligence, screwed up his eyes and looked at George even more suspiciously. He somehow instinctively knew what the answer was going to be.

'Never 'eard of it,' came the dispiriting reply.

'Dor*min* Road, actually, sergeant.' George ventured to correct constable Penrose. The superior officer stroked his chin for a moment, consulted some invisible oracle in the sky (apparently the sky is a favourite resource of policemen seeking evidence, clues and information usually undisclosed to the casual seeker after the truth) and finally pronounced:

'No. Never' eard of it.'

At this point both policemen were looking at George suspiciously as though, George felt, he might be some congenital idiot and even possibly dangerous. He decided the best thing to do would be to retreat while he still possessed his freedom, strike out on his own and perhaps enquire of some passer by or tradesman he felt sure to encounter on the way. He thanked them both for their help and began to proceed in an orderly fashion towards a junction in the mid-distance which he perceived to be fairly busy. Still feeling uneasy, although guilty of no crime to his certain knowledge, he glanced back (just to make sure they weren't following him should he be contemplating some housebreaking or other larcenous activity in the neighbourhood) to see them both standing at the spot where he had left them and both performing leg bends in perfect unison. He momentarily had a vision of rows of policemen in the early stages of training at police school, all bobbing up and down and rocking to and fro, hands clasped behind backs thus perfecting this very necessary and fundamental aspect of solving and preventing crime.

By this time it was nearly quarter past seven. Although the sun was now lower in the sky, it was still stiflingly hot and humid. After being suffocated by nicotine fumes and enduring fruitless encounters with the employees of the London, Brighton and South Coast Railway; then officers of the Metropolitan Police, George felt in need of some refreshment. His hopes of seeing his new home before nightfall were rapidly diminishing and if he were destined to spend the night roaming the streets of Streatham like some land-locked Flying Dutchman at least he wouldn't expire from dehydration.

In recounting this woeful tale we feel that it might occur to the reader to ask why on earth George went into the office on the day he was moving house. Well, the truth is that his hand was rather forced. An old client who put a lot of business George's way was up from Manchester just for the day and wanted to see him particularly about a new issue of stock his firm was contemplating. Of course George would rather have been at home helping to supervise the move but had to tell his wife that he simply *couldn't* get out of this important meeting. Rather to his surprise she seemed almost relieved. George really couldn't think why.

The 'George and Dragon' on the corner of the junction looked inviting. The saloon was quiet and the bar clear with the landlord, a large, ruddy-faced man, polishing glasses while awaiting his customers. There was Bass's Ale on draught and George ordered a pint. After he'd managed to wash away some of the taste of the tobacco smoke he enquired of the landlord whether he knew Dormin Road. He eyed George suspiciously, polishing a beer glass as though it was a valuable piece of Georgian silver. 'Never 'eard of it,' he said and George's heart sank. He was beginning to wonder whether Dormin Road was just a figment of his imagination. Perhaps he had just dreamed that he was moving that day and that he really did still live in Lower Sydenham. ''ang on a mo,' continued the landlord as he placed another glass carefully on the shelf behind the bar, 'I'll ask 'arry. 'e'll know. *'arry!*'

'*'ello?*' came a disembodied voice from the vicinity of the public bar.

'Where's Dormouse Road?'

'Never 'eard of it.'

'It's Dor*min* Road actually,' said George, almost apologetically. The disembodied voice materialised and 'arry appeared.

'Dor*min* Road?' 'arry repeated, looking at George quizzically.

'Yes, I shouldn't think it's far from here,' he said hopefully.

'Oh, I know it. It's them big posh 'ouses near Tootin' Bec Common. Fair old trot from 'ere squire.' 'arry gave George a sort of sympathetic look which seemed to say: 'You'll peg out in this heat before you get to the end of the road.'

The subtleties of 'arry's physiognomy, however, passed George by; At last! he thought. He was getting somewhere. Well, figuratively speaking at least.

'Tell you what squire,' 'arry went on, 'Alf's in the bar. Local cabbie. 'e'll take you if 'e 'asn't got a fare at the mo. *Alf!*'

'*'ello.*'

'You free?'

'Yeah.'

'Got a fare for yous. Out near Tootin' Bec. Dormin Road.'

'Never 'eard of it.'

(Here we go again, thought George.)

'Yes you 'ave. Them new 'ouses. Big uns. By the Common.'

Alf came through from the bar. Thus ensued a tripartite discussion between the landlord, Alf and 'arry regarding the best way to get to Dormin Road, there being, apparently, several various and alternative routes, each with its advantages and disadvantages depending on the time of day, the day of the week and whether it happened to be raining or not. This high level conference went on for some minutes during which time several pints of Bass were consumed punctuated by an interlude during which several bottles of Allsopp's Celebrated India Pale Ale were opened and drained. None of these beverages came George's way, despite a cordial invitation from the landlord, which he declined courteously (if he ever did get home that evening he didn't want to arrive smelling of beer; there would be general *disapproval*), although by this time he was beginning to feel a bit thirsty again, the pervading taste of tobacco having returned to his parched throat. Eventually, however, a suitable route was decided upon which called for a final round of Bass. 'I'll bring the cab round guv,' said Alf, turning to George in triumph.

The cab was a motor and George sank thankfully into the back seat. With a bit of luck he should be home before sunset. The cab lurched forward and died. Much cursing from Alf. Much swinging of the starting handle. Much silence from the engine.

George ordered another pint of Bass.

About half an hour elapsed and there was no sign of Alf who had gone off in search of assistance. The air in the George and Dragon was getting hot and the saloon was beginning to fill up. George decided to stroll down the road in the hope of seeing Alf return or even another cab that he might hail but the area, which had been busy an hour or so before, was now quite deserted.

The reader will probably not be surprised to learn that we have now caught up with our story and have reached the point at which we opened the tale a little while ago. George was in a quandary. He had been deserted by the Constabulary, not to mention officials of the railway; spent a confused hour in the company of innkeepers, their associates and cabmen and was now marooned among the endless labyrinthine roads of Streatham which, to him, all looked the same. Whichever way he looked rows of houses stretched out before him: an endless sea of red brick and slate. Behind every front door happy families were sitting down to their evening meal, husbands were kissing wives, children were greeting their fathers with open arms, dogs and (perhaps) cats wagged their tails with happiness and canaries sang sweeter than a Swedish Nightingale. George was hot, tired, hungry and thirsty. Savoury aromas of dinners cooking wafted occasionally in the air. The thought crossed his mind that if he stayed out much longer he might be arrested for vagrancy. Then he remembered that the only P.C. in South London was rooted to the spot outside the station. Not much chance of that, then. He breathed a sigh of relief. He began to trudge (a mode of perambulation all but foreign to George. He usually walked at a fair clip) almost aimlessly along the hard, unforgiving pavement when something extraordinary happened.

George was not a man given to strong drink but he could usually manage a pint or two of ale without any ill effects. However, the sight before him as he wearily turned the corner into the next road caused him to stop in his tracks. For a moment he thought he was seeing double and wondered whether the Bass was stronger than usual or even that he had been affected by the heat, exhaustion and exertions of the day which had combined to cause a temporary ocular hallucination. Walking towards him were two identical young ladies, arm in arm, as if mirror images of one another.

On seeing him, as if to confirm his suspicions of hallucinatory tendencies, they raised their arms, broke into a smile and exclaimed in unison, 'Daddy, *there* you are!'

'We've been sent out to look for you,' said Alex taking his left arm and kissing his cheek.

'Mummy was getting worried,' said Vicky taking his right arm and kissing the other cheek. His beautiful daughters. What a surprise to see them, and how silly he felt not recognising them straight away!

'Oh, had to stay a bit late at the office,' he said with as much nonchalance as he could muster. 'But you've walked a long way, and in this heavy weather.'

'Nonsense, daddy,' said Alex.

'We're practically on the doorstep,' said Vicky.

'But it's a fair old trot to Dormin Road,' said George.

'Daddy, what on earth are you talking about?' said Alex, frowning.

'That was the house you and mummy didn't like.' In perfect unison.

'We liked this one, do you remember?' said Vicky; 'Number 3, "The Limes", Scattersdale Avenue, SW,' joined in Alex as they stopped right outside the gates.

Oh, what a fool he felt! Of course they'd decided on Scattersdale Avenue. He'd signed the lease not ten days since. He couldn't imagine what was going on in his mind to think that they'd moved to Dormin Road. He could only put it down to the heat which hadn't let up for days now. He was not good in hot weather. It didn't agree with him. Oh, he didn't mind the odd warm day as long as there was a bit of a breeze blowing but when it got like a bally blast furnace hitting you as soon as you opened your front door in the morning or came out of the office at night then he was afraid he began to wilt. He couldn't imagine how those chaps out in the colonies managed. Yes, they'd got fellows who pull punkahs and move the air around a bit but it wasn't the same. It was still hot air wherever you moved it to. No, it was cool and bracing for George every time.

Even before their marriage George had thought of his dear wife Rosalind as the most organised and *capable* of women. For the last two weeks she had rarely been seen without a list in her hand. Towers of crates had been piling up all over the place and furniture had been wearing neatly hand-written labels with: 'Kitchen; Dining Room; Drawing Room', etc., etc. You see the idea. If it had been left to George there would have been the most unholy muddle and things would have been scattered all over the country instead of arriving at Scattersdale Avenue in a neat and timely manner. True to form, as he got in she came to greet him with a peck on the cheek. As cool and unflustered as usual, despite the weather and the exertions of the day.

'We've found him,' said Alex, leading him by the hand out through to the back garden.

'He was wandering about near the pub,' said Vicky. He said he had to stay late at the office but I bet he was lost really. Come on, admit it, daddy, you were lost weren't you?'

'He was on his way to Dormin Road, weren't you, daddy?' added Alex getting him into deeper and deeper trouble.

'George, dear, why on earth were you going to Dormin Road?' said Rosalind, frowning. 'We crossed that one off the list a fortnight ago. Don't tell me you'd forgotten?'

'Oh, do stop going on at me,' he said wearily. 'I'm suffering from heatstroke and sunstroke as well I shouldn't wonder. I nearly collapsed on the train and a police constable was about to call an ambulance. You're lucky to see me at all this evening, I should say.'

'Oh, poor George. Revive you with a glass of beer did he?'

It was the second pint of Bass that did for him. He'd sign the pledge.

Tomorrow.

CHAPTER TWO

~ Domestic Bliss

Saturday 22nd July 1911

There cannot be many readers who have not experienced the dubious pleasures of moving house. It has the reputation, quite deservedly, of being the most *trying* business. George had managed to 'escape' to the office on moving day itself but was not immune to being rocked by all the ripples, large and small, that are created by such an uprooting. However, after about a week he felt that he had more or less recovered from the trauma of moving from Lower Sydenham which had been the family home since before the twins were born. He'd managed to sort out the season ticket difficulty, got used to the different railway route into and out of the office and was even on nodding terms with the ticket collector at Streatham Common station, not to mention constable Penrose (who had, at last, apparently convinced himself that George was not an habitual recidivist and who never seemed to stray far from his spot).

The weather was still unbearably oppressive and he was glad to get out of the City in the evenings. He couldn't remember when they'd last had some significant rain, and the fresh greenery of the early spring had been replaced by yellowing leaves and brown scrubby grass. He had taken to getting up early after fitful humid nights and been glad of some relatively cool fresh air before the sun got too high in the sky which had been virtually cloudless for weeks. Occasionally a little puff of cotton-wool cumulus would form but would disappear almost as soon as it had arrived. The sky remained, from dawn to dusk, a deep, steel blue. The air was heavy and still and when something of a breeze did blow up it was hot and scorching; a penetrating, unforgiving Sirocco.

There was quite a decent garden at the back of Number 3 'The

Limes', Scattersdale Avenue SW. (George had no idea why it was called 'The Limes'. He was not at all sure what a lime tree looked like but there were no trees of any description within the immediate vicinity or boundaries of the house.) Bigger than the one at Sydenham at any rate. The house hadn't been up long enough for much to have been established but he was looking forward to doing something with it eventually. Mucking about in the garden, even though he didn't really have much of a clue as to what he was actually doing, gave him a certain pleasure when it was not too wet, dry, cold or hot; one, or a combination of which, it usually was, this being England, but he supposed it gave people something to talk about 'over the garden wall'.

Although he'd wandered about a bit in the garden several times during the cooler evenings, he hadn't found anyone to talk to yet 'over the garden wall', left or right. Whoever they were he hoped they were decent sorts and that there were no small boys who took perverse delight in firing pea-shooters at him like his nemesis next door at Lower Sydenham. A dried pea fired at you at close range stings like billy-o as George could attest with great and painful conviction. The twins may have driven him to distraction at times while they were growing up but at least they never took to pea-shooters. On the whole George tended to agree with Mr Grimwig in 'Oliver Twist' – There were only two types of boys: mealy boys and beef-faced boys. George couldn't tell for certain which type his assailant resembled; the little blighter always managed to go to ground before he could catch him out.

He'd taken the house on a long lease – five years, with the option to extend – which would take them up to Midsummer Day 1916. He'd be 60 in August of that year and entitled to draw his pension from Fysh, Fysh, Iceberg and Fysh. The girls, hopefully, would be married by then (not that he wanted to see them go) and, anticipating a smaller household and reduced income, together with his dear wife Rosalind, they might take a house in the country.

George had always regarded himself as something of an architectural enthusiast. At one time he had taken out a subscription to 'The Builder' magazine and had been so absorbed by an article discussing the various merits and deficiencies of the English Bond as opposed to the Flemish Bond that he salvaged several hundred London commons from two adjoining walls that had collapsed at the bottom of the garden in Lower Sydenham with the aim of rebuilding them, incorporating both styles to test the theories of the article. Both fell down; the English Bond lasting just days longer than the Flemish Bond. George attributed both failures to inferior mortar. On the advice of Rosalind he did not renew his subscription to 'The Builder'.

George's keen eye for architectural detail had noted that his new house was built in 1908 and so was quite *modern*. It was certainly more spacious, lighter and airier than Lower Sydenham. He'd had a chance to have a good poke about and had just about got his bearings. Double fronted with large bay windows either side of the porch, which was reached by a low flight of five steps, the brickwork was a deep, satisfying red (English bond with blue-grey headers) embellished with a little tasteful decoration here and there; courses of brick of a lighter hue running round at first floor level and some pleasing decorative but restrained brick patterns over each window. All the woodwork was white and the rainwater goods were in black cast-iron. The roof was slate, punctuated by dormers on the top floor. There were three chimney stacks, two on each flanking wall and one at the back where the house extended at right angles, each topped off with a considerable number of pots. There was a large frontage, laid to gravel, with two gates wide enough for a cart, carriage or motor. Laurel hedges had been planted and were establishing themselves well. Saplings of some variety (perhaps these were 'the limes'?) had been planted on both sides of the Avenue for its entire length and, although still in the very first flush of youth, promised a shady colonnade in the years to come. The house agent described it as a 'Superior modern detached villa situated in a convenient position, with pleasant and sunny aspects. Arranged over three floors, two half landings, attic and cellar. Reception room, drawing room, dining room, breakfast room, kitchen, scullery, cold room, laundry, eight bedrooms, study, two bathrooms with separate offices. Fitted with the most modern and up-to-date conveniences. Electric light in all rooms, water heating and cooking by piped gas. Conservatory, ground floor office, boiler house, outhouse, large gardens to front and rear and space for a motor house.' A pretty fair description George supposed, although he had his doubts about the water heating.

Of course when one moves, lock stock and barrel, to a new house there are bound to be *difficulties*. The first of which is that one's furniture doesn't fit, there's too much or too little, there are carpets and curtains to think about and the catering arrangements are always a trial. Then there is the allocation of bedrooms. There is a popular parlour game played at parties organised for children called 'musical chairs'. The reader will surely be familiar with the concept, however, for the benefit of those who have not encountered this potentially traumatic experience, a brief description may not go amiss: The idea is that several chairs are placed in the middle of the room, a jaunty tune is played on a gramophone or piano and the children run excitedly around the chairs until the music is suddenly interrupted at which point the children rush to find a vacant chair. There is always one chair fewer than the number of children participating and so each time the music stops one child is 'out' until there is only one chair and one child left who is triumphantly declared the winner, whereupon he or she is rewarded with a sticky bun. We feel exhausted just describing it.

However, it is on the basis of this game that the novel idea of 'musical bedrooms' was apparently conceived. The subject was first raised on Saturday morning. George had at last dropped off for an hour or two after a particularly warm and humid night when there was a fairly sharp prod in his back.

'George.'

'Hmm.'

'George.'

'Hmm.'

'*George!* Are you awake?'

Another prod. At moments such as these it is futile to protest that one is, in fact, sound asleep.

'George, listen. I've been thinking about the bedrooms.'

'Yes, dear. They're lovely.'

'*No*, George! I mean, I don't think they're right.'

'What's wrong with them?' he managed, still half asleep.

'Well, you remember in Sydenham?'

'Yes.'

'Well, the sun set in the west.'

George acknowledged that it was, indeed, the accepted custom.

'But we were in the east.'

George found it generally a good plan not to disagree with Rosalind although, at this particular moment, he was somewhat hazy as to the significance of this celestial observation. However, light, as it were, at that juncture, dawned.

'George, dear, you sleep much better away from the side where the sun goes down and it's much nicer in the morning when the sun comes up streaming through the windows. It's very dark in here because the sun's shining into the other side of the house.'

'Well, we can't go back to Sydenham,' said George, still not fully attentive. 'The house is let and I've changed my season ticket.'

'*No*, you goose!'

A sharper prod.

'I think we should move to the bedroom overlooking the garden. It'll be much brighter in the mornings and it won't be so far for you to get to the office.'

This latter remark sailed so far over George's head he did not attempt to enquire the reasoning behind it.

Unimpeded and undeterred, Rosalind continued: 'Will you speak to Pickfords on Monday? But don't arrange for them to come before Wednesday because Waring's are delivering more bedroom furniture on Tuesday and I need to supervise where it all goes.'

George wondered how Rosalind could be so enthusiastic so early in the morning. 'Wickfords. Paring's,' he muttered under his breath.

He thought that this would be the end of the bedroom manoeuvres but, no, not a bit of it. Half an hour later he was just spreading some rather decent marmalade on a slice of toast when Alex and Vicky appeared. 'Good morning, you two,' he said in as cheery a way as he could muster after a disturbed night's sleep. 'I hope you slept well. Better than I did at any rate.' Sympathy for their father's disturbed night came there none. Instead there was a complaint.

'Mummy, daddy, the bedrooms aren't right,' said Vicky intercepting some toast which had been destined for George's plate. He groaned inwardly.

'I'm pained to hear it,' he said. 'Would this be because the sun does not describe a perfect geometrical arc through the correct windows at the proper and respectable hours of dawn and dusk?'

'Don't be silly, daddy,' said Alex depriving him of another slice of toast which had just arrived directly from the kitchen.

'George, don't be so grumpy,' said Rosalind, pouring him a cup of tea. 'What is it darlings? What is it that's not right?'

'We've tried very hard, honestly, but it's no good. I don't like the wallpaper and Vicky said the paint made her feel ill, didn't you Vicks?' said Alex, giving her sister a prod.

'Makes me feel ill,' echoed Vicky who, despite having made it downstairs, appeared to be still semi-comatose and relapsing rapidly.

'But it's not new paint,' said George. 'Any paint odour would have dispersed long ago.'

'It's not the smell, daddy, it's the *colour*,' said Vicky, suppressing a yawn.

'How the deuce can the colour make you feel ill?' George said with some surprise and not a little exasperation as yet another slice of toast failed to make it safely to his plate.

'Now, George, you know that Vicky is artistic,' said Rosalind pouring hot water into the teapot. 'She's very sensitive to colour aren't you dear?'

'It's sticky *brown*, daddy. *So* old *fashioned*.'

'It's the varnish,' he said. 'House is plastered with it. Everywhere you look. See?' George pointed to the breakfast room door.

'But it's so old *fashioned*,' came the echo from Alex.

'It is rather dark, George,' said Rosalind. 'Perhaps we should get the decorators in.'

'Oh, yes, mummy,' said Vicky, suddenly discovering some enthusiasm at the prospect of spending her father's money. 'Then they can change my wallpaper too!'

'But think of the cost!' George remonstrated feebly, at the same time knowing that he was fighting a losing battle.

'I'm sure it won't be that expensive, George,' said Rosalind, dear, sweet simple optimist that he knew her to be. 'And the girls can move into the two spare bedrooms temporarily before Clementine and Celandine move in.'

Clementine and Celandine. The names hit him like a thunder-bolt out of the blue. Rosalind's sister and her daughter. He'd almost forgotten about them. How could he be so silly? They were the main reason they'd moved from Lower Sydenham in the first place. An even more audible groan.

With all the to-ing and fro-ing he was glad to escape to the office on Monday. He had taken an earlier train in the hope that it would be cooler and less crowded and had to admit that the journey was not unpleasant. The heat, however, remained merciless during the day and well into the evening. On Tuesday he left early and on Wednesday he stayed a little later in the hope of avoiding the worst of the tropical sun but neither plan was very successful. The afternoon of the former was broiling and fearfully humid, the latter wasn't much better with no air moving and, to make matters worse, the train ground to a halt just after it had left London Bridge, and, when it finally did get going again after twenty minutes or so, crawled at a snail's pace the rest of the way. There was a different ticket collector at Streatham Common that evening and, on enquiring casually the reason for the delay, he was met with, 'Blowed if *I* know, guv.'

***

On Thursday evening George arrived home to see, to his mild consternation, a man apparently sitting on top of a tall pole which had mysteriously sprouted by the hedge in the front garden during his absence. He passed the time of day with him in as casual a manner as he was able to summon up given that he was in the last stages of heat exhaustion, the day having been particularly fierce and his office window, which he had managed to free on Wednesday, having become mysteriously stuck again. (George's strong suspicions lay towards Warbeck and Simnel in this regard and he made a mental note to speak to them about it, telling them in no uncertain terms that they'd better watch out if they valued any sort of future at Fysh, Fysh, Iceberg and Fysh.)

The house appeared to be deserted but there was a pleasant draught blowing through and presently he heard voices coming from the back garden.

'Oh, there you are dear,' said Rosalind greeting him with a peck on the cheek. 'Come and have some iced lemonade.' For a moment he thought the sun had gone to her head but, sure enough, bobbing around in the glass were two or three lumps of ice. As if to read his thoughts like some celebrated music-hall magician she went on, 'Mrs McGillycuddy next door has an ice-making machine. We met quite by chance by the front gates earlier. Isn't it wonderful? If this lovely weather continues we really must think about getting one.'

More expense.

'Rosalind,' said George after nearly swallowing a particularly large lump of ice, 'There is a man sitting on a pole in the front garden.'

'Yes, dear,' said Rosalind with an air of nonchalant indifference while brushing the shoulders of his jacket. 'He's from the General Post Office.'

'Then he's clearly lost his way,' said George. 'I doubt he'll make many deliveries if he insists on staying up there.'

'Oh, no,' Rosalind went on, filling his glass again, 'he's putting in the wires.'

'Wires? What for?'

'The new telephone, of course.'

'What new telephone?'

'The one we're having installed. You remember, you agreed to it before we moved.'

Yet more expense. He did vaguely remember something of a conversation regarding telephones but had dismissed it from his mind pretty soon after. Telephones were useful in business, of course; they'd had them at the office for some years now, but he failed to see the need for one in one's home. The infernal thing would be going off at all times of the day and night. A man's home is where he can relax; retire from the world of business and commerce. He couldn't see why anyone would want to be conducting conversations with all and sundry. And it would be of no use to Rosalind and the girls. What could they possibly have to say on a telephone?

***

The following Monday the decorators were due to start. George viewed the prospect with mild foreboding but attempted to put the matter to the back of his mind while he was at the office. He had made a rather half-hearted effort to put a brake on the operations by examining closely the terms of the lease in the hope that it forbade alterations of the sort envisaged. He was, however, thwarted and somewhat disconcerted to note that, not only was decoration allowed, it was positively encouraged.

For the previous week the house had been littered with samples from Liberty, Morris, Jeffrey, Sanderson and sundry other companies and every post seemed to bring an avalanche of catalogues and communications from the decorating fraternity of south west London. On Saturday morning Rosalind informed him that Messrs. Zebrani & Stripp, General Builders and Decorators, had been graciously awarded the contract and would he mind signing the necessary paperwork please?

'They are most reputable and come very highly recommended, George. Mrs McGillycuddy had them in to re-decorate the whole house and she hardly knew they were there.' George was about to remark that the reason for this was that for a good deal of the time they probably weren't there, but thought better of it.

A partners' meeting had been called for 11 o'clock. One of the items on the agenda was the conduct of the firm's account at Capital & Counties Bank. There had been one or two serious errors in accounting recently due to some slap-dash paying in and, sadly, the trail, yet again, was leading to the desks of Messrs.

Warbeck and Simnel. As they came directly under George's command he undertook to assure the other partners that he would take the matter in hand. This item on the agenda had just concluded when there was a knock on the boardroom door and Simnel poked his head in.

'Excuse me gentlemen. Begging your pardon for interrupting but there's an urgent telephone call for Mr Chesshyre.'

'Who is it, Simnel?' asked George with a degree of exasperation.

'I believe it's Mrs Chesshyre, Mr Chesshyre. She said it's most urgent and can you come to the telephone immediately.'

George made his apologies and followed Simnel back to his office. 'George Chesshyre,' he said lifting the receiver.

'George, dear, is that you?'

'Yes of course it's me Rosalind. Is everything all right?'

'Oh, George, it's really nothing to worry about. I thought I'd ring you up because now the telephone's been installed it's so convenient to speak to you during the day and not have to worry about waiting for you to come home in the evening before I can tell you.'

George sighed and closed his eyes. He hoped this was not going to become a regular occurrence. 'Rosalind, dear, it's really lovely to speak to you of course but I *am* very busy and I've just been called out of an important meeting.'

'Of course, George, I'm terribly sorry to disturb you but I thought I should let you know that Mr Stripp has turned off the gas.'

George sank down into his chair like a rapidly deflating gasholder. 'Well, as long as he turns it back on again I don't think we need to worry,' he said.

'Yes, but George, Mrs Sprackett is worried that she won't be able to do cutlets for dinner and suggests a cold collation.'

George replied that a cold collation would serve admirably especially as the mercury in the thermometer was threatening to burst out of the top of the glass at that point.

Further intimations were flowing down the line. 'Mr Stripp says he can turn the gas back on if it's absolutely necessary but he'd rather not because of possible explosions and anyway you'd probably prefer beer to tea in this hot weather wouldn't you?'

A cold bottle of Allsopp's Celebrated India Pale Ale floated in a vision before him. 'Well... well as long as there's some gas in the beer at least,' he said, rather pleased with his little off-the-cuff witticism. 'Rosalind, you must do what you think best, dear. Tell Stripp just to get on with it. Now I really must go, dear. I shall see you later and I shall look forward to whatever Mrs Sprackett can rustle up for us. I'm sure it'll be splendid. It always is. Goodbye, dear.'

'Goodbye, George. Shall I hang up the speaking-tube thing now?'

'Yes, dear. Put it back on the hook.'

'Perhaps you should hang up first, dear.'

'Rosalind, why don't we both hang up the – speaking-tube things – together?'

'Oh, that's a good idea. I didn't want to think that you thought I was rude if I hung up first.'

'Rosalind, I shall count to three and then we can both hang up the tubes together.'

'Oh, yes George! What a good idea. How clever you are!'

'Right, here goes – One – two – '

'George.'

'Yes, dear.'

'How will I know that you've hung the speaking-tube up?'

'Because I shall have – well – you won't be able to speak to me any more.'

'Oh. But then you won't be able to speak to me, either.'

'Yes, dear. That's the whole idea.'

'But what if you suddenly thought of something you wanted to say to me and had forgotten?'

'Then I should ring you back.'

'Oh, yes. Of course. How silly of me. Why don't you do that now?'

'Do what?'

'Ring me back.'

'But why? I'm already talking to you.'

'George, you'll have to tell me later on. I haven't time to chat now even though it's lovely. Oh, I'm so glad we've had the telephone installed! Will you ring me again tomorrow?'

'Ros—' The line went dead. He put the 'tube' down and sank back further in his chair. He hoped that this was not going to be the start of a daily report of domestic difficulties and goings on. He knew this telephone business would lead to trouble. He should have to nip it in the bud!

By this time he'd really had enough of Stripps, Spracketts and cryptic telephone conversations and decided to take an early lunch. The afternoon was mercifully quiet with no more interruptions. Even Warbeck and Simnel were subdued. He'd given them a large pile of stock transfer forms to complete in relation to an issue of Midland Railway 2½% Unsecured Loan Stock 1941 and told them they couldn't go home until they'd finished at least half of them.

By the time he got home Messrs Zebrani and Stripp had departed for the day but evidence of their presence was, despite the sincere testimonial of Mrs McGillycuddy, everywhere to be seen. There were trestles and stepladders in the hallway, several large tins of paint on the first landing and much sheeting draped, apparently haphazardly, over doorways and sundry pieces of furniture.

He was met with the customary peck on the cheek and a glass of lemonade but no ice. 'Mrs McGillycuddy is most upset, George. Her ice-making machine has stopped working but she has spoken to the shop that supplied it and given them a severe reprimand. She used our telephone, I hope you don't mind, George.'

He raised half an eyebrow. 'Do you mean to tell me that Mrs McGillycuddle hasn't got a telephone of her own?'

'No, George and it's McGillycuddy,' Rosalind corrected him. 'She says she wouldn't have one in the house. She says that she can see no reason why anyone would want to have a telephone in their house because you never knew who would ring it and it would never do to have strangers ringing you to whom you hadn't been introduced. She says it would not be proper.'

He was too hot and exhausted to pursue this peculiar line of reasoning so, taking his glass of warm lemonade, he stumped upstairs to change into something cooler.

'Don't *stump*, George,' called Rosalind after him. 'Vicky has a bad headache.'

***

By half past seven he had cooled down sufficiently and was relaxing in the conservatory. Vicky and Alex had appeared from wherever they'd been hiding amongst the besheeted labyrinthine pile. Alex was waving a fan furiously in front of Vicky. Mrs Sprackett had been busy with her 'cold collation' which was appearing, by degrees, on the conservatory table.

'I thought we'd have dinner out here tonight, George, as it's so warm again,' said Rosalind, putting a slice of corned beef on his plate. He was rather partial to corned beef especially if it was accompanied by some good, hot mustard. There were some cold potatoes and radish, boiled beetroot, lettuce and spring onions as well. Mrs Sprackett had made some of her special recipe mayonnaise which complemented the collation admirably. He had uncorked and decanted a pleasantly light claret that he had been keeping in the cellar which, mercifully, had stayed cool despite the tropical atmosphere above.

The second glass of claret was slipping down nicely together with another slice or two of corned beef when Rosalind produced a letter from her handbag. He thought he detected a momentary look of nervousness on her face. This was unusual because Rosalind was the most composed of women and invariably a calm and dependable pair of hands in a crisis, urgent telephone calls excepted.

'George, dear,' she began nervously. 'I received a letter to-day from Clementine.'

He groaned.

'Would you like to read it?'

'Oh, lor. Must I?'

'I think you ought.'

Apprehensively he took the envelope, unfolded the single piece of paper and read:-

'Deolali

20th May '11

My Dear Rosalind,

I hope you are well. Everything is settled here. Celandine and I embark on the 27th and are due at Southampton on 7th August. It's taking rather long because the ship goes round the Cape and not through the Canal. V. disagreeable. Cook's arranged it especially so cannot argue. Will get the boat train and will wire later when I know times. Tell George to meet us at Waterloo. Are tolerably well under the circumstances. Not looking forward to cold weather. I hope your new house has good heating. Much love to Vicky and Alex.
Your loving sister,

Clementine

PS I hope George has shaved off his moustache. It did so frighten Celandine.'

He went in search of another bottle of claret.

CHAPTER THREE ~

~ Discord

—❧❧—

Monday 7th August 1911

1871 was notable in the Parliamentary Year for introducing and enshrining in law the 'Bank Holidays Act'. This most worthy and benevolent law proclaimed that the first Monday in August be declared a holiday for all and that the joyous and grateful masses would throng to the seaside (on special trains benevolently laid on by the railway companies) whereupon the joyous and grateful masses would frolic on the golden sands and swim in the deep blue sea; eat cockles and mussels and other molluscs too disgusting to mention; laugh uproariously at pierrot shows and return home on the benevolent trains deliciously tired and deliriously happy to spend another gruelling twelve months down a mine or scrubbing clothes below stairs for fourteen hours a day.

The Act did not go so far as to declare that the weather should remain fine for the duration; the sun must shine, uninterrupted, from rise to set; no rain must fall nor dark clouds dare to appear over the horizon and the temperature must not fall below a balmy 72 degrees. Honourable and Right Honourable Members in drawing up this most benevolent piece of legislation could not, while sitting in the Commons and the Other Place, envisage a scene other than that before described.

Readers who live in Britain may permit themselves a sardonic smile at the notion of an August Bank Holiday free from wind, rain and cold but the sorrowful truth is that more often than not these are the climatic conditions endured by the joyous throng. The day before will be tropical; the day after will be tropical. But on August Bank Holiday Monday a deep depression will centre itself over the British Isles, deposit several hours of unrelenting rain, then evaporate as quickly as it had appeared.

August Bank Holiday Monday, 1911, however, was positively blistering from dawn to dusk. George awoke with a sinking feeling. Under normal circumstances he would be enjoying a relaxing lie-in and a leisurely breakfast followed by a stroll to the park with Rosalind and the girls; a Bank Holiday lunch (Mrs Sprackett always did something special on a Bank Holiday) followed by a snooze and an informal tea / dinner in the late afternoon. However, today was not a normal Bank Holiday. Not only was it witheringly hot from the moment the sun made an appearance, he was faced with the wearisome task of braving the Bank Holiday crowds at Waterloo to meet Clementine and Celandine.

He ran through the arrangements in his head as he washed and shaved. Despite Clementine's edict, he had declined steadfastly to shave off his moustache. The sheer *effrontery* of the woman. Frightened Celandine indeed! He was very proud of his moustache. Some had remarked that, with his military bearing and aquiline nose, he bore an uncanny resemblance to Edward Elgar. He mentioned this to Rosalind once who seemed to think the notion hilarious in the extreme and said something about him being an unfathomable enigma. Of course George realised that that was just her little musical joke.

He had taken the precaution of engaging a taxicab. He didn't relish the prospect of the train journey to Waterloo amongst the madding (maddening) crowd and then running the risk of there being no cabs to be had at the terminus. This had initially posed something of a problem. Not knowing the area well he wasn't familiar with the local cabmen. Then he remembered Alf whom he had encountered at the George and Dragon. He'd called in on the off chance on his way home during the previous week to make enquiries. Sure enough, he was in the bar. George told him of his situation and, after Alf had assured him that his cab was now fully and reliably operational, arranged to be picked up at the house at ten o'clock the following Monday. True to his word, at ten on the dot he drew up outside.

'Mornin' guv. Luvly day for it!' George felt a wave of annoyance wash over him at this cheery optimism. A hurried breakfast had given rise to slight dyspepsia and the prospect of a rattling cab ride did little to settle his stomach.

'I wish I could share your enthusiasm,' he replied as they pulled away. In George's experience which, we have to say, was not particularly extensive, there tended to be two types of cab drivers: the taciturn and the garrulous. Alf was of the latter variety, a condition which George could not with certainty attribute to Allsopp's Celebrated India Pale Ale although the possibility crossed his mind despite the early hour. By the time they approached Waterloo there had been an almost continuous monologue covering, amongst other things: The coronation; how wonderful Asquith was; votes for women (bad); the weather ('Luvly, ain't it?'); votes for women (good); the fortunes of the MCC; how dreadful was that Asquith?; aeroplanes (would never catch on); the prospects of Crystal Palace in the forth-coming season; suffragettes ('I'd put 'em over my knee!'); aeroplanes (the coming thing); the weather ('Too bloomin' 'ot for me, guv!'); suffragettes ('They've got a lot of go in 'em!'); the price of children's shoes ('Shockin', guv. 'alf a nicker a pair an' I've got three of the perishers!'); and, finally, the fate of his onion patch, ('Water 'em every night, guv, but they're still the size o' marbles!')

Waterloo was seething with humanity. If there was a worse day to have to complete the task in hand George didn't know of it. There were lines of taxicabs, motors and horse-drawn, vying for space and position. If things continued to go on in this fashion, in ten years time London would be at a standstill. The motors were belching out smoke and the engines in the station likewise. A blue haze hung in the air and the atmosphere was choking and stiflingly hot. He yearned suddenly for the relative quiet and fresh air of his Streatham back garden. (Beef-faced boys with pea-shooters notwithstanding.) Vast hordes of people were milling about, some purposefully, some apparently aimlessly. Harassed porters struggled with overloaded trolleys and long queues snaked, serpent-like, outside every ticket window.

With instructions to Alf to find a suitable spot and wait, he fought his way towards the departures and arrivals board. Pulling out of his pocket the wire received a few days before he read:-

'Arrive Waterloo 7th 11:40 am stop C stop'

The station clock showed 11:38 as he scoured the arrivals board for information regarding the boat train. For a fleeting moment he had the notion that he should be pleased if there were no intimation of its arrival; that Clementine and Celandine had actually remained in India; that this was all a bad dream and that at any moment he would awake from a peaceful snooze in the back garden. However, he was very quickly disabused of this notion by the sound of a porter shouting: 'Boat train – Platform One!' By some fortuitous serendipity he found himself actually standing very close to the entrance to Platform One and, looking down the track, saw a large green engine slowly approaching. It reached the buffers, stopped, then let out a sort of long, mournful sigh.

He knew exactly how it felt.

Tuesday 8th August 1911

George had taken the precaution of letting the office know that he was staying at home on the Tuesday. He felt it would be wise in order to recover from August Bank Holiday Monday. He was, however beginning to question the sagacity of this decision even though the nagging dyspepsia had returned and was making him rather tetchy. Clementine and Celandine had been under his roof for almost exactly twenty-four hours and he felt that he had aged twenty-four years. He could not go into the drawing room on account of the fact that a fire was commanded to be lit almost the instant they stepped over the threshold. In addition to this they were wearing overcoats! Goodness only knows what they'll be like when the weather actually does turn cold, he thought.

Clementine (or 'Lady Disdain' as he had, for some years, referred to her as, owing to her contemptuous regard for him; he was never, in her eyes, good enough for Rosalind) had spoken not two words to him since they had met at Waterloo and Celandine appeared to him to be in a state of perpetual catalepsy which he put down to either: the weather, Mrs Sprackett's valiant attempt at kedgeree, or the terrifying sight of his Elgarian whiskers. (He suspected the kedgeree which had been pretty fearful that morning with far too much boiled egg.)

'George, dear, you have to make allowances,' said Rosalind as they sat in the conservatory with a pot of tea after lunch, the refugees still in a state of hibernation. 'Their whole world has been turned upside down,' she went on. 'What with Bertie dying so unexpectedly like that it's left them dreadfully bereaved and shocked.'

George leaned back in his chair, his hands behind his head. 'Yes, you're right, old girl,' he said, pursing his lip as he reflected. 'Poor old chap was only, what fifty one? Seemed a pretty decent sort the times I met him. It's the climate out there, you know. Suits some but not others. Drives 'em mad. I certainly couldn't stand it. Wouldn't be surprised to learn that he'd done himself in. Either that or she did for him.'

Rosalind nearly dropped the teapot. '*George!* What a *dreadful* thing to say! You know that the doctors said it was his heart. Clemmie said he seemed to have a lot on his mind during the months before he died.'

'Probably wondering whether he could do for her first,' he said, warming to the homicide / suicide theory. 'I suppose she'll have a pension?' He stirred his tea and shooed a wasp from the sugar bowl.

Rosalind was outraged. 'George, I shan't tell you again. Stop being so rude! If you go on like this I might just do for you!' She looked at him askance, her face softening into a smile. 'Anyway it's too soon to be thinking about pensions. You're very mercenary at times, you know George. I imagine there will be one, but we must be tactful. I'm sure she'll tell us in time.' The wasp buzzed around her head. 'George don't shoo that wasp in my direction. She didn't say much at all about finances when we were arranging for her to come and live with us. We need to help them both as much as we can, George.'

'All right,' he said, sipping his tea, on top of which was floating some curdled milk. (Drat this hot weather!) 'I'll do my best. But they'll have to learn to speak. I presume they do speak English?'

'*George!*'

'Well, I don't know. Clementine walks past me with her nose in the air and I swear that if Celandine's eyes get any bigger they'll pop out of her head.'

'*George!!*'

Saturday 12th August 1911

George awoke to find a large ginger cat sitting at the end of the bed, staring (in the way that cats do) at him. This was, to say the least, rather unnerving. They did not, to his certain knowledge, possess, nor had they ever, possessed a cat so from whence this marmalade feline had hailed was a mystery. He had little experience of cats but had noticed, on the occasions he had encountered one, that they had an eerie habit of staring at you almost as though willing you to back down and look away first. He had to admit that it was a rather beautiful cat with a large proud head and magnificent whiskers. It flicked its tail in a desultory fashion then yawned in a way which indicated to him that it was bored and sought some excitement elsewhere. By this time Rosalind had stirred.

'George, there's a cat at the end of the bed.'

He replied that he was, indeed, cognisant of the animal's presence.

'Is it yours, George?'

'Of course it's not mine! Do you think that I go about at night kidnapping strange cats and planting them on the end of the bed?'

'Well, where's it come from, then?'

'How the deuce do I know? I just woke up and there it was, staring at me. Look, it's still staring at me. It hasn't given you so much as a glance.'

'I expect it likes you.'

'How can it possibly like me? It doesn't know me from Adam.'

'Perhaps it thinks you're a mouse. You do look a bit like a

mouse sometimes when your front teeth stick out. I've told you before, George, you really ought to see the dentist about those two front teeth.'

At this the cat decided he had had enough and that presumably George was not a mouse, yawned again, jumped off the bed and sauntered out through the open bedroom door with his tail in the air as though he owned the place.

George was looking forward to a leisurely, quiet breakfast. The girls hadn't yet come down and Lady Disdain and Celandine were, as far as he was aware, huddled under six blankets with a roaring fire in their respective bedrooms. He shuddered to think of the coal bill next winter. A new type of marmalade had appeared on the dining room table and he was just about to spread some on his toast when a marmalade head of the feline variety popped up across the table from him. It had a kipper in its mouth. Just then there was a dreadful commotion in the kitchen. It may be opportune at this moment, lest the casual reader should be alarmed at the following intimations, to introduce Mrs Daisy Sprackett, who has so far remained in the wings although we have been made aware of her cold collations and fearful kedgeree; plain cook (her own description although she was capable of producing feasts of delectable quality) housekeeper, professional firebrand and keeper on a short leash of Polly and Dolly (officially parlour and kitchen maids but whose duties were frequently interchangeable) who, at this moment, were standing in the kitchen doorway, looks of horror and extreme amusement on their countenances respectively. George had the utmost respect for Mrs Sprackett as did Rosalind and the girls. She'd been with them since the twins were born and had run the household with a rod of iron despite frequently difficult and exasperating circumstances. In all the years George had known her, her appearance hadn't seemed to change a bit. To liken her to Peter Pan would be rather stretching things but he remembered when she joined them she was of indeterminate age and she maintained that quality to the present. George supposed she would be about five foot three but her presence and forcefulness belied this. She was a very well built woman and her habit of wearing clothes of a voluminous nature only served to enhance the effect. Always with a spotless apron and mob cap, red hair, a ruddy complexion and piercing green eyes combined with a fiery temper; it led him to believe that there was some Celtic blood coursing through her veins but in her speech she was pure 'cockney', although whether the first sound ever to reach her ears when she entered this world was the tuneful peal of St Mary-le-Bow remained a mystery. It is the convention that cooks, whether married or not, assume the title 'Mrs'. This is probably because by the time they attain that elevated position in a household they are of mature years and believe that 'Mistress' will carry more weight with local tradesmen and the public in general than 'Miss'. In Mrs Sprackett's case the title was genuine, there having been, at one time, a Mr Sprackett whose untimely demise was sometimes discussed and bewailed at considerable length, usually when sweet sherry was involved.

However, we must return to the subject of the brouhaha which has caused Mrs Sprackett to fly out of the kitchen in a temper most terrible.

'Lord bless us and save us there's a ket in my kitchen! Blow me if it ain't stole a kipper right out of the pan!'

'Mrs Sprackett whatever is the matter?' asked Rosalind, as she came into the breakfast room. Mrs Sprackett pulsed visibly. For a moment George was seriously concerned that she might explode.

'A ket. Big ginger varmint. Right 'ere in my kitchen as bold as brass if you please. I don't 'old with kets in the kitchen. Beggin' your pardon, mum, but 'e stole a kipper as I was fryin' for the master's breakfast.'

'George, you really must do something about that cat.' said Rosalind rounding on him while making placatory gestures to Mrs Sprackett.

'But—' He hardly had time to protest that he had only just become aware of its presence when Vicky and Alex came chattering in.

'Oh, what a beautiful cat!' They said virtually in unison, apparently unconcerned or surprised by the sudden appearance of the kipper eating feline and the commotion he was causing as if it were a perfectly normal occurrence and happened quite regularly on Saturday mornings. 'Is he yours, daddy?' asked Alex.

This must have been the morning for asking ridiculous questions. 'Yes,' he said, summoning up a ridiculous answer. 'He came by the first post. I've just unwrapped him.' This remark went unacknowledged so he carried on buttering another piece of toast.

'Can we keep him mummy?' asked Vicky.

'Look, Mrs Sprackett, he's eating a kipper!' exclaimed Alex, wide-eyed and pointing at the obvious.

Mrs Sprackett was again approaching imminent detonation. 'Gordon Bennett! I *know* 'e's eating a kipper! 'e stole it from the pan as I was makin' for your father's breakfast!'

'I expect he's hungry,' said Vicky sympathetically. 'He looks a bit thin.'

House-breaker and kipper-stealer he may have been, but for a vagrant feline he looked remarkably well-fed to George.

'Well, 'ungry or not 'e shouldn't go about a-stealin' people's kippers, that's all I can say.' Mrs Sprackett stood her ground defiantly. 'If 'e's 'ungry 'e should go and find a mouse.'

Rosalind gave George a sideways look. Mrs Sprackett went back into the kitchen, grumbling. Polly and Dolly, who had been enjoying the spectacle immensely from the safety of the doorway, beat a hasty retreat.

'Well, I vote we keep him!' said Alex. 'I'm sure he's a jolly good mouser.'

'When he's not eating my kippers,' said George.

'Don't be such a grouch, George,' said Rosalind. 'I'm sure Mrs Sprackett has some left-over kedgeree. There's Finnan Haddie in that'

George was not impressed. 'Oh, Lor, Ros. I can't face any more of that bloomin' kedgeree. Gave me dyspepsia yesterday and anyway, Finnan Haddie is not the same thing at all as a breakfast kipper.'

Rosalind was not to be swayed. 'For goodness sake stop complaining, George. If you hadn't let that cat into the house we wouldn't be having all this trouble now. I'll go and get you some Epsom salts. You can put some in your tea'

Vicky and Alex, oblivious to these exchanges, were whispering together in the corner. 'We're going to call him Tarporley!' announced Vicky, triumphantly.

George was beginning to think that he had entered some kind of Alice in Wonderland parallel universe. As it turned out, he wasn't far wrong.

'Don't you see, daddy? We've adopted him so he's a Chesshyre cat!' said Alex.

'Yes', said Vicky. 'We had a friend at school, you remember, Agatha Askey? We used to call her Agony Aggie because she could be such a pain sometimes. Anyway, she was from Tarporley. "It's in Cheshire, you know," she used to say with her nose in the air. "My pa's in salt."'

'My kipper's in Tarporley,' said George feeling quite proud of this witty remark which, however, drew blank stares from Vicky and Alex. He looked across at Tarporley. The kipper had, indeed, disappeared and all that was left was a bone and a big ginger grin.

CHAPTER FOUR ~

~ A Rational Man

—— ❧ ——

'Deep in the sun-searched growths the dragon-fly
Hangs like a blue thread loosened from the sky'

Dante Gabriel Rossetti ~ *'Silent Noon.'*

Sunday 13th August 1911

George had often thought that Sunday was the wrong day for religion and church and suchlike. It seemed such a peaceful day and you really ought not to have to rush around getting dressed up in order to sit on an uncomfortable plank of wood listening to some old duffer droning on and on about some obscure prophet from Ecclesiastes or Ezekiel or one of those other interminable books of the Old Testament. This morning he felt it more acutely than usual. The air was heavy and humid, the sky overcast. He'd had a fitful night and had been walked over several times by Tarporley who had made more entries and exits to the bedroom than the entire *dramatis personae* in Henry IV. Parts One *and* Two.

It was while he was shaving that he had the idea. He remembered Vicky and Alex babbling on about 'rational dress'. This was during their 'bicycling phase' (which didn't last long because neither of them could get the hang of balancing and would invariably fall off before reaching the end of the road). George had the vague idea that it was all George Bernard Shaw's idea. Or it might have been William Morris. Anyhow, it was all wrapped up with the 'aesthetic movement' or some such. Not a bad fellow, Shaw, thought George, although he would have to take issue with vegetarianism. Man is an omnivore. Cats are carnivores, horses are herbivores but man is an omnivore. However, that as it may be. Each to his own and if Shaw was happy with nut cutlets and lentils who was George to argue?

Rational dress is all about convenience and comfort. He normally wore a wing-collar to church, as he did to the office, but that morning he was feeling daring. He would wear a *soft* collar to church. What's more he would wear a light linen jacket and no waistcoat. He was aware that he had caused a stir as he entered the breakfast room.

'George, are you feeling all right?' asked Rosalind, frowning. 'You're not suffering from dyspepsia again are you, dear, because, if you are, I can get some Epsom—?'

George cut her short with an airy wave. 'Never felt better,' he replied with a self-satisfied smile.

'But you're not *dressed*, George.'

'*Au contraire,*' he replied as he sat down and buttered some toast. 'I have decided to follow in the footsteps of George Bernard Shaw.'

'George! You haven't become a *socialist?*'

'Worse than that,' he replied, feeling very mischievous, 'I'm thinking of becoming a *Methodist.*'

'Oh, George, please don't say such things, even in jest.' Rosalind was very orthodox.

'Rosalind, my dear, I've had enough of this blessed tropical heat. It's bad enough during the week but I don't see why I should have to suffer it on a Sunday as well. It's more than a man can stand.' This proclamation seemed to quell her disapprobation and apparently convinced her that he had not, in the heat of the night, turned into a political revolutionary or dangerous recusant.

When one moves to a new area all sorts of things have to be considered, not the least of which is finding a suitable church to attend. Since moving to Scattersdale Avenue SW the Chesshyres had tried out: St Michael's (too high); All Saints (too low); St John the Divine (too catholic); and St Mark's (too far). On Friday evening George had come home from the office having made it through another blistering week. Rosalind greeted him with a peck on the cheek. 'Poor George. You look worn out. Go and change and then come out into the garden. There's some ice-cold lemonade waiting.'

George barely grunted an acknowledgement and stumped upstairs.

'Don't *stump*, George. Vicky has a headache.'

Ten minutes later George stumped back down and out into the garden where he sank into a vacant deck chair. A glass of lemonade, ice bobbing on the surface, was thrust into his hand. 'Ah, ice,' he said. 'I take it you've seen the McGillycuddle woman again?'

'Yes, George. And it's McGillycuddy. I do wish you'd remember, George. She brought a jugful round just now. You've only just missed her. What a shame.'

George thought he'd had a narrow escape. 'Why is she bringing ice round Ros? Is she still trying to get you to buy one of those machines?'

'No, of course not, George. Don't be so cynical. She brought it round to say thank you. She came round earlier to use the telephone. She was most apologetic but she wanted to ring her sister in Dundee. I told her not to even think of it and that she could use the telephone at any time when she needed to. It took an awfully long time to make the connection but it was worth it in the end because they had a nice long chat. They must have been talking for well over an hour because I heard the clock in the drawing room strike twice. Oh, George, I'm so glad we had the telephone put in. You see, it's turning out to be very useful isn't it?'

George had turned very pale.

'Anyway,' Rosalind went on, not the least bit deterred by George's ghostly complexion, 'you would never guess, but we had a nice long chat too and I happened to mention that we were trying out all the churches in the area but hadn't yet found one to suit and she said she attends Holy Trinity in Ribblehead Road. She's been going there ever since it was built and that she wouldn't go anywhere else. "The sermons are so *uplifting*," she said. "I always come out of there feeling spiritually uplifted and positively a *new woman*, Mrs Chesshyre," she said. "Do you know,

Mrs Chesshyre," she said, "I intend to be buried there and have picked just the spot." '

At that moment George would quite cheerfully have escorted her there and sat her down on a nearby bench while he dug a deep hole.

Holy Trinity Church, Ribblehead Road, SW was, thankfully, only a ten minute stroll from them. Very *modern,* the foundation stone dated 21st June 1906 and built in the 'Arts and Crafts' style. (William Morris again. 'Rational Dress' should go down very well here.) The sign in the churchyard proclaimed the vicar to be the Reverend Algernon Humpidge, BD, MA (Oxon).

George's one concession to conformity was to wear a straw boater (he resisted the temptation to stick a card on it stating 'In this style, 10/6') removing it on entering the church which was pleasantly cool after the broiling air outside. There was a good turnout and he looked out over a sea of hats, highly decorative (and some truly monstrous) examples of the milliner's art, festooned copiously with flora and, he shouldn't be surprised, not a little fauna. He could have sworn he saw something move amidst the concoction on the head of the woman sitting in front of him. His hopes for some sort of sartorial rationality were somewhat depressed.

If Holy Trinity was modern, then the Reverend Algernon Humpidge was decidedly ancient. George thought him at least as old as Westminster Abbey and should have quite believed it if he were told he'd come over during the Norman Conquest.

'Good gracious,' he whispered to Rosalind who was acknowledging a greeting from across the aisle from Mrs McGillycuddy. 'Look at him. D'you think he'll make it through the service? I bet if we're using "Hymns, Ancient and Modern", they'll all come from the first part of the book.'

'Ssssh, George. People will hear you.'

How young men get into the professions they end up in is a subject worthy of careful study. Some go into the army or the navy if they can face the prospect of being shot dead or drowned. We understand that a fulfilling and stimulating career can be developed especially if you get into the position of ordering men around and preferably doing this from a position where you are unlikely to be blown up or sunk. Some go into the law where they spend endless days wrestling with torts and affidavits and charging extortionate fees for writing two line letters and giving five minute consultations. Some go into medicine, a profession somewhat akin to the law except that instead of bankrupting clients by means of the Chancery Courts and Circumlocution Offices, they go one step further and send them to the Poor House having tortured them half to death during their 'treatment'. Some go into banking and accountancy where they are given in charge of enormous sums of money a good proportion of which finds its way into their own bank accounts which they are able to pore over with some satisfaction provided their eyesight has not deteriorated from adding and balancing countless ledgers late into the night. The young man who has looked over all these options and has been exercised by none of them may turn his mind to more spiritual things and consider going into the Church. Whether he believes in God or not is fairly irrelevant. A country living, a commodious rectory, a biddable congregation, a wife to organise everything while he sits in his study and composes pious sermons, looks over his butterfly and stamp collections and smokes an agreeable English Mixture is an attractive proposition to any chap provided the Bishop stays away and there is not the prospect of too many baptisms, marriages or funerals to upset the daily routine. Of course money is likely to be a bit of a problem but if there is an allowance from the Pater and the prospect of a not insignificant inheritance somewhere along the way, not to mention what his good wife can bring to the union, a tolerable to comfortable existence is there to be had. George, as we have already intimated, was a stockbroker. That most mysterious of professions which has its roots in Coffee Shops, South Sea Bubbles and links with other disasters such as Overend Gurney. George's career was, we are thankful to say, not punctuated by such traumatic events; some might say his working life had been rather humdrum. But that was the way George preferred it. He had no use for dubious adventure and liked everything to be well-ordered and predictable.

George arrived in the world early on a wet Friday morning in May 1856. The delivery was unremarkable, there having been two sisters born before him. The doctor had been roused from his bed but arrived too late to do little more than pronounce George healthy, with everything where it should be and working as it was supposed to. He was visited and cooed over; played with by his sisters as though he were a doll; dropped once or twice but to no apparent ill effect and generally thrived in a somewhat chaotic household with his schoolmaster father and piano-teaching mother. At school he was good at figures and won little prizes for his efforts. At the age of twelve he was accepted, on liberal terms, by his father's school where he excelled at mathematics and music but was something of a duffer at history and Latin. This rather clouded his chances of going up to one of the great universities and so, when the time came, he was obliged to consider his calling. All the above professions were considered and discarded. 'Going into the Church' was the one that caused him most trouble. From the age of ten he had been a chorister at St Benedict's, a High Anglican church which celebrated mass and where the vicar was an adherent to Tractarianism and was an ardent follower of Newman. The organist possessed a large collection of Tallis's works and these were played regularly, Sunday after Sunday. There was talk of George reading theology but the Latin was against him. A family friend had connections in the City and, after a certain amount of correspondence, George was taken on by Messrs. Fysh, Fysh, Iceberg and Fysh in the summer of 1878 to learn the art or mystery of stockbroking. He took to it immediately and was soon calculating discounts, percentages, stamp duty, commissions and dividend yields while watching the markets closely in Home Rails and Gilts. He rose quickly to become a senior dealer in 1905 and a full partner in 1909.

But we have become diverted from our story. We must return to George sitting in his pew amid glorious manifestations of millinery. The Reverend Algernon Humpidge BD, MA (Oxon) was about to deliver his sermon. George was keen to know the subject of the homily but from where he was sitting it came over as a long drawn out moan. The pitch varied a little from time to time and occasionally there was a staccato crescendo (if such a thing is permissible in music) but for the duration, which was considerable, and saw George nodding off from time to time, no intelligible, uplifting or upbraiding words reached his ears.

As far as George was concerned the best part of the service was the organ. It was obviously a very good quality instrument and no expense had been spared on its construction and installation. It produced a deep rumbling bass which vibrated through the air and made his feet tingle at times. He did love a good bass. The organist was excellent and not afraid to open the throttle. During the collection he played Tallis's 'Third Mode Melody' from 'Archbishop Parker's Psalter', the theme of which, George had been reading in the latest number of 'The Musical Times' (a periodical approved by Rosalind as no bricks were involved) Mr Vaughan Williams had apparently used in his new 'Fantasia'. The ethereal melody wove ghost-like through the aisles, nave and chancel alike and followed George around, haunting him for the rest of the day. He could quite imagine himself back in Tudor England as he gazed around the church trying to ignore the extraordinary Sunday get-ups of the 'fashionable' Streatham set. Tallis was probably wasted on this lot. Went over their heads he should think. A pity. A bit lower and it would have knocked their silly hats off.

Parker's Psalter, at any rate, put him in a good mood for lunch. Mrs Sprackett had acquired an exceptional joint of topside and the thought of it roasting away while The Revd. Algernon Humpidge droned on and on kept him going. Mrs Sprackett normally attended evensong with Polly and Dolly (The Unholy Trinity) and so didn't accompany George, Rosalind and the girls to the morning service except at Easter and Christmas.

Fragrant aromas of roasting beef assailed his nostrils as he opened the front door. This sybaritic olfactory experience was somewhat tempered, however, by the sight of Lady Disdain and Celandine, who had apparently risen from the heat of Hades to take the air of Scattersdale Avenue, Streatham, London SW.

Before George had time to acknowledge their elevation to the land of the quick yet another great commotion arose in the kitchen. A ginger streak flashed past him closely followed by Mrs Sprackett brandishing a rolling pin.

'Blow me down that ket's been in my kitchen again!'

'What *are* you talking about, woman?' said Lady Disdain icily. Celandine had turned as white as a ghost.

'That Tarpaulin, that's what!'

'Why on earth have you got a tarpaulin in the kitchen?'

'On my kitchen table. I jest turned my back for a minute to baste the joint and when I turned round it 'ad it's great ginger 'ead in my mixin' bowl. Them Yorkshires'll 'ave to be throwed out now. Lord bless us what a waste!'

'George, what *is* the woman gibbering about?' Lady Disdain glared at him.

'*George,* what on earth's going on?' Rosalind, too, glared at him as she came in, slipping off her gloves. The likeness between the two sisters was remarkable when confronted with a situation befitting the description 'high drama' ('kets in the kitchen' meeting the required qualities) and was none the less disconcerting for that.

'Daddy, Tarporley's run up a tree and won't come down!' Two more sisters pointing the finger of blame at him.

George stumped up the stairs and refused to come down.

***

George found it best when domestic altercations were raging to stay out of the way if at all possible. The thought of Mrs Sprackett brandishing her rolling pin in the same room as Lady Disdain filled him with horror and so he retired to his study, his *sanctum sanctorum*, while the tempest blew itself out.

He stood looking out over the garden for a minute or two. Towards the back was an old elm which the builders had thoughtfully left standing while the area was being developed. Its leaves were yellowing already in protest at the fierce, unyielding heat of the sweltering summer. He wondered whether it would recover next season. He longed for some rain. Steady, gentle rainfall that the ground would greedily soak up like a parched man in the desert who comes across an oasis after being lost for days.

Rain – soft, refreshing, life-giving rain. Would they ever get it again? He couldn't remember when he last saw the streets awash, down-pipes overflowing, umbrellas everywhere. There had been talk in the newspapers of water rationing; supplies turned off for several hours a day. Reservoirs were running low and so was groundwater. Perhaps in September the weather would turn. Cooler nights. 'Season of mists and mellow fruitfulness.' This weather couldn't last much longer could it? He looked up at the sky. The overcast morning had become a burning afternoon; the sky a harsh, brilliant blue, the sun beating mercilessly, an incandescent orb piteously baking England into a brown, barren land.

He'd slipped off his jacket, undone the collar and rolled his sleeves up in a defiantly rational way. Things had quietened down in the kitchen and the glorious aroma of roast beef was again working its way around the house. He sat down for a moment at the piano that had been rather unceremoniously dumped there by the removers ('We couldn't think where else to put it, George and it did clutter up Lower Sydenham, you must admit') and eyed the yellowing keys. An old Broadwood upright. It had seen better days and badly needed tuning especially after its recent upheaval which seemed to have unsettled it. He played a chord. A dusty, old-fashioned, undamped sound but not entirely unmusical. From memory he played a few bars of 'Silent Noon', not inappropriate for the time of day if you were able to ignore the mayhem going on below. The chords echoed round the study and died away into silence. It was then that he became aware of a presence. Some sixth sense told him that he was not alone during this 'silent noon'. Turning round a wan, whey-faced wraith stood looking at him.

'Hello Celandine,' he said, smiling, somewhat taken aback but trying not to show it. She stood there in the doorway for a moment looking startled. Then she fled, silently. He went over to the doorway but she had disappeared. Somewhat unnerved he sat back down on the piano stool. Lady Disdain and Celandine had been with them for a fortnight now but whereas LD never lost an opportunity to display her fervent dislike of him, Celandine's presence had barely registered. She was such a slight child, pale, her features almost gaunt, she seemed to float around the house half-seen and unheard. She appeared at mealtimes, although overshadowed by LD, but ate very little, disappearing again with no noise, unnoticed by anyone. George was vaguely troubled. He should have to speak to Rosalind about her.

Monday 14th August 1911

They'd been at Scattersdale Avenue now for just a month and George felt they were settling in well. The girls had had their bedrooms newly decorated by Stripp who, despite his initial misgivings, had done a very good job. The new colour schemes had not, so far, induced nausea, headaches, beriberi, plague (of the bubonic or pneumonic variety) or incited ridicule amongst those sensitive to such things. He could not, however, guarantee that such maladies would not evidence themselves when the bill came in. Little homely appointments were appearing, supervised by Rosalind who had a most artistic eye and was a devotee of what she called *Art Nouveau*. Probably French, George thought, and very *modern*. Vases with swirls and curlicues and other startling devices had taken up residence in many rooms. These designs were also, by degrees, appearing on Rosalind's and the girls' dresses, apparently to the disapproval of LD whose attire remained stubbornly severe. Vicky had taken to wearing a *saree* on occasion which George thought most becoming and gave the house something of an exotic air. He thought that this would make LD feel at home but no, not a bit of it. Disapprobation was kept somewhat at bay by reminding LD that Vicky was *artistic* but this was, apparently, not a good enough excuse for bringing the neighbourhood into disrepute.

Meanwhile, the house was light and airy and, even in those furnace days, by keeping doors and windows open, it was possible to induce a relatively cool breeze at times. A good choice by Rosalind and no doubt far preferable to Dormin Road if he'd ever found out where it was. (One day, while in a brown study, George realised that 'Dormin' was the reversal of 'Nimrod'. As the great-grandson of Noah he wondered if he might be prevailed upon to make it rain.)

Things were quiet in the office. The market had gone into its usual summer lull, even more so that year given the oppressive weather. Never was 'Sell in May and go away' more appropriate. By four, with very little trading, he decided to come home. The train was fairly empty and he dozed off as they rattled through the August haze. Everyone was out in the back garden when he arrived. The heat had tempered slightly by five and jugs of lemonade were a welcome sight as he sank onto an available chair, loosening his collar as he did so. Lady Disdain was nodding off and so was not aware of his arrival. Vicky and Alex were sprawled on the grass, each engrossed in a book. Rosalind gave him a peck on the cheek in greeting and poured him a glass of lemonade. It was a scene of perfect domestic bliss (well, as long as LD stayed asleep). Only Celandine was missing. He drank the lemonade, ice bobbing on the top again (George hoped that this didn't mean there had been more lengthy telephone calls to Scotland) and then went inside to change. As he neared the bedroom he could hear his piano being played. Somehow, he instinctively knew immediately who was in his study. The little wraith was sat at the piano stool. She had found a book of easy studies that Vicky and Alex had worked on when they were quite young and a pretty Bach gavotte was being coaxed rather hesitantly from the keys.

Suddenly she stopped. She had sensed him in the same way as he had sensed her previously. Her hands froze and her body stiffened noticeably. He didn't want to startle her further so crept away and shut his bedroom door quietly. The music didn't restart and he didn't see Celandine again for the rest of the day.

***

'Hurt no living thing:
Ladybird, nor butterfly,
Nor moth with dusty wing,
Nor cricket chirping cheerily,
Nor grasshopper, so light of leap,
Nor dancing gnat nor beetle fat,
Nor harmless worms that creep.'

Christina Rossetti 'Sing-Song'

Saturday 19th August 1911

The day started with typical clamorous uproar. Tarporley came in through the bedroom window at about half past six (heaven only knows how he gets up there, thought George) and jumped up onto the bed thus ruining any semblance of a weekend reverie that he might have hoped for. He had developed a habit of walking up and down on George's chest and legs, then padding with his front paws, purring loudly. George didn't have the heart to push him off. He never went near Rosalind who remained blissfully ignorant of his presence. After about fifteen minutes of this performance he would jump down and wander off, presumably to see who else he could annoy at that ungodly hour. George was thankful that Mrs Sprackett kept her bedroom door tightly closed and had so far remained immune to these feline visitations. Mrs Sprackett and Tarporley had settled down to a mutual, if wary, respect for one another. Despite her avowed abhorrence of 'kets in the kitchen' George had noticed that a bowl of milk appeared regularly outside the back door.

Now fully awake but without the energy or will to get up, George mused over recent events. Despite the addition of Lady Disdain and Celandine, not to mention Tarporley, to the household, he felt quite pleased with himself and more and more settled in his new home. One of the advantages of living in a modern house is that it has all the latest conveniences built in. Not the least of these is piped gas for water heating and cooking. There was a boiler just off the kitchen which was lit early every day and provided copious quantities of hot water for all the washing and bathing that seemed to go on interminably for the rest of the morning. The lighting of the boiler was a duty delegated to either Polly or Dolly, depending on who got there first. Polly and Dolly were delightful girls who came with them from Sydenham. They occupied the attic bedrooms and were usually the best of friends except when they had had a row and then the whole house knew about it but it soon blew over. George supposed them to be about Vicky and Alex's age and were kept busy running errands, going to the local shops, helping Mrs Sprackett in the kitchen and generally ensuring that the house ran efficiently.

The lighting of the boiler was not for the faint-hearted. George had already had first-hand experience of this. A temperamental piece of equipment, it was rather aptly named 'The Acme Mighty Thermoboil No. 3', and was manufactured by the 'Acme Thermoboil Company Limited, New Furnace Works, Halifax'. In order to fire up the 'Thermoboil' you had to find a piece of newspaper and roll it up. A 'Swan Vesta', admirable match though it may be for many uses, is not long enough to poke into the firing hole. The rolled up newspaper, suitably alight, is thrust into the lighting orifice after the gas tap has been turned on. You then wait with bated breath. If you're lucky, the boiler will light with a soft 'whoosh' and you can retire in the satisfaction of knowing that you had coaxed it into life and would soon be enjoying a hot, relaxing bath. However, should the 'Thermoboil' be in an unco-operative mood, the burner will remain unlit and you have to douse the lighter before it burns your hand. You then have to start again with a fresh piece of paper, remembering to turn the gas off temporarily while you recommence the exercise. Turning the gas on again you hesitantly push the lighted paper into the hole. Nothing. Your heart sinks. Meanwhile the kitchen is beginning to fill with the smell of unburnt gas. You open the door to dissipate the noxious fumes and worry that either: a) you will poison yourself with coal gas or, b) you will blow the house up at the next attempt. Never mind. Third time lucky. You steel yourself, turn the gas on, thrust the flaring paper into the hole and curse under your breath; 'From Hell, Hull and Halifax, good Lord deliver us'.

Suddenly there is a blue flash and a deep, resonant boom which rattles the windows. The 'Thermoboil' has been roused! You wipe the sweat from your brow and go in search of a steadying drink.

That morning the 'Thermoboil' was, apparently, a reluctant riser. Raised voices could be heard far below in the kitchen as Polly, aided and abetted by Dolly, battled against the *crème de la crème* of the 'New Furnace Works'. A low thud, a rattling window sash, two high-pitched screams a perfect third apart and a blood-curdling yowl from Tarporley announced finally that the 'Thermoboil' had sprung to life. On balance George felt that coke, although more labour intensive, was far less injurious to the nerves. It might be imagined that this would be the end of the story. Not a bit of it. Once the 'Thermoboil' has got going it starts to rattle the pipes, making the devil of a din. Sometimes George could swear it was sending secret Morse code messages to its fellow 'Thermoboils' all over South West London.

However, despite his criticisms and misgivings, he had to say that the 'Thermoboil' did a jolly fine job of supplying copious amounts of hot water. It had recently occurred to him that he was sharing the house with eight women, all of whom made inexhaustible demands on it. The 'Thermoboil', therefore, was called upon to work very hard and he really didn't blame it for going into a sulk occasionally.

There were two bathrooms in the house, one off the first half-landing and a second on the first floor proper. The architect had been very generous with the fittings; George had rarely seen baths of such massive dimensions with brass taps that gushed hot and cold water so abundantly and forcefully it was like having your own private Niagara Falls. Both bathrooms were also equipped with shower facilities directly over the bath. They had their own separate taps which you had to adjust carefully before venturing under in order to ensure that you were not scalded or frozen to death.

Despite being as two peas from a pod, Vicky and Alex were as different as chalk and cheese when it came to getting up in the morning. Vicky was usually an early riser (except when suffering from wallpaper-induced nausea) but Alex was a lingerer and took ages to come round. George had finally given up any hope of enjoying an extra half an hour in bed not long after the 'Thermoboil' had come to life and was sitting in the conservatory with a cup of tea which Dolly had made for him when there was a piercing scream from somewhere inside the house.

'Lord bless us what was that?' said Dolly, nearly dropping the teapot.

George ran in and up the stairs as fast as he could at his age to find Vicky standing trembling outside the bathroom door on the first floor.

'Oh, daddy, it's *horrible!*' said Vicky, her eyes as round as saucers.

'What is? What on earth is it?' he said, unsuccessfully trying to conceal the alarm in his voice.

'In there,' she pointed to the bathroom door. 'In the bath!' At which she fainted clean away and collapsed into his arms.

By now the whole house was awake and aroused and had come to see what all the commotion was about. George was surrounded by a sea of anxious faces and even Lady Disdain looked concerned.

'What is it?' asked Alex, rubbing her eyes, and was actually so concerned she had persuaded herself to get out of bed. 'Is Vicky dead?'

'Vicky, darling what's happened?' asked Rosalind, gently shaking her and anxiously looking for signs of injury.

'The girl's had a fit!' came the opinion from Lady Disdain. 'Sal volatile! Quickly!'

Polly and Dolly were peering anxiously through the banisters.

'Who's Sally Volatty?' said Polly, looking around her.

'We ain't got no Sally,' said Dolly, eyes fixed on the bathroom door. 'P'raps it's a burglar.'

'Well, blow me!' said Polly. 'Fancy a burglar comin' in 'ere an' takin' a bath! Bloomin' cheek I call it!'

'It's that bloomin' Tarpaulin again ain't it?' said Mrs Sprackett who had come up from the kitchen, rolling pin in hand.

Amidst all the panic and confusion no-one had taken notice of Celandine who had slipped quietly into the bathroom. 'It's just a little spider,' she said looking up at Vicky who by now had regained consciousness. 'I didn't hurt him. I put him out of the window.'

CHAPTER FIVE

~ Being Counted

—⁂—

'Shout, shout, up with your song!
Cry with the wind for the dawn is breaking.'

Ethel Smyth and Cicely Hamilton
'The March of the Women'

Sunday 20th August 1911

The following morning Vicky had recovered sufficiently to accompany the family to church. Much to George's disappointment the acoustic quality of Humpidge's sermon had not improved and he was again forced to endure the eerie moan which ebbed and flowed, waxed and waned for the best (or worst) part of an hour. Just when he thought it was coming to an end as the moan declined in pitch and volume and sounding for all the world as though it was winding up, it started again with renewed vigour much to the delight of the hats who seemed to think it and Humpidge a spiritual tonic of biblical proportion.

If it wasn't such a bind he'd go back to St Matthews in Sydenham. The vicar's sermons were boring but at least he could hear them. Still, the organist was in rattling good form again and they had a rousing 'For All the Saints' from the English Hymnal which was a deal better than the dreary, old-fashioned stuff they were subjected to more often than not at Sydenham.

There was still no let-up in the weather. The sky was a deep azure with not a hint of a cloud anywhere. George was beginning to wonder if they were ever going to get any rain again. The trees were already beginning to turn, and crisp, brown leaves were underfoot everywhere. Vicky, (None the worse for her encounter with the gargantuan burglarious arachnid which was at least half an inch across) Alex and Rosalind were as brown as berries. Strangely, Lady Disdain and Celandine remained deathly white.

He couldn't really imagine how this could be so. How they had escaped the effects of the tropical Indian sun was a mystery.

Mrs Sprackett had excelled herself again with another prime piece of topside. This time there were no kitchen disasters and the Yorkshires had risen to perfection. King Edward potatoes were early, no doubt due to the weather, and had crisped up beautifully. Sunday lunch was usually the chance for some animated chatter and discussion and today was no exception. After a lot of babbling about autumn fashions the conversation somehow turned to the subject of censuses.

'Daddy,' said Alex, 'Do you remember when you had to fill in the census papers?'

George replied that he did, indeed, recall the fateful day on which their presence in the house would be recorded for all time.

'Well,' Vicky took up the thread. 'Did you have to put animals down?'

George had to admit that, despite vast experience, he still struggled with some unexpected lines of questioning.

'Hmm? Put animals down?' he said, only half paying attention as he opened a bottle of Bass. He thought he may have got rather on the wrong tack here, but realised it at once and decided to have a bit of fun. 'I've never had to put an animal down,' he said airily. 'Never had any pets. Won a goldfish at the fair once but it only lasted a day. Chap at the office had to have his dog put down. I asked him if he was mad, and he said, "Well, he wasn't very pleased about it!" ' He was rather proud of this witticism but it was apparent that his enthusiasm was not shared by the rest of the gathering.

'Don't be silly, daddy,' sighed Vicky. 'That's a dreadful joke and we've heard it hundreds of times before.'

'What we mean is,' Alex continued, speaking slowly as though addressing a congenital idiot, 'do you have to put animals on the census form if you have them, like a pet or something?'

'Yes, for instance,' Vicky went on, 'if we had Tarporley then would you have had to put him on the census papers?'

George sighed in a mock-patronising way. 'Of course,' he said, carefully pouring the Bass which was forming a magnificent head.

'He would be undoubtedly head of the household. *Chef de la famille*. Name – Tarporley Chesshyre. Age – over twenty-one. Occupation – Chief mouser and *bête noire* of Mrs Sprackett.'

'Humph,' came the retort from Lady Disdain staring at him icily over her half-moon pince-nez. 'I've never heard such rubbish. Filling the girls' heads with nonsense. Putting cats on census forms, indeed. Rosalind, I don't know how you put up with it.'

'Years of practice,' said Rosalind coming to his defence. 'Who's for more broad beans? There's plenty left.'

Spurred on by LD's disapproval George got into his stride. 'Chap at the office was telling me that on census night, a suffragette hid in the Houses of Parliament.'

'What on earth for?' asked Rosalind, spooning some broad beans onto Celandine's plate who was watching in horror.

'So that she could say her address on census night was the Houses of Parliament. Sort of protest. Can't vote but broke through the barrier, figuratively speaking. Apparently she locked herself in the broom cupboard when everybody had gone home.'

'Gosh, yes! I read about her in the Daily Mirror!' said Vicky.

'I wonder what they said when they discovered her in the morning,' said Alex.

'Probably had a bit of a brush with the law,' said George. 'Still, I expect they swept it under the carpet.'

A chorus of groans. 'Don't be *silly*, daddy,' came the response in unison.

'Humph. Rode off on her broomstick, I shouldn't wonder,' was the imperious response from Lady Disdain. (Humour was wasted on her, thought George, although he had higher hopes for Celandine. He had just caught the glimmer of a smile as the ghastly broad bean encounter was momentarily forgotten.) 'Rosalind, I'm surprised at you, allowing the Daily Mirror in the house.'

'Just wait till she sees my copy of "Das Kapital",' said George under his breath.

Monday 21st August 1911

Another tropical day. George arrived home that evening feeling like a damp rag that could be wrung out at will. He had taken to having a warm bath immediately on return from the office. Fortunately the 'Mighty Thermoboil' was functioning splendidly and a long, deep, soak was a blessed relief after the City of Hades which was what London had come to resemble in recent weeks. Despite keeping a wary eye for lurking arachnids he was pleased to note that no further wildlife appeared to have made its way into the bathroom for which he was grateful because sudden, unexpected screams and screeches are wearing to the nerves.

Those watery and soothing interludes, further softened by whatever bath salts might be found on the shelf, at the end of an arduous day, and before facing the predictable trials and tribulations of the evening, had enabled him to reflect somewhat philosophically on the nature of things. For instance, it had only occurred to him recently that he was the only male in a household made up completely of women. The only ally he had was Tarporley and there seemed to be some uncertainty about his gender. Of course, for some men his situation might appear to present something of a nightmare. Some of the chaps at the office seemed to lead truly hen-pecked lives and dreaded going home in the evening. They looked forward to escaping to the office in the morning and then sometimes to their club, if they had one, afterwards. If not they sought solace in a public house and would anaesthetise themselves with a whisky or two before braving the domestic situation awaiting them. He couldn't really imagine what that must be like. He had the most wonderful wife in his dear Rosalind and his beautiful daughters were, despite displaying a frequent aversion to rationality, a constant delight to him. He was even beginning to take to Lady Disdain. She had shown signs of thawing recently and had even been known to pass the time of day in a not uncivil manner. Their little wraith, Celandine, remained something of an enigma, however. He had the feeling that she'd come out of her shell given the right encouragement. As if by coincidence events that evening proved influential in bringing this about.

'George,' Rosalind said as he got into bed, 'Clemmie and I had an interesting chat to-day.'

George groaned. 'Interesting chats' usually meant trouble. 'Ros, I'm not shaving off my moustache. I'm sorry if it upsets Celandine but I'm sure she'll get used to it given time.'

Rosalind sighed. 'Don't be ridiculous, George. It had nothing to do with your moustache and I'm sure they've barely noticed it. Clementine hasn't mentioned it at all.'

'Well, I hope it's got nothing to do with their bedrooms. They've got jolly good aspects and I'm not getting Stripp in again to redecorate. They'll have to put up with them as they are.' He punched his pillow which emitted a feather or two.

'George, will you *listen?* They're perfectly happy with their bedrooms, in fact Clementine remarked how tasteful they were and how she was so grateful to us for making them so welcome after losing Bertie so tragically like that.'

'Well, we've done our best, old girl,' he said, pushing Tarporley off his shoulders whence he'd landed after leaping off the bedhead in the vain hope of catching a feather. 'I just hope they appreciate it. I worry about Celandine, though. She seems so withdrawn and quiet. Not afraid of spiders, though. Vicky said it was a big fellow. Still, I suppose they grow 'em big in India. Big as dinner plates some of 'em. Poisonous, too. Plucky little soul I'd say.'

Rosalind shivered. 'George, *please* don't talk about spiders. You know Vicky and I don't like them. We were actually discussing Celandine. She told Clemmie how she'd discovered your piano and was afraid you were cross with her for going into your study and playing it.'

George raised an eyebrow. 'Good heavens no,' he said. 'I'm glad she's found something that interests her. She seems to wander round like a lost sheep much of the time. Did she have lessons while she was in India?'

'She did. Clemmie said she was doing very well and her teacher was very pleased with her but of course all that stopped when they had to return to England.'

'Well, she can take it up again here,' said George, pushing Tarporley off his chest for the third time. 'We'll find her a teacher. Shouldn't be difficult. Plenty of superannuated old bats about who'd jump at the chance of earning a few bob.'

'Yes, George, that's exactly what Clemmie and I thought although we wouldn't have put it quite so – so – *colourfully*. But there is something of a problem.'

'Oh?'

'It's the piano.'

'In my study, you mean? Well, we can get it shifted into her bedroom or downstairs if you like.'

'No, George, it's not where it's situated, it's the piano itself.'

'Oh?'

'Yes. It won't do.'

'Won't do?'

'Clemmie raised her hands in horror when she saw it.'

'Well it is a bit decrepit, I suppose, needs tuning of course, but it's all right for learning on, surely?'

'Apparently it's only fit for firewood.'

'Only fit for firewood? I'll tell you what, I'll make a bonfire out of it and stick her on the top!'

'*George!* That's a dreadful thing to say!' Rosalind looked at him in mock horror but couldn't suppress a laugh. 'Listen, I think it would be lovely to have a music room. There's plenty of room downstairs and if we had a nice new piano Vicky and Alex could take it up again. Clemmie thinks we should get a Bechstein.'

'What?!' he nearly fell out of bed. 'A Bechstein? Have you any idea how much they cost?'

'It would be an *investment*, George. Just think of all the enjoyment the girls would get out of it.'

'I shall be ruined! I shall end up in Carey Street!'

'Oh, nonsense, George. Clemmie said she'd contribute to the cost when Bertie's life insurance comes through and Mrs McGillycuddy says that the Bechstein is the only piano she'd have in the house. She's had three you know.'

'Oh, I might have known she'd be involved somewhere along the line,' he said holding his head in his hands.

'And, of course, if we are going to attract a good class of teacher we'd need a good piano. It would set the right tone.'

'Well, it's setting a blooming discord with me, I can tell you.'

'Oh, don't be such a *grouch,* George. You'd enjoy playing it as well.'

'That's if I ever get a look in and I'm not imprisoned in the Marshalsea for bankruptcy.'

'George you've been reading too many Dickens' novels. I told Clemmie you'd have a look round their showroom while you're in town. It's in Wigmore Street.'

At that point Tarporley wandered in again and sat on the end of the bed looking at him.

'Oh, George don't let him walk all over you,' said Rosalind as she closed her eyes and suppressed a yawn.

'Humph. Why not?' he said. 'Everybody else seems to.'

'George, don't be such a *grouch!*'

Saturday August 26th 1911

Never let it be said that George was one to let the grass grow under his feet. He had to admit that the idea of getting a new piano, although initially filling him with horror at the thought of the expense, did quite rapidly enthuse him and he entered Bechsteins's showrooms on Tuesday afternoon with quite a spring in his step. He had sold some Great Western stock, which he had been holding for some time, and had made a respectable turn. He could reinvest it when Clementine's share of the cost of the piano came through. He had taken the initiative and decided that if they were to have a new piano it would be the best in the showroom. Rather rash, he knew, on reflection, but he *would not* be outdone by Mesdames Disdain and McGillycuddy. Just they wait until they saw it installed in the 'music room'. There would be gasps of astonishment. There was a gasp of astonishment all right when he looked at the price labels. No matter. A good piano they wanted and a bloomin' good piano they were going to get!

An hour and a half later he was the newly impoverished owner of a Bechstein Concert Grand in figured rosewood and his current account at Capital & Counties Bank was 295 guineas lighter.

***

There was a buzz of excitement running through the house that morning as the arrival of the magnificent instrument was awaited. George had taken great care to measure all the entrances and doorways that it would have to fit through and had satisfied himself that it would be manoeuvred into position with consummate ease.

Of course it wouldn't. At half past eleven Pickfords' special piano moving van drew up outside and six men alighted.

At twelve o'clock the piano, wrapped and swathed in protective hessian, was standing on its side on a trolley in front of the porch. A ramp had been put into position over the steps to the front door. The foreman was scratching his head. 'It'll *nearly* go, Mr Chesshyre, but I'm afraid the front door's going to have to come off. See, if we twist it slightly to clear the lintel it fouls the door.'

At a quarter past twelve the front door was propped up against the side wall and the Bechstein had advanced as far as the inner hallway whose door also 'had to come off'.

At half past twelve there was more scratching of heads. 'It'll *nearly* go, Mr Chesshyre, but it won't quite clear the music room door. It'll have to come off.'

At a quarter to one the music room door was off. 'It's not *quite* there, Mr Chesshyre. It's the door frames, y'see? They're very deep. We're going to have to take them out. Don't worry, we'll do a good job and put 'em back so as you won't know they'd ever been disturbed.'

At half past one the frames had been levered out and were propped up next to all the other doors which had 'had to come off'.

At a quarter to two, as if by some miracle, the Bechstein was in position, the right way up, and the wrapping removed, releasing a heady smell of new wood and French polish. It was truly an imposing sight. There was even a matching new stool to go with it. Pickfords' men were as good as their word. By half past two the frames had been reinstalled and all doors were back on their hinges with not a sign that any disturbance had taken place. George slipped the foreman a generous gratuity with his grateful thanks and instructions that he should stand his men a round or two at their favoured hostelry. As they drove off he was aware of a hushed gathering in the music room.

'Oh, daddy, it's *beautiful!*' said Alex approaching with deference and stroking the polished rosewood reverently.

'Oh, I can't wait to try it!' said Vicky walking round it, awe-struck at its magnificence.

'It's wonderful, George,' said Rosalind. 'And it looks just right in this room. Oh, we'll have some musical parties to remember in here!'

'What do you think, Clemmie?' George asked. 'Better than the old Broadwood, eh?'

She eyed it up and down critically. 'I'd prefer it if it was ebonised. Rosewood's too modern for me. Still, I suppose it'll have to do.' At that moment George had never been closer to carrying out his Broadwood threat but managed a synthetic smile. He turned to Celandine. The little wraith stood transfixed, hands clasped together. She didn't say a word but her eyes were as round as saucers. He wasn't sure whether this was the result of overwhelming delight or extreme trauma. 'Now, we have to be patient,' he said with an air of authority. 'The man at Bechstein's said we have to let it stand and settle for a couple of days. Then on Monday the piano tuner is coming to tune it to concert pitch and make sure everything is all right.'

Magic spells are easily broken and even the presence of a new Bechstein was not enough to impress Mrs Sprackett and keep her from the warpath.

'Beggin' your pardon, mum, but I can't keep this haddick warm much longer. Luvly bit o' haddick it is too what I got special from 'im in the 'igh Street. It'll go 'ard and then it won't be worth eatin' and then it'll end up in that Tarpaulin as I shouldn't wonder!'

Heaven forfend, thought George, that Tarporley should get a taste for 'haddick'.

CHAPTER SIX ~

~ **Notes from Boston**

———ℰ ℈———

Monday August 28th 1911

George took the day off in order to be at home when the piano tuner arrived. In the meantime it had dawned on him the reason why the piano had been so difficult to get into the house. When he had measured up he had failed to realise that it would be brought in on a trolley and, of course, the extra height meant that it wouldn't clear the lintels as he had expected. Never mind. He kept this secret to himself. He didn't want Lady Disdain getting wind of his incompetence or he'd never hear the end of it. There had been enough tut-tutting as it was when doors and fittings were being dismantled. However, everyone had been most obedient and had resisted the temptation to play even the merest grace note on the keys.

Listening to a piano being tuned is a rather peculiar experience. Some very unmusical and discordant sounds emanate from the instrument and it is not difficult to imagine that it is being tortured so mercilessly that it will never be persuaded to sing harmoniously again. However, we must defer to the greater expertise of those well versed in the art or mystery of piano tuning and leave it to them to achieve the triumphant and wondrous successor to Bach's well tempered clavier.

The tuner's name was Finkelstein and had been engaged on George's behalf by Bechstein's showroom. He was a man of few words and George left him in the company of Tarporley, who had apparently developed an intense interest in pianos, sitting patiently a safe distance away from the tuning operations, audibly reacting in a manner eerily reminiscent of the sounds being produced by the tuning process which, George sensed, was somewhat annoying to Finkelstein who glared at Tarporley quite frequently. By mid-day the tuning forks had been packed away and the Bechstein was declared fit for use. A further appointment was made for a month's time to ensure that everything was well and settling down nicely. George couldn't resist sitting at the stool and playing a few bars from memory. The tone was rich and deep, the keys beautifully weighted, even and responsive. Chords filled the room and shimmered as they died away. The difference between this and his old Broadwood was astounding.

Lost in his initial reverie he was, for a moment or two, unaware of the quintet of heads that had popped up in various places around the piano. Now it had been given a clean bill of health and declared fit for the Albert Hall, it was being subjected to close scrutiny. Alex was looking down at his feet. 'Daddy, it's got three pedals. Why has it got three pedals, daddy?'

'Ah, well, you see,' he said, sitting back and stretching expansively, pleased to be able to offer his sage explanation for this piano-esque curiosity, 'this piano was made in the Isle of Man. As you know, everyone on the Isle of Man has three legs and so is fully equipped to take advantage of the three-pedal Bechstein.'

'Do they *really* have three legs, Uncle George?' asked Celandine, saucer eyes widening by the second.

'Oh, yes,' he said, sitting back and smiling, eyes half-closed and fingers intertwined. 'It's a wonderful sight to see the Isle of Man pianists when they get going on a particularly dazzling bit of Chopin, their three legs going up and down like Billy-o.'

'*Do* they Auntie Rosalind?'

'No, of course not. George stop filling the girls' heads with such rubbish.'

'Of course, it can get a bit difficult at dances,' he went on, undeterred. 'What with six legs whirling around instead of the usual four they can get into a terrible tangle and end up in a heap on the floor. Mind you, the Manx cat is a sight to behold; three legs and no tail, they tend to go round and round in circles rather a lot. Once, when I was playing the piano at a dance in the Isle of Man—'

'George!'

***

Of course the main purpose of acquiring this very expensive leviathan was to allow Celandine to continue her studies. It followed that they should somehow or other engage a teacher. Scanning the local paper yielded very little of promise. There was an old chap in Sydenham that George knew of who gave lessons but as he was nearly ninety and deafer than Ludwig van, he didn't hold out much hope for him as a possible candidate. Besides, he was too far away. It was while he was in church the day before listening to Humpidge's usual drivel that he, in between thoughts of apostasy, had the idea of speaking to the organist to see if he knew of any suitable teachers in the area. At the end of the service he went in search of him to try to 'beard him in his organ loft' as it were. 'Jesu Joy of Mans' Desiring' was wafting gently around the church as he approached the organ screen. As the last notes died away, he made his presence known. He cleared his throat. 'Excuse me,' he said. 'Might I have a word?'

The organist turned round, a little startled at this intrusion into his reverie. 'Of course, sir. How may I be of assistance?' He stood up as he spoke. A tall, thin, academic looking young man of about twenty-five. He wore round, metal-rimmed spectacles. At first George wasn't quite sure but he got the impression he wasn't English.

'I'm sorry to disturb you,' he went on, 'George Chesshyre.' He held his hand out to him.

'Eugene Rickenbacker. I'm glad to know you, sir.' He responded to George's offered hand.

Of course. It suddenly dawned on him. This young man was an American! 'I must congratulate you on your fine organ-playing,' he said.

'Why, thank you kindly, sir.' He smiled. 'It's a fine instrument, sir. It has all the latest appointments and is powered by electricity sir.'

'Extraordinary!' said George. 'You don't have to rely on someone pumping the bellows, then?'

'Oh, no indeed, sir. You can play this organ for as long as you please and there is no-one to complain about getting aching arms. The Reverend Humpidge has been very kind letting me practise on it and I repay him by playing for his services on Sunday, him not having a regular organist right now.'

'Ah, I take it you're a music student, then?'

'Yes, sir. I'm studying for my doctorate at the Royal College of Music right here in town.'

Clearly George was in the presence of genius and was a little over-awed at this young man's prodigious abilities yet he seemed very unassuming and almost shy. He thanked him for his time and turned to go when he suddenly remembered the reason for introducing himself. The young man had begun to gather his music together when George said rather hesitantly, 'I say, I don't suppose you know of a good piano teacher in the local area?'

Eugene stopped his gathering and frowned. 'Why, no sir, I'm sorry to say I do not. I'm not really that familiar with the neighbourhood.'

'Ah, no matter,' said George. 'I shall have to continue my hunt. My niece has recently returned from India and her mother's keen for her to continue her studies.'

'Well, sir,' said Eugene hesitantly, 'I do a little teaching. Just to help with school fees a little. I'd be glad to meet with the young lady with your permission, sir.'

George was truly taken aback. It hadn't occurred to him that this young man could teach or even that he'd consider it. If he was studying for a doctorate at the RCM he surely wouldn't want to get involved in some pretty elementary key-bashing. However, he wasn't going to let an opportunity slip through his fingers. He'd ask him to come back to the house after the service the following Sunday. 'Come to lunch,' he heard himself say. 'You can try out my new Bechstein.' At that moment he knew he had the right man. The mere mention of the word 'Bechstein' caused him to stop in his tracks, his eyes widened and a big smile spread across his face.

'A Bechstein, sir?'

'Yes,' said George, nonchalantly. 'Concert Grand. Brand new. Of course I looked at Steinways and Bosendorfers but Bechstein is the fellow for me. Wouldn't have any other make in the house.'

There was a big smile on George's face too as he opened the front door. The others, tired of waiting, had left church before him and were already gathering in the dining room where the promise of a roast chicken was about to be fulfilled. He savoured the moments before he delivered his *coup de theatre*.

'George, there you are. Where have you been? We thought you'd got lost again, I was about to send the girls out to look for you,' said Rosalind as she broke off from speaking to Mrs Sprackett.

'Got lost? What on earth do you mean?' said George, pretending to be annoyed. 'Can't get lost coming back from church. I do know where I live.'

'Well, you didn't not long ago. I had to send Alex and Vicky out to find you that time.'

'Ridiculous. Of course I knew where I lived. Momentary aberration, that's all.' At that moment, to everyone's amazement, Vicky and Alex who had been giggling together in the corner suddenly broke into song:

> 'Dillied and dallied,
> Dallied and dillied,
> Lost me way and don't know where to roam.
> Oh, you can't trust a copper like the old time specials
> When you can't find your way home!
> Stopped off to have one at the George and Dragon
> Now I can't find my way home!'

'Very funny,' said George sarcastically as the hilarity subsided. 'If you're so bloomin' clever I'll pack you both off to perform in the music halls. See how you like that, performing every night in front of a rowdy crowd.'

'Ooh, can we daddy? We know lots of songs, don't we Vicks?'

'Ooh, yes! Let's do that new one. One, two three …'

> 'Our parlour wanted papering,
> And pa said it was waste,
> To get the paper hangers in
> And so he made some paste.
> He bought some rolls of paper,
> Got a ladder and a brush,
> And with our Mother's nightgown on
> At it he made a rush –

When father papered the parlour
You couldn't see pa for paste,
Dabbing it here, dabbing it there
There was paste and paper everywhere,
Mother was stuck to the ceiling
And the kids were stuck to the floor,
You never saw a bloomin' family
So stuck up before!'

'Really!' said LD who had been listening in the wings. 'I've never heard anything so low and vulgar. Celandine, cover your ears!'

Celandine was too busy covering her mouth and trying unsuccessfully not to laugh.

'Rosalind, I can't think where those girls pick up such things. If they carry on like this they'll end up in the workhouse and no man will look at them.'

'Oh, Clemmie, it's just a bit of fun,' said Rosalind, laughing. 'And you have to admit they do sing very well.'

'They'd be far better off applying themselves to singing something more uplifting.'

'What I should like to know,' said George, 'is where you two heard such songs in the first place.'

'Oh, here and there,' said Vicky airily.

'Round and about,' said Alex dismissively.

Now George was a pretty astute fellow and not much got past him despite being habitually made fun of. No-one realised it but he saw a fleeting but knowing look exchanged between Alex and Vicky and Polly and Dolly who had been watching the goings-on from the safety of the kitchen doorway.

'Well, wherever you've been, you're here now,' said Rosalind bringing them all back to reality. 'Are you ready to carve the chicken?'

In George's experience the chicken was a tricky little customer. It differed from the usual Sunday joint in that it was roasted whole and was therefore comprised of many different angles, curves and elevations. Of course you'd have difficulty roasting a whole pig or cow or sheep in a modern kitchen which is why those animals are already cut up into convenient joints ready for the oven. But a chicken is different. It is small enough to be roasted whole and the entire bird is presented on a dish ready to be expertly divided up. Therein lies the difficulty. With a joint of topside, for instance, everybody gets pretty much the same cut. It's the same at the beginning as it is at the end and there are no quarrels amongst the hungry throng. But with chicken things are very different. There's breast meat, leg meat (whole or carved) wings, white meat, dark meat, skin, no skin, a wishbone, stuffing – the list is endless. The squabbles can be fearsome. A potential culinary cacophony can easily get out of hand and, of course, you are to blame when diners don't receive the cuts they wanted or think they deserved. Then, in addition, you have to remember that the chicken may well have to do duty for a cold lunch the next day; it's bones might be needed for stock or soup if there's enough left and a chicken sandwich late at night with a glass of single malt finishes the day off splendidly.

Through long and bitter experience, George had found that the best way of dealing with this potential conflict was to get the thing carved up on the sideboard and its constituent parts placed on a warm serving plate. Then everyone could help themselves thus avoiding any personal opprobrium. By this method he usually ended up with a leg, which suited him fine, together with some of Mrs Sprackett's delectable sage and onion stuffing which wasn't universally popular amongst those with a more delicate sense of taste; Mrs. Sprackett sometimes included a fairly powerful measure of garlic in the recipe, an idea she had picked up from a friend who had served in the kitchen of a French lady.

'What *were* you doing after we'd left the church, George?' asked Rosalind as the great division of the chicken concluded.

'Aha!' he said with an air of self-satisfaction. 'I had a little chat with the organist.'

'I hope you didn't ask him if you could have a go, daddy,' said Vicky as she pulled the wishbone with Celandine who had turned very pale at the prospect of having to make a wish. 'We haven't forgotten how you got your shoe stuck in the pedals at St Matthews.'

He ignored this attempt at defamation. 'It seems he teaches the piano, he's much in demand and, after considerable persuasion on my behalf he has agreed to visit next Sunday afternoon for a trial lesson. Celandine has her piano teacher!' He beamed at the little wraith who was holding the victorious half of the wishbone. A little colour had come back into her cheeks. She didn't have to reveal the nature of her wish.

'Oh, that's wonderful, George,' said Rosalind. 'How clever! I would never have thought of that! Isn't that exciting news, Clemmie?'

'Humph,' was the not unexpected response from Clementine. 'I suppose he's expensive?'

'We haven't agreed terms yet,' said George. 'We can discuss it when he comes next week. I've invited him to lunch.'

Another "Humph". 'Very rash. We know nothing about him. He could be masquerading as a piano teacher for all we know.'

'Clementine, he has very high qualifications,' said George with an air of condescension. 'He's studying for his doctorate at the Royal College of Music.' He beamed with satisfaction around the table.

Yet another "Humph". 'Student, is he? Well, he can't be much good if he's not qualified. He'll be a ruffian I'll be bound.'

'Clementine, he has impeccable manners. And – he's an American.'

'I don't like Americans. I knew one once. Loud and common.'

'Well, I assure you this one is neither loud nor common. He's a very reserved young man.'

'And does he have a name – this impeccably reserved young man?'

'Of course. His name is Eugene Rickenbacker.'

A stunned silence. Then peals of laughter so long and loud that Tarporley, who had been gazing longingly at the chicken, ran out of the house and hid in the hedge, only reappearing when he was sure that the commotion had died down and it was safe to do so.

Tuesday August 29th 1911

George was glad to get home that evening. Another baking, sweltering day and he was looking forward to his customary soak as soon as he got in. As he walked up the driveway he was surprised to see a bicycle propped up against the porch. The mystery was soon solved when he went through to the conservatory and saw Humpidge sipping tea and eating cake. George presumed the bicycle to be his but how he managed to ride it at his considerably advanced years was a further mystery and he looked forward to watching him depart on it in due course.

'Ah, George, there you are.' The customary greeting and peck on the cheek. 'We have a visitor. The Reverend Humpidge has called in to see us. Isn't that nice of him?'

'SPLENDID! SPLENDID!' said George, shaking his hand and wearing a forced grin. 'I'M VERY PLEASED TO MEET YOU VICAR. NO, DON'T GET UP.' Humpidge had somehow managed to wedge himself into a chair that was far too low for him and he resembled a beetle unsuccessfully trying to right itself as he tried to extricate himself from his sitting position.

'HOW D'YOU DO, CHESSHYRE?' he said and George was pleased and relieved to be able to understand him. In fact he spoke so loudly and clearly that he thought the whole of Scattersdale Avenue heard.

'VERY WELL, THANK YOU, VICAR. I HOPE MY WIFE IS LOOKING AFTER YOU.'

'There's no need to shout, George,' said Rosalind aside, giving him a poke.

'But he's shouting at me.'

'He probably thinks you're deaf, George.'

'Me, deaf? I thought he was deaf.'

'Just speak normally, George.'

Meanwhile Humpidge was occupied with a slice of Mrs Sprackett's Victoria sponge. 'Eh? Oh, yes. Capital. Splendid cake. Had two slices.'

George was relieved to note that the cake seemed to have had the effect of lowering the volume by quite a few decibels. 'We always enjoy your sermons, don't we dear?' he said ingratiatingly, wringing his hands and smiling grotesquely.

'Very uplifting,' agreed Rosalind with an altogether sweeter and more genuine smile.

'And inspiring,' added George.

Humpidge looked pleased. 'Capital!' he said 'Thought I'd better look in as you're new. Wife's been telling me you come from Swindon.'

'No, *Sydenham*, vicar,' corrected Rosalind.

'That's right,' Humpidge frowned. 'I went to Swindon once. Got lost. Wrong train. Look here, my organist, what's his name, Rabbitsplicer, tells me he had an interesting conversation with you, Chesshyre. Teaching you the organ, I hear.'

'No, vicar, he's going to teach our niece, Celandine. The piano.' This was obviously going to be difficult.

'Ah, yes. That's right. Splendid fellow. Austrian, you know. Wouldn't think it. Speaks English. You'll get on well with him. Organ's at your disposal old man. Electric bellows, you know. I don't understand it myself but I suppose we must move with the times, eh, Chesshyre? Well, I must get on. Excellent cake. Had two slices!'

George and Rosalind helped him out of his chair and he tottered out to where his bicycle was parked. To George's astonishment he mounted it expertly and rode purposefully up the street with a wave and barely a wobble. If only Vicky and Alex had been around to see how it was done.

Wednesday August 30th 1911

Something of a vexing question had been at the back of George's mind for a while. All the business with Clementine and Celandine had caused him to take his eye off the ball regarding Vicky and Alex. Two lovelier girls you could not wish to meet. They had grown into elegant, well-mannered (usually), polished young ladies and were an absolute delight to Rosalind and him. The problem was they didn't actually *do* anything. Rosalind had reminded him the other day that it would soon be their twentieth birthday. This caught him up short in his tracks. He had the vague notion that they were about fifteen or something like that. Then he began to think about it and realised that they hadn't been to school for what really must have been several years. He broached the subject with Rosalind when he got home that evening.

'Where are they who must be obeyed?' he asked, taking off his jacket in the hallway.

'If you mean the girls,' said Rosalind with mock disapproval, 'they've gone next door to Mrs McGillycuddy's. She invited them in to look at her new aquarium. The finest in the district, apparently.'

George said he should have been disappointed if it had been anything less. 'Well, I hope they don't come back wanting any goldfish,' he said. 'They wouldn't last five minutes here with Tarporley lurking about. I haven't forgotten the kipper fiasco. What's that smell?'

'Curried chicken with boiled rice. Mrs Sprackett thought it would be a nice treat for Clemmie and Celandine. Come through to the conservatory. We're having dinner out there again as it's such a lovely evening.'

He grimaced and followed dutifully. 'Well, I hope it's not too hot. Nearly blew my bloomin' head off last time.'

She turned, smiled and pushed him playfully. 'Don't be such a *grouch*, George. Mrs Sprackett assured me it wouldn't be too hot because she knows Celandine has a delicate constitution.'

A long face. 'Really? What about my constitution? Last night's liver and onions were repeating on me right up until this afternoon. I had terrible indigestion last night as well.'

A frown and a poke. 'Oh, George don't go *on* so. You're becoming very grumpy recently.'

George went on, undeterred. 'Wouldn't surprise me to learn that I had an ulcer. I don't suppose we've got any Epsom salts?'

'There's some in the medicine cupboard. You can have a dose after dinner if you still feel liverish.'

'I feel liverish and *onionish*. I wish this blasted weather would break. Oh for a crack of thunder and a jolly good downpour.'

'I'm sure it will, George. It's the beginning of September tomorrow. It's bound to start getting cooler soon. Clemmie was saying that we need to get Celandine enrolled in a suitable school.'

'I thought she'd left school.'

'Of course not. Clemmie wants her to continue her education over here. She had a private tutor in India.'

'Oh. I suppose she'll have to go to a private school over here then? More expense.'

'Of course. Clemmie said she can pay for the fees when Bertie's life insurance pays out.'

George wasn't convinced. 'Hmm. Sounds like there's going to be a lot of calls on Bertie's life insurance. It's got to cover half the cost of the piano, don't forget. Makes me wonder whether she really did do him in in order to get her hands on the spondulicks.'

'Oh *George!* Please don't keep saying that. You do have some wicked thoughts sometimes you know.'

'Well, you have to wonder, don't you? You're not trying to do the same thing to me are you? Slowly poisoning me with antimony like that poor fellow over in Balham a few years ago. Is that what you're doing? Antimony in the curried chicken? No wonder I feel liverish.'

'George, you're impossible. Strychnine in your cocoa's more my style. Much quicker and I wouldn't have to wait ages to get my hands on your life insurance.'

'Aha! But how do you know I've got any?'

'Because you signed the cheque for the renewal premium last week.'

'Touché, Ros old girl! I think I'll make my own cocoa tonight.'

Rosalind triumphant, George deflated.

At this point all thoughts of education, frightful bills and fearful homicides were put aside as Mrs Sprackett appeared with the curried chicken followed closely by Dolly carrying the rice.

Mrs Sprackett beamed. 'Now I do 'ope as 'ow you enjoys this, mum. I made it nice an' mild and not too 'ot so as the young miss can eat it comfortable like if you gets my meaning.'

George was sceptical.

Rosalind was not. 'It smell delicious, Mrs Sprackett. I'm sure we shall all enjoy it,' she said taking the lid off the tureen.

Mrs Sprackett was in a reflective mood. 'Sprackett, my late 'usband, Gawd rest 'is soul, used to enjoy my curried chicken once in a way. "Daisy, old gel," 'e used to say, "Your curried chicken is the best I've tasted this side of Poundacherries." Twenty five years in the Poona 'orse, 'e was. Course, it killed 'im in the end. First winter back in England 'e got the *newmownila*. Dead within a week 'e was. Oh, it do seem 'ard, don't it mum? Dolly! 'urry up with that rice.'

This monologue was delivered without the apparent need for a reply and Mrs Sprackett scuttled back into the kitchen on the pretext of checking to see whether the blancmange had set.

George was a great believer in giving credit where it was due and he had to say that the curried chicken with rice was superb. Not hot but nicely spiced and with a selection of home-made chutneys from recipes in Mrs Sprackett's secret volume of culinary spells. She really was the most excellent cook and any household would be lucky to have her. By the time he'd finished a suitably cool bottle of Bass he'd forgotten all about his dyspepsia, not to mention life insurance and dying horribly from unspeakable poisons.

Vicky and Alex had returned from Mrs McGillycuddy's chattering excitedly about fish and even Clemmie showed signs of interest. Celandine had dug up a book of Chopin études from somewhere and was studying it intently, apparently not moved by things of a piscatory nature. All this had quite put him off his stroke and diverted him from the subject he had intended to bring up. Nevertheless, it would have to be addressed sooner or later.

CHAPTER SEVEN

~ Old Mortality

—e·9—

'Far from the madding crowd's ignoble strife
Their sober wishes never learn'd to stray;
Along the cool sequester'd vale of life
They kept the noiseless tenor of their way.'

Thomas Gray *'Elegy in a Country Churchyard'*

Thursday August 31st 1911

There was sad news when George arrived at the office. Hector Grantley looked in to tell him that Sam Kitcat had died. George had known Sam for many years. He was a senior partner in the firm but had taken early retirement due to ill health. He'd left town and moved out into the country; George had rather lost touch over time. The funeral was the following Thursday and he thought he ought to go. He'd get Simnel and Warbeck to sort out the details. Give them something useful to do instead of throwing paper darts around the office when they thought he wasn't looking.

George normally got into the office about nine and today was no exception. It was a quiet morning, unremarkable except for the news about Sam. At about half past ten Mrs Gotobed arrived with his cup of tea and two Bath Olivers. Mrs Gotobed had been with the firm since the Battle of Waterloo and was fiercely loyal. An enthusiast of the 'one-way conversation' school, she would talk 'at' you for about five minutes, usually about the state of her health. On this particular morning she informed George that she had a 'headache in her side'. As the monologue persisted uninterrupted, George was unable to sympathise. Mrs Gotobed rattled off as quickly as she had arrived, the 'headache in her side' apparently causing no impediment of perambulation.

George stirred his tea. He'd arranged for his desk to be moved so that it was no longer in the full glare of the sun during the afternoon. The window was still stuck fast and no blinds or shutters had reappeared. He dipped a Bath Oliver and took a satisfying bite. (Rosalind deplored this as 'vulgar' and Lady Disdain thought it beyond the pale so he was confined to practising this proletarian habit at the office.) Sitting back in his chair he entered something of a brown study. He mused for a moment or two over the name of the firm. The firm he had served for several decades. It occurred to him that a peculiarity of stockbroking firms was that many of them were named after people you'd never heard of. Take his firm for instance: Fysh, Fysh, Iceberg and Fysh. He'd never met anyone connected remotely with the firm with any of those names. Even when he joined back in '78 the most decrepit and crusty old partners were Benjamin Panmure and Luke Dreyfuss. He'd never come across a Fysh, salt or freshwater, neither had he met, nor known of, an Iceberg.

Of course everything had got so *fast* these days. They'd had telephones in the office for several years and at first they seldom rang but George noticed recently that they had developed a tendency to go off far too often during the day. It could be quite a nuisance when you were trying to concentrate on some particularly tricky dividend calculation, unravelling some blunder of Warbeck's or Simnel's or endeavouring to decipher some arcane investment request from a new client. On top of that Rosalind had taken to telephoning him frequently in order to consult him about some aspect of the evening's menu or to tell him that the 'Thermoboil' had got into a sulk; everyone was frightened to go near it and did he think he could come home early to put it right?

Then there were the typewriters. Goodness didn't they make a clatter! At first they just had one or two and they were tucked away in a side office but now they had a typing *pool*. The previous week he had counted ten young women bashing away and making the devil of a din. What with that and the electric telegraph machine rattling away, sometimes you could hardly hear yourself think. He tried to keep the door to his office closed as much as possible but with the almost infernal hot weather he had to try to encourage as much of a draught of fresh air as possible blowing through the office.

The typists were ruled with a rod of iron by Miss Antrobus and they were not supposed to talk to each other but they found ways round that. A lot of chattering went on when she was out of the room and smirking and cheeky looks abounded if George happened to pass by. It was singularly puzzling how often Warbeck and Simnel appeared to find it necessary to consult one or more of the young women, the results of which usually culminated in peals of not very well-suppressed laughter.

He'd finish in 1916 but might decide to wind things up before that. Every day London seemed to get busier and more crowded. There was noisy, smelly motor traffic everywhere, the trains were packed and more and more young women seemed to be coming into town. When he started it was unusual to see a woman in the City but now they were everywhere. Not that he objected. It was quite right that women should be independent and have careers. He wished Vicky and Alex would take a leaf out of those modern, go-ahead girls' books. The suffragette business was getting a bit out of hand, though. He had accidentally got caught up in a 'rally' recently and got some strange looks from the Pankhurstians. He just hoped the government would jolly well hurry up and give the women the vote then perhaps they'd all get a bit of peace.

Of course, it wasn't just the young women who had 'modern' ideas. Young chaps seemed to have forgotten how to behave with decorum and show respect for their elders. It wasn't like that when he was young. If he had spoken to his superiors in the way Warbeck and Simnel sometimes spoke to him he'd have been out on his ear. He blamed the music hall. Some of the acts were all right but there were some very low comedians and sometimes their 'jokes' found their way into the office. He wouldn't have been at all surprised if it was these that were making the typists laugh.

No. On the whole it was all getting too fast for him. Rosalind had said he was an old fogey and that he should move with the times. Well, the times could move on perfectly happily without George Hector Chesshyre, thank you very much. After Sam's funeral he'd take the opportunity to have a look round at the countryside. It might just be the spot where Rosalind and he could settle down quietly. Things didn't move so fast in the country. They did things differently there. That would suit him down to the ground. If Lady Disdain decided to stay in London, well, so much the better.

Sunday September 3rd 1911

There was an unusually prolonged period of washing and bathing this morning. Instructions had been given to Polly that the 'Thermoboil' was to be lit a whole hour earlier than usual. Much grumbling ensued from this edict and Polly was told roundly by Mrs Sprackett that: 'If she didn't like it then she could bloomin' well look for a position elsewhere and see as 'ow she'd like that. Saucy madam.'

George found it impossible to get into either bathroom for his morning shave. During the week he had no difficulty because there was not much stirring amongst the household until after he'd left for the office, but this morning there was rushing and bustling and taps going full bore, curl papers stuck everywhere and exotic perfumes wafting throughout the house from not long after sunrise.

He decided that it would be prudent to get out of the way and let them all get on with it. He had a leisurely breakfast without all the usual Sunday mayhem which had rather conveniently removed itself to the upper floors of the house. Of course all this frantic activity was for the sole benefit of Eugene Rickenbacker who was joining them for lunch. George hoped he knew what he was letting himself in for and would not be so smothered with attention that he would be frightened off and head for the next sailing back to New York.

George was disturbed to note that the scene in the churchyard after the service was quite unseemly. Humpidge was ignored and Rosalind, Vicky, Alex and even Celandine practically mobbed Eugene as he came out of the church. Only Clementine remained detached and aloof but even she let slip a clandestine show of interest when she thought no one was looking. Poor Eugene looked flustered and had turned bright pink. George felt duty bound to rescue him. He somehow managed to insert himself between him, Vicky and Alex and led him to a temporary place of safety. Eventually things calmed down and they made their way back to the house, Eugene, despite George's valiant efforts, entrapped at either arm by Vicky and Alex.

Things were no more serene back at the house. A state of chaos reigned in the kitchen. There was a banging and clattering of pans, raised voices from Polly and Dolly and orders being shouted by Mrs Sprackett. Eugene stood in the hallway looking bemused and clutching his hat which he had dutifully and respectfully removed on entering the house as befits all well-bred Americans and not common at all. George half expected him to make a run for it. What on earth did he think he'd let himself in for? He didn't have much time to plan his escape for within moments Vicky and Alex were herding him into the dining room.

'We're so excited you could come, Mr Rackenbicker,' said Vicky.

'We've been looking forward to it all week!' said Alex.

'Are you really American, Mr Reckenbocker?' asked Vicky.

'Yes, ma'am,' said Eugene as he was ushered towards the dining table.

'Do you know any Red Indians?' asked Vicky, hopefully.

'No ma'am. No Red Indians in Boston to my knowledge.'

'Perhaps he knows Buffalo Bill,' said Alex to Vicky.

'Do you know Buffalo Bill, Mr Rockinbecker?' asked Vicky.

'Never had the pleasure, ma'am. And, please, call me Eugene.'

A short outbreak of giggling.

'Do you like roast chicken, Eugene?' asked Vicky.

'Why, yes ma'am. Thank you ma'am.'

'Oh, good. Mrs Sprackett's cooked a really big one to-day. I saw it yesterday when it was delivered. But you mustn't mind daddy. He's hopeless at carving chickens, isn't he Alex?'

'Oh, yes. Hopeless! The last time we had one it shot across the table and landed in Aunt Clemmie's lap!'

A shocked look from Eugene. Peals of laughter from the girls.

At that moment Polly came into the dining room. 'Beggin' your pardon, mum,' she said addressing Rosalind who was trying rather unsuccessfully to placate Clementine after the chicken outrage, 'but Mrs Sprackett would like to know as 'ow Mr Knickerbocker is particler, like, to honion soup.'

'Just bring the tureen through, Polly; I'm sure Mr Rickenbacker will enjoy it.'

'Very good, mum. Only Mrs Sprackett is most concerned, like, because she forgot she put quite a lot of honion in it and she didn't know as 'ow Hamerican gen'lemen likes honions or not.'

'I'm sure it will be excellent, Polly.'

'Very good, mum. It's just that Mrs Sprackett 'ad the notion, like, that honions might give 'im the hindigestion like as 'ow the master was afflicted most terrible bad the other night.'

George sighed. If they were going to have this much fuss and trouble over the bally soup he dreaded to think how the rest of the lunch would progress. As it turned out, however, they got through the soup without incident, the chicken behaved itself and didn't fly off anywhere, and, despite aspersions cruelly cast regarding George's carving skills, everyone received the cut requested to their complete satisfaction. Space was somehow found for a superb apple tart and custard and even the cheese board proved popular with some excellent strong Cheddar and a ripe, tangy Stilton. Bass & Co provided the beer with a light Sauternes ('A very good year,' according to George. 'Too sweet,' according to Lady Disdain) for the ladies. A jug of Mrs Sprackett's noted lemonade was enjoyed by Celandine who had, again, been victorious in a wishbone duel with Alex.

With everyone full from the feast and no apparent unwanted side effects from the dangerous onions it was approaching three o'clock before the subject of piano lessons was broached. Surprisingly it was Celandine herself who brought the subject up. 'Excuse me Mr Rickenbacker,' she said, gravely, approaching his seat. 'Would you play one of these for us, please?' She held out the book of Chopin études she had been studying previously.

Eugene looked startled for a moment having been deep in conversation with Vicky and Alex about freshwater fish and whether a trout could be kept in a goldfish bowl. 'Pardon me, miss; why, I'd be happy to, if I have the kind permission of your mother and uncle.'

George beamed and swelled visibly. What a capital chap Rickenbacker was. His manners were beyond reproach and he'd seldom encountered such politeness. He wondered whether all Bostonians were so cultured. Warbeck and Simnel could certainly learn a lot from him. He cast a condescending smile towards Clementine as if to say: 'What do you think of my loud and common American now?' She returned his smile with a glare. 'What a splendid idea!' said George, not the least put out and anxious to hear the new Bechstein put through its paces. 'Why don't we all go through to the music room? Perhaps Mrs Sprackett will arrange some coffee for us.'

The Bechstein had been slumbering quietly since it had been tuned. Having been allowed to settle for a few days, it was a magnificent sight as George opened the music room door. He could see immediately that Eugene was impressed. 'Sir, this is a beautiful instrument,' he said. 'May I?'

'Of course, feel free.' said George, reverently propping up the top board and lifting the fall board to reveal the keys.

'Will you play this one, please?' asked Celandine, handing the book to Eugene. He smiled at the little wraith and took it without a word; placed it on the music stand and began to play Étude Op. 10, No. 3. 'Tristesse'. The combination of Chopin, Eugene and Bechstein was verging on magical. The gorgeous melody came to life under Eugene's fingers. The Bechstein breathed and spoke in sweet, shimmering tones. It was almost as though the Warsaw genius was in the room with them that hot, sultry September afternoon.

The last notes died away and everyone stood transfixed. George's bank account might have been lighter by 295 guineas but at that moment it was worth every last penny.

George had heard it said that the experiencing of certain events in one's life could give the impression of making time stand still.

This was surely one of those moments.

'Humph. You'll never play like that. Not in a month of

Sundays.' Clementine looked contemptuously at Celandine who had been standing there in a reverie of her own. Her face fell and she dissolved into tears. George had never felt more capable of murder in his life.

CHAPTER EIGHT ~

~ Beer and the Deity

—❧❧—

'Here in the country's heart
Where the grass is green,
Life is the same sweet life
As it ere hath been.'

Norman Rowland Gale
'The Country Faith'

Wednesday 6th September 1911

George was writing a post card by oil light in his room at the 'Pig & Whistle', Chipping Loosely, somewhere in Gloucestershire. It really had been the most *trying* day. He had made a grave error in entrusting Simnel and Warbeck to look into the travel arrangements for him regarding Sam Kitcat's funeral. When he had got into the office the previous morning and had asked Simnel (Warbeck hadn't been seen since the previous Friday) whether he had looked up the train timetables for him he affected to remember nothing of the request. 'But I'll get onto it straight away,' he said. An hour later a piece of paper appeared on George's desk. On it was written, '11:47 or 1:14 from London Bridge. Arrive 1:06 or 2:38. Good hotels in the town; convenient to the railway station. A Telegraph Station.' Obviously copied verbatim from Bradshaw's so presumably reliable, thought George. His opinion of Simnel softened slightly. Half an hour later he poked his head round George's door to tell him that he had booked him into 'The George' for two nights and was this agreeable to him? He had apparently underestimated the boy and thanked him for his initiative. He would have a leisurely journey down, attend the funeral the next day, not have to worry about rushing back to town and travel back on Friday morning ready for the weekend.

Of course George didn't like having to attend funerals. They could be the most *difficult* affairs especially if the deceased had a large family and had expired prematurely. However, Sam was a confirmed bachelor and he didn't anticipate a large turnout. He expected it to be a fairly quiet ceremony and that it would all go off quite smoothly without the customary wailing and gnashing of teeth. He hesitated to think it but he had almost been looking forward to getting out of town for a couple of days. The heat showed no signs of letting up and he felt sure the air would be fresher and cooler down in the country. (It wasn't.) Rosalind was willing to accompany him but after discussing it they decided it would be best if she stayed at home to keep an eye on things. Goodness knows what mayhem might ensue in their absence and he wouldn't have been able to relax and enjoy the funeral properly not knowing what the girls and Lady Disdain might get up to. Then he was fearful for the safety of his new Bechstein. He had given Celandine *carte blanche* to play it whenever she wanted to and he knew she would treat it with the respect and reverence it deserved but he had grave reservations about the twins and what plots they might have hatched. For all he knew he might return to find an aquarium installed on top and Tarporley trying desperately to get his paws on a freshwater trout.

'Glad confident morning!' Browning's words rang round his head as he set off for London Bridge. He had decided to catch the 11:47 and resisted the temptation to go into the office first. Things were still pretty quiet but would probably buck up about the middle of the month. Still in a buoyant mood he made his way to the ticket office.

'First Class return to Stroud please,' he said breezily to the booking clerk.

He frowned. 'Never heard it called that before,' he said.

'I beg your pardon?' said George.

'Strood. Never heard it called "Stroud" before.'

'But it is "Stroud"; I don't want to go to "Strood".'

The clerk looked at George in a sort of self-satisfied way, reminiscent of ticket-collectors and stationary police constables. 'Well, there's no "Stroud" on this line,' he said, enjoying having the upper-hand in the discussion. 'Are you sure you don't want to go to Strood?' He half-closed one eye and moved closer to the window.

'Positive. Stroud. It's in Gloucestershire.' George met the clerk's gaze and moved closer in. He hoped he wasn't about to enter into another Dormin Road state of confusion.

The clerk pursed his lips and drew breath. 'Just a moment, sir.' He consulted a large volume of time-tables. Pages were flicked back and forth and a moistened finger moved quickly up and down unseen columns innumerable times.

'Ah!' he said finally. George was aware of a long, impatient queue forming behind him. 'Here we are. "Stroud"; It's on the Great Western. You need to go to Paddington, sir.' Another self-satisfied beam shone through the window.

George seethed. Simnel had better keep out of his way for the next few months.

He couldn't be bothered to work out how to get to Paddington; besides, his case, although small, was getting heavy and the weather was getting hotter as it approached mid-day, so he managed to hail a cab at the station entrance and sat back with some relief as they crossed London Bridge and negotiated the City *en route* for Paddington. Luckily the driver was of the taciturn variety and he was spared the political, social and sport monologue so beloved of Alf, entertaining though it was.

When they arrived at Paddington he repeated the exercise of an hour earlier. 'First Class return to *Stroud* please,' he said to the second booking clerk. He made this request with some trepidation in the fear that he was about to be sent off to Euston or St Pancras or Gare du Nord.

Fortunately there were no awkward queries or even a raised eyebrow and the clerk punched a ticket immediately and decisively. '21/11, please,' he said.

'What time is the next train?' asked George, opening his wallet and handing over a white fiver.

'2:16. Change at Swindon.'

'Isn't there a straight through one?'

'Not until 4:58, sir.'

This was going to turn out to be a long day, thought George.

Luckily the train was already standing at the platform and he found an empty compartment about half way along. It was a corridor train and very comfortable after the suburban carriages he had been used to. The pleasant but parched countryside passed by rapidly and just before half-past three the train slowed and drew into Swindon. He was rather sorry to leave his compartment which he had occupied all to himself from Paddington but now had to hunt down his connection to Stroud. On enquiry he discovered it departed just before four so he stretched his legs for a few minutes after negotiating the underpass which led to his platform. He suddenly remembered how Humpidge had got lost here and supposed he could understand how such a thing could happen. Swindon was an extensive station with many platforms. He watched, fascinated, at the several arrivals and departures that drew in and out even in the short time he had to wait.

George thought the Great Western engines to be handsome beasts. Many of them were painted in an attractive mid-green and there was much copper pipework and burnished brass. Polly and Dolly would have their work cut out cleaning that lot. As he waited, a London-bound express pulled in with an engine named 'Polar Star' at the head. It's nameplate with individual brass letters glittered in the afternoon sun. There was a hustle and bustle as passengers alighted and others embarked, then there was a sharp whistle and 'Polar Star' moved off smartly with a purposeful bark from her chimney. George thought how wonderful it must be to be an engine driver, being in control of so much pent-up power and unleashing it at will. 'Polar Star' had just disappeared over the horizon when a goods train hove into view. Its engine was black and grimy, a volcano of dirty smoke shooting from its chimney. As it passed at about ten miles per hour with a deafening roaring and clanking, the driver and fireman working furiously to keep the beast moving, their faces blackened and full of perspiration, George decided that, on the whole, he preferred the stockbroker's life.

Soon his own train approached the station. He wondered whether its engine, too, would have an evocative name. It did. As it drew slowly in he could barely believe his eyes. He was about to board a train for Stroud pulled by No. 2907 – 'Lady Disdain'. Was there no escape?

Despite her unfortunate name, 'Lady Disdain' proved to be a willing performer and they bowled along at a respectable clip. The landscape was flat and rather featureless but pleasant enough although the relentless sun had taken its toll and there wasn't much evidence of 'England's green and pleasant land'. Eventually they plunged into a long tunnel and emerged into a steep-sided valley. Heavily wooded, with houses apparently growing out of the hillside, they threaded their way through a curious mixture of bucolic charm and smoky mills. They drew to a halt at Stroud and, following the signs to the town, George crossed the footbridge in search of a cab. As he was no longer to stay at the 'George' in Strood some two hundred miles away he would have to make some pretty hasty alternative arrangements. Fortunately there was a cab rank in the station forecourt and several were lined up in anticipation of the train from Swindon. Managing to secure one he enquired of the driver whether he knew Chipping Loosely.

'I do, zur,' came the reply.

'Is it very far from here?' asked George.

'About three mile, zur,' he said.

'Good. Could you take me there, please?'

'I can, zur.'

He settled back in the cab for the second time that day. Soon they had left the town and were heading down a leafy country lane. He leaned forward in his seat. 'I don't suppose you know of any hotels near Chipping Loosely?' he asked as they started to climb a perilously steep looking hill.

'Ah. I don't, zur. Not 'otels. There be the pub, "Pig and Whistle"; they'll put thee up I expect. Long as they bain't vull. Course 'e might be vull. Then again 'e might not be. Can't rightly say. Put you up if 'e bain't vull.'

'Good,' George replied, feeling a little more hopeful. 'If we could go there perhaps you could wait while I make enquiries.'

'Right you are, zur. Course, 'e might be vull. Can't rightly say.'

They continued to ascend what, at times, seemed more like an

Alpine pass. On several occasions they drove round bends so sharp and steep they almost turned back on themselves. George thought it was rather disconcerting.

'This is a very steep hill,' he remarked.

'Ah. It be, zur. Can't go very far round yer without goin' up a steep 'ill.'

'I hope you've got good brakes!' said George somewhat nervously.

'Oh. Ah. They be, zur. Can't go very far round yer without good brakes.'

As the engine laboured and they negotiated yet another steep bend of such acute angle George felt sure the cab would die and topple over, he reflected on what Alf would make of it. There were no hills to speak of around Streatham, at least nothing remotely resembling the terrain they were currently travelling over. There was Streatham Hill, of course, but somehow it didn't seem as formidable as this dusty, narrow track. His driver, however, seemed perfectly at ease and swung the steering wheel expertly as they made their way to the top of that bit of the Cotswolds.

After what seemed to George like an age as they ground slowly ever upwards, the road flattened out and they were amongst open fields again. Dry stone walls lined the route and there seemed to be an awful lot of sheep. Soon a church spire came into view and they drew up outside the 'Pig and Whistle'.

'I'll just go in and make enquiries,' said George.

'Right you are, zur. Course, 'e might be vull.'

George had to lower his head in order to get through the entrance doorway. It led into the bar area which had an air of the 'Marie Celeste' about it. The only sign of life was a tall grandfather clock in one corner ticking solemnly away the hours. After a moment or two there were sounds of life somewhere out in the back and a large man appeared drying a glass. He looked at George with some suspicion.

'Good afternoon,' he said. 'I was wondering if you have any rooms available.'

'Ah. I might,' said the large man, still looking at George with suspicion. 'I shall 'ave to check, zur.'

There was much puffing and blowing as he searched for something under the bar. Eventually he re-emerged, holding a dusty volume which he examined closely while alternately scrutinising a key rack on the wall behind him on which were hung three sets of keys. 'Well, blow me, zur!' he said after much page turning and head scratching. 'You're in luck. I got rooms available. That's a bit o' luck, bain't it?'

George replied that it was, indeed, most fortunate.

'Course, I could a bin vull. It's a bit o' luck that I bain't vull, bain't it?'

George again confirmed that he could not remember when he had last felt so blessed with good fortune. He was quite prepared for these serendipitous celebrations to continue and was contemplating inviting the cab driver in to share in the happy discovery that there was room at the inn when a shrill voice from somewhere offstage burst the bubble of their jubilant moment.

'Amos!'

'The wife.' Amos looked at George with a mixture of resignation, trepidation and an expression which said: 'I'm sure you understand.'

Without waiting for an answer, 'the wife' came through to the bar. A look of thunder turned into a sunny afternoon on seeing George. 'Oh, hello, sir. I didn't realise we 'ad guests. Amos, why didn't you tell me we 'ad guests?'

'Gentleman's only jus' come in my dear.'

'Your husband was just checking to see if you had any rooms available,' George said helpfully.

'Course we got rooms available!'

'I was rather afraid you might be full.'

'Course we ain't full. Amos, wot you bin tellin' 'im?'

'I 'ad t' check, my love.'

''ad t' check? My sainted aunt! When was the last time we 'ad a guest stayin'? Eh? You tell me that! 'ave you seen anyone a-trippin' in an' a-trippin' out? 'ave you took up any 'ot watter t' the bedrooms? 'ave you bin a-helpin' a guest up and down the stairs with their bags? 'ave you sat down of an evenin' an' partaken of victuals with me in the kitchen an' 'eld a conversation with a guest? Now you tell me that Amos Clutterbuck an' you think 'ard before you answer me and go a-lookin' in that book to see if we got rooms available!'

'It don't do no 'arm t' check, my sweetness.'

At that point the door opened and the cab driver came in. 'Beggin' your pardon but be you a-stoppin' then, zur?'

George was momentarily lost for words. He looked first at Amos, then his wife who was looking daggers at Amos. 'Ah, I think so,' he finally managed.

'Because if 'e's vull I s'pose you'd be lookin' t' go somewhere else,' the cab driver said helpfully.

'And perhaps 'e don't want t' go anywhere else,' Mrs Clutterbuck turned her naked vitriolic attention to the cabbie. 'Perhaps 'e'd like t' stay 'ere where we got rooms available. Perhaps the gentleman is tired an' thirsty an' 'ungry an' would prefer not to go anywhere else. Perhaps the gentleman would prefer to stay in a nice quiet room that's available with a comfortable bed. Perhaps the gentleman would prefer to avail 'imself of the comforts an' services of the Pig an' Whistle. Why should any gentlemen want to go somewhere else when 'e can avail 'imself of the comforts an' services of the Pig an' Whistle, that's what I should like to know an' you just think 'ard before you answer that question Ezekiel Farthing!'

'It don't do no 'arm t' check, Mrs C.'

And George thought the 'George and Dragon' was lively!

As his cab disappeared into the distance George suddenly realised that he *was* tired, hungry and very thirsty. Mrs Sprackett had cooked him a very substantial breakfast; 'Seein' as 'ow you're goin' to a funeral which is very tryin' to a person an' the grief exhausts the brain terrible bad'; but chasing around London, five assorted conveyances and ascending perilous, contorted hills had exhausted the body even worse. He was by now anxious to sample the 'comforts and services' of the 'Pig and Whistle' having ascertained beyond doubt that rooms were available and he dared not incur the wrath of Mrs Clutterbuck by intimating that he might prefer to stay elsewhere. His fears were unfounded, however, because her demeanour towards him was sweetness and light.

Having booked him in for two nights she disappeared again after instructing Amos to show him to his room. George followed him as he was bid. Amos puffed and groaned as he ascended the steep, narrow and tortuous stairway which reminded George of the road to the pub itself.

'Mind thy yud, zur,' he turned and said as they got about half way up.

'I beg your pardon?' said George.

'Mind thy yud. Tis low up yer.'

Too late. By the time George had interpreted 'yud' to mean 'head' he had banged it against the doorway at the top of the stairs.

'Yer tis. This do you zur?' Amos, oblivious of George's painful encounter with the lintel, showed him into a surprisingly large bedroom which contained a very substantial looking brass double bedstead, a chest of drawers, a dressing table overlooking the low window and a big old oak wardrobe.

George glanced around approvingly but could not help wondering how they had managed to get all that heavy furniture up the narrow staircase. 'This will do me very well, thank you,' he said.

'Right you are, zur,' Amos said and turned to go. 'If thee bist wantin' anythin' jus' let I know.' His slow, heavy footsteps creaked on the stairway and George put his case on the bed ready to unpack. Pulling his watch from his waistcoat pocket he realised it had just turned six o'clock. He was tired, hungry and thirsty so, taking care to 'mind his yud' he went straight back down to see about something to eat. Entering the bar he surveyed the beer pumps. Mine host was still engaged in drying glasses. 'What can I get you, zur?' he said putting the glass down.

'Do you have draught Bass?' George enquired. (No danger of Rosalind's disapproval out here.)

'No zur. Godsell's 'ouse, we bist.'

'Godsell's?'

'Yes, zur. Godsell's Brewery. Down in the town. Finest beer in the district. By 'eavenly appointment, zur. What does it say at the entrance to the Pearly Gates?'

George was beginning to think the crack on the head had affected his brain. 'I've no idea,' he said, frowning.

'God sells beer!' Amos grinned.

'Ah, yes! I see!' The kindly light shone. 'Most amusing! Ha ha ha!' The *bonhomie* was not entirely false. He must remember this joke and tell Humpidge. A pint of Godsell's Best Pale was pulled expertly and George thought it was some of the best beer he had ever tasted. The cellar had kept it cool and there was a beautiful balance of malt and hops. All he needed now was something to eat. Amos seemed to anticipate his request.

'Come far then, zur?' he asked, taking up his polishing duties again.

'London,' George replied.

'Ah. Thee bist 'ungry, then.'

George took this to be an observation that he required some solid sustenance. 'Indeed I am,' he said, rather proud that he was getting the gist of the local dialect.

Now, Mrs Sprackett was a very good cook and her meals were always delicious and the portions plentiful but what was put in front of George half an hour later very nearly equalled her best. Amos had invited him to share their evening meal. As George took his seat in the kitchen, an enormous rack of beef was brought to the table and Amos set about carving it. Slice after slice was piled on his plate followed by a mountain of roast potatoes, peas, carrots and a Yorkshire pudding almost as big as the county itself. His protestations fell on deaf ears as he was told that, 'As thee's come all the way from that London thee must be 'ungry and thee bist better make a proper job on't!'

Another pint of Godsell's went down very easily indeed but he had to insist on just a small helping of steamed jam pudding and custard. Country air does appear to stimulate your appetite but there are limits.

It was midnight before he got to bed. The evening meal lay rather heavy on his stomach but there was no sign of dyspepsia. Of course that must have been due to the one or two (or maybe three or four, he couldn't remember exactly) glasses of Haig he had enjoyed while relaxing in the lounge and wondering at the stillness of it all. It was so quiet. There was no noise and no hustle and bustle. No rushing crowds hurrying hither and thither. Just the occasional sound of a cow mooing in the distance broke the evening silence. Yes, this was the sort of place Rosalind and he could retire to. She was bound to love it.

Thursday 7th September 1911

The next morning three large sausages, an equal number of bacon rashers, two large slices of fried bread and a fried egg appeared on George's breakfast plate.

It was delicious.

The funeral was at mid-day so he had a chance to have a bit of a poke about the village. There was a green with a pump, several low-gabled Cotswold stone houses grouped around it, a narrow street (wherein resided a baker and butcher), a small Post-Office-cum grocer, a lych-gate leading to the church and a large vicarage covered in ivy. The 'Pig and Whistle' was the only public house and there was no sign of a village school. In fact there was not much sign of life anywhere. At a quarter to twelve he took his place in the church which was pleasantly cool after the heat of the day, by then building to its usual intensity outside. High up in the steeple a muffled bell began to toll and the organist was quietly playing a piece George did not recognise.

Suddenly, silently, he was surrounded by people. The cortege passed slowly down the aisle followed by a woman covered in black attended by two younger women. They took their places in the front pew and the service began. The vicar, even though he must have been all of twelve years old, spoke clearly and movingly and his short sermon was a masterclass in how to retain the attention of the congregation. He must speak to Humpidge about this when he returned, he thought.

Then began the slow procession to the churchyard. The final offices were given and Sam was lowered into his eternal resting place. The congregation began to disperse and he was just starting to wonder what to do next when the black-clad woman approached him. 'Excuse me,' she said. 'Are you Mr Chesshyre?'

'I am, indeed,' George replied not knowing whether to smile or frown at this solemn moment.

'I'm Caroline Fitzpatrick, Samuel's sister. I'm so glad you could come.' She smiled and held out her hand.

'I'm very pleased to meet you,' he said. 'Although under very sad circumstances. Please accept my condolences.'

'Thank you,' she said, her eyes momentarily downcast. 'Not unexpected, I'm afraid. Samuel had been ill for some time as I think you know.'

'Yes,' he said; by now managing to master the art of smiling and frowning at the same time in a sort of sympathetic manner. Rosalind would probably have termed it more pathetic than sympathetic. 'It's been some years now since he left the firm,' he went on regardless. 'I'd rather lost touch, I'm afraid. But I didn't know that he had a sister.'

'Oh, I came along quite a few years later. Something of a shock to our parents, I think.' She smiled as if recalling her childhood days. 'Sam often spoke of you in his more lucid moments. I hope you will come back to the house with us?'

The vexing question of what to do next was instantly solved. He hadn't really relished the thought of going straight back to the 'Pig and Whistle' and the prospect of some gargantuan mid-day feast being immediately laid before him. The sausages were still lying heavy on his stomach, excellent though they were. 'Thank you,' he said. 'I should be honoured.'

She turned and began to walk towards the lych gate. George was steered in the same direction by a discreet arm entwined with his. Rather forward, he thought but perhaps perfectly allowable under the circumstances. Lady Disdain would have reached for the 'Sally Volatty' had she been present. 'The girls will have gone on ahead to get things ready,' she said.

'Your daughters?'

'Yes, Morgana and Guinevere. Of course I love them dearly but they're a bit of a handful at times.'

Morgana and Guinevere? Morgana and *Guinevere?!* Good

Lord! What sort of present-day Arthurian legend was he getting mixed up in here?

'I sympathise,' he said, retaining, with some difficulty, his composure. 'I've got two of my own, Vicky and Alex. About the same age, I should think. He put two and two together. 'Your husband is not with you?' he asked, looking around, half hoping to be rescued but wary at the same time of suddenly coming face-to-face with some red-faced Excalibur wielding warrior.

'Gosh, no. He died some years ago.'

'I'm very sorry to hear it,' said George.

'Huh! I'm not. He was a pig.'

He wasn't quite sure how to respond to this rather unexpected statement although a vision of three giant breakfast sausages suddenly passed through his mind.

Sam's house was just behind the church and hidden from view by a copse of oak. A large, handsome Georgian property called, as he found out later, Chipping Grange. A wide gravel drive led up to the entrance and the creamy Cotswold stone glowed in the afternoon sun. The interior was cool and Caroline showed him into the large, high-ceilinged drawing room where the customary funeral tea was laid out. A selection of sandwiches was complemented by plates of baked meats and several stands of dainty fancy cakes. A decanter each of port and sherry catered to those in need of fortification. Several mourners together with the adolescent vicar had arrived at the same time as him and were milling about eyeing the generously laden table. To George's great surprise the vicar poured himself a very large port and knocked it back *tout de suite*. Two young ladies were making some final adjustments as if fine tuning an old and valuable violin.

'Come and meet my daughters,' said Caroline, steering him towards the table. 'Mr Chesshyre, this is Morgana and this is Guinevere.'

'Delighted to meet you,' he said, by now having perfected his rather fixed, sad-pleasant smile. 'What unusual names you both have.'

A little unsuccessfully repressed giggling.

'How do you do, Mr Chesshyre. Daddy was convinced he was descended from King Arthur,' said Morgana, the taller of the two.

'We always had to have our holidays in Cornwall,' said Guinevere.

'Ah! Did he discover the Holy Grail?' asked George, trying to behave normally in these slightly bizarre circumstances.

More giggling. 'Gosh, no,' she said. 'He'd go off tramping for miles and just end up with holey shoes!'

'And holey socks!' added Morgana. 'You never saw such spuds!'

'He got arrested in Tintagel once. The police thought he was a vagrant!' said Guinevere.

An uncontrolled outburst of mirth. George could see that these two would get on well with Vicky and Alex. God forbid they should ever get together.

'Girls!' Caroline chastised them, rather unconvincingly. 'A little more decorum, please. Remember where you are.' A plate was suddenly thrust below George's nose. 'Cucumber sandwich, Mr Chesshyre?'

'Please, call me George,' he said, taking one. 'Thank you. I think it's about all I can manage after the breakfast I had this morning.'

'Oh, where are you staying?' The cucumber sandwiches had disappeared and were replaced with a plate piled high with miniature sausages. Was there no escape?

He was about to say 'Pig and Whistle' but thought it might appear indelicate so just said: 'The pub in the village.'

'Oh, the 'Pig and Whistle'. You were lucky to get in there. He might have been full.' An almost indeterminable raising of one eyebrow and a Mona Lisa smile.

'Ah, you know the landlord, then?' he said, not picking up the inference. 'He did have to check to see if he had vacancies.'

'He's *always* got vacancies,' said Caroline, scornfully. 'I think the last time anyone stayed there was when the old queen died. *He's* all right but that wife of his is a bit of a tartar. Are you going back to London tonight?'

'No, tomorrow morning.'

'Then you must stay here with us tonight. There's plenty of room and I'm sure you'll be much more comfortable.'

'But I couldn't possibly impose upon you – '

Caroline was not to be rebuffed. She held her hands up in protest. 'I absolutely insist. We're staying on for a few days to sort things out. Besides there's a mountain of paperwork and I'd be really glad of your advice about some of it.'

'In that case I should be delighted.'

'Spendid! That's settled then.'

'I must go and square things at the pub,' he said. 'To be honest, I wasn't really looking forward to spending another night there. Oh, it's clean and comfortable enough you know but the meals they insist on putting before me are, well, you know – *formidable*. I share your opinion about the landlord's wife too. She is a bit of a dragon, isn't she?'

That's two inns he should have to apologise to. He made a mental note to write to the 'George' in Strood when he returned.

Conditions at Chipping Grange were, indeed, more spacious than those at the 'Pig and Whistle' and there was also much less chance of sustaining concussion from the low ceilings and doorways. He explained the situation to Amos Clutterbuck, collected his case, sampled a final pint of Godsell's best and paid him for two nights. He seemed pleased with this and said he was welcome back any time he was in the district. 'If I bain't vull.'

Friday 8th September 1911

George had an excellent night's sleep. The bedroom was large and airy with a panoramic view over the valley below. Chipping Grange had been the subject of some modernisation in recent years and he was very thankful for a long hot soak in the bath the previous evening. He had not been away 48 hours but was already missing the familiar comforts of Scattersdale Avenue. He had had a quick look through the paperwork Caroline had mentioned but there was too much to make any real sense of it in the time available. He suggested she get it all packed up and sent on to him. He'd have a good look through and refer anything he thought necessary to the firm's solicitor.

'What a good idea. You are kind. Good gracious, we're practically neighbours!' said Caroline as he gave her his card. 'We're in Tulse Hill! What an extraordinary coincidence!'

George was taken aback. Somehow he'd formed the notion that she lived in the village. 'Tulse Hill? Really? Good Lord. Why, that's virtually on the doorstep.' Suddenly he heard himself issuing an invitation. 'You must come soon and meet the family. Rosalind and the girls would be delighted.'

Caroline smiled 'Oh, we'd really look forward to that!'

'Excellent! So shall I.' He beamed, pleased with himself and glad of the chance to repay Caroline's hospitality. 'Now, I really must see about getting back to London,' he said, pulling out his watch. 'I need to get to the station. Is there a telephone I can use?'

'Not here, I'm afraid but there's one in the Post Office.'

'Ah. Thanks. I'll toddle round and organise it.'

The cab was duly summoned and, after saying his goodbyes which were accompanied by some rather over-effusive hugs, he was making the perilous journey back down the mountain pass within the hour. As luck would have it there was a train due although he would, again, have to change at Swindon. Soon the familiar sight of a copper-capped chimney glinting in the sun appeared round the bend on the approach to Stroud station. He was somewhat relieved to see that 'Lady Disdain' had not been commandeered for this duty; instead, and with somewhat satisfying irony, his green goddess was called 'Lady of the Lake'. She did sterling service to Swindon where, after taking great care not to get lost, 'Morning Star' took over and whisked him to Paddington. A cab off the rank and he was back in Scattersdale Avenue by five. There was no-one about so he opened a bottle of Bass and sat out in the conservatory where he promptly fell asleep. When he awoke there was hustle and bustle going on all around him. He was too tired to recount the details of his adventures and no-one seemed to be very interested anyway. An early night and the weekend ahead of him.

CHAPTER NINE

~ Costly Knowledge

—e·ɔ—

Saturday 9th September 1911

The notion had occurred to George many times during his life, but, in particular since he got married, and, even more so after having children, that he was, in fact, invisible. Were this to be true it would explain why no-one took a blind bit of notice of him; why he was invariably ignored during discussions concerning such grave matters as the arrangement of furniture; the style of curtains, carpets, etc.; and fairly trivial matters such as spending more money than the bank balance would allow; whether or not he was putting on weight (invariably he was) and the girls' future, this latter topic, as we have seen, being of particular interest and concern to him as they, beyond his notice, appeared to have advanced in years from about fifteen to almost twenty during which time he could swear he'd only celebrated one birthday.

Of course, when the subject of money, and in particular extracting a large amount from him, cropped up, he suddenly became visible. He had hardly had time to recover from his solemn country duties than he was being harassed at the breakfast table. A large kipper, which had escaped the clutches of Tarporley, had just gone down very well and he was in the process of sampling a new kind of marmalade when an elaborately printed and illustrated brochure was thrust within his purview.

'George, look at this. Isn't it splendid?' said Rosalind, beaming.

'What is it?' he asked, rescuing his toast which had been obscured by volumes of paper.

'It's Celandine's new school.' said Rosalind. 'Isn't it lovely?'

He took a cursory glance. 'Yes, jolly good. When does she start?'

'On Monday week. She's very excited.'

George couldn't honestly imagine Celandine getting excited

about anything. Every time he saw her she appeared to be terrified. He had stubbornly resisted shaving off his moustache but he really couldn't believe she hadn't got used to it by now.

'George, I need you to write a cheque.'

'What on earth for?'

'The school fees, of course.'

'*What?*'

'The school fees. They're due at the beginning of term.'

'But why do I have to pay them?'

'Now George, don't be difficult. You know it's only until Bertie's life insurance comes through.'

'Why can't she go to the local elementary school?'

'I don't think there is one.'

'There must be!'

'Celandine's too delicate. She needs to be nurtured carefully.'

'I'll go and get my watering can.'

'*George!*'

'All right, how much is it going to cost me this time to advance further down the road to bankruptcy?'

'Fifteen guineas.'

'Oh, well, I suppose that's not too bad for the year.'

'Per term.'

'*What?*'

'Then there are extras.'

'*Extras?*'

'Violin.'

'How much?'

'Four guineas.'

'Per term?'

'Per term.'

'Anything else?'

'Piano.'

'But she's having lessons from Eugene!'

'Compulsory.'

'How much?'

'Four guineas.'

'Per term?'

'Per term.'

'Is that it?'

'Not quite.'

'Go on.'

'Dancing.'

'Dancing?'

'She needs dancing for when she comes out.'

'Comes out where?'

'Into society, of course. George, you're hopeless. No man will look at her if she can't dance.'

'What about cooking? Wouldn't that be cheaper? Chaps would certainly look at her if she could cook.'

'Cooking comes next.'

'Compulsory?'

'Of course.'

Suddenly the kipper, which had gone down very well a few moments ago was lying very heavily on his stomach and he feared an imminent attack of dyspepsia. He sighed wearily. 'Rosalind, if I am going to invest enough capital in Celandine's education to float a medium sized company I should like to know a bit about it. Where is this *crème de la crème* of educational establishments?'

This faint demonstration of interest, though purely pecuniary, was probably, in hindsight thought George, a mistake. It served to double Rosalind's enthusiasm and she pulled up a chair next to him, put her hand on his arm and continued with a peculiarly feminine gusto in the manner women do when trying to persuade their husbands of the sheer excitement and absolutely positive necessity of what they're trying to convince you of and you know that it is pointless to resist because the topic will be raised again and again at carefully timed strategic intervals until you give in.

'Well, you wouldn't believe it,' she went on. 'It's just ten minutes walk from here. Clemmie and I just happened to raise the subject with Mrs McGillycuddy recently and she highly recommended it. Both her nieces attend and their mother wouldn't send them anywhere else. "They *mould* the girls, Mrs Chesshyre," she said.' George had a momentary vision of Mrs. Sprackett's rabbit-shaped blancmange mould and tried to imagine Celandine with long ears, buck teeth and whiskers. 'We visited yesterday when you were away,' Rosalind continued enthusiastically. 'The Headmistress is called Miss Oswaldwhistle and she was very welcoming. She took immediately to Celandine and she wasn't too frightened of her.'

'Well, that's a relief,' said George. 'I can understand how she might have been intimidated by Celandine.'

'George, don't be such a goose. Look, here's the prospectus. Why don't you read it?'

As it was being waved energetically in front of his nose he felt that he had no option. Reluctantly he picked it up. It was very elaborately printed and must have cost a fair old bit to produce.

"The Laurels' School for Girls.

Principal – Miss Lettice Oswaldwhistle (Lady Margaret Hall, Oxon)

'The Laurels' is a day school for girls aged 12–18. It is situated in large and charming grounds in the borough of Streatham, South London where the climate is agreeable and temperate, yet refreshing and invigorating; a boon to young ladies of delicate or nervous disposition.

Miss Oswaldwhistle is assisted by a fully qualified staff and teaching is by the most up-to-date methods using the best English and Continental systems.

The object of the school is to give care and individual attention which it is impossible for larger schools to provide.'

The prospectus droned on about how wonderful it was and how it would admirably equip girls for 'life's great adventure', all for fifteen guineas per term not including extras.

He tore a blank cheque out of the book and handed it to Rosalind. 'Here you are,' he said wearily. 'Fill it in and I'll sign it.'

Sunday 10th September 1911

George had the most peculiar dream during the night. He was stuck on a hill somewhere and there was a train chasing him. Although he couldn't see clearly he just knew it had the face of Lady Disdain and was bearing down on him while he desperately tried to escape. A very vivid and unnerving experience which stayed with him until after breakfast.

The weather had become oppressive and overcast. He shouldn't have been surprised if they had a thunderstorm before long. The heat had been going on for weeks and he was thoroughly fed up with it. The whole country was as dry as a tinder box and there were grass fires breaking out all over the place. The water shortage had become acute although thankfully they were not affected. Heaven only knew how much they got through during the week. It was useless to encourage economy. Everyone insisted on having at least one bath a day and the 'Thermoboil' was kept hard at work.

He gave church a miss that morning on the pretext that he had developed a headache. This wasn't entirely untrue. The heavy weather had rather got him down and he couldn't face another of Humpidge's interminable rambles. He had the house to himself apart from Mrs Sprackett, Polly and Dolly who were busy in the kitchen. He was not easily given to napping during the day but he felt so weary he gave in and went for a lie down in the bedroom. He thought the events of the past week had caught up with him, rather, and he needed a bit of time to recover. A quiet afternoon and evening.

CHAPTER TEN ~

~ **Monsoon**

—ஒ ஒ—

'But when I came to man's estate,
With hey, ho, the wind and the rain,
'Gainst knaves and thieves men shut their gate,
For the rain, it raineth every day'

William Shakespeare *'Twelfth Night'*

Monday 11th September 1911

George was recovering from an extremely trying day. The previous evening had been unbearably oppressive and, about five, the sky began to darken. He had noticed tall thunderclouds building from late morning on and there was the odd rumble in the far distance. The glass had dropped a long way during the day but it didn't seem to come to anything, however, and they went to bed at about eleven. He eventually managed to drop off and slept fitfully. A bit of a breeze blew up and he got out of bed to pull the sash down at about four o'clock. He lay awake for a while listening to Tarporley making an odd chattering noise out on the landing. He'd been behaving oddly all day running in and out of the house and sitting on the stairs, watching every passing body through the banisters, something he very rarely did. He wasn't sure at first, but after a minute or two, yes, there it was, the sound of raindrops on the window pane. What a comforting sound. Rain. It was raining at last. He couldn't remember the last time they'd had any rain. It must have been weeks. Months, even.

He had always rather thought the expression 'the heavens opened' to be a bit theatrical. However, what happened next, just as he was dropping off, was verging on Armageddon. There was a blinding flash followed almost instantly by the most tremendous crash of thunder which rocked the whole house. Simultaneously it began to rain with a force and velocity he had never encountered. More lightning. More cracking, booming, thudding and rolling around the sky. With each crack, the rain seemed to intensify. On and on it went. By now the whole house was awake. Clementine was running around like a mad woman. 'Cover the mirrors! Cover the mirrors!' she screamed. Celandine was standing outside her bedroom door, pale and petrified. Vicky and Alex stood on the landing in a tight embrace, both with the same terrified expressions. Rosalind was rushing around closing every open window she could find. Mrs Sprackett appeared on the stairs, curl papers flailing, 'Lord bless us if it ain't the end of the world! I knew as it would come to this. It's the 'eat. It ain't natural! It's a visitation on our wickedness, that's what it is and no mistake!'

Suddenly there was a piercing scream from the top of the house. Polly's door was flung open and she ran down the stairway, soaking wet and leaving pools of water behind her. 'The ceiling! The ceiling!' she screamed. George ran up to her room to find water pouring in through a hole in the ceiling which had collapsed.

'Quick! Buckets!' he called out. 'Buckets! Anything, saucepans, anything to catch the water!' He couldn't be sure how long this state of mayhem went on. Everything became a blur of saucepans and buckets, filled with water then tipped out of the window before being returned to be filled again in an instant. The electric light in the hall and stairway which was the only source of illumination flickered ominously. The rain hammered relentlessly in monsoon quantities never relenting for a moment. Then, just as the first rays of dawn were appearing, it stopped as quickly as it had begun. The cascade of water slowed to a trickle and finally became an intermittent drip. As the light strengthened he was able to survey the room. An area of plaster about two feet square had come down revealing sodden lathwork above. Polly's bed was soaked as was the carpet. The only saving grace was that the bed, being directly below the collapsed ceiling, had soaked up much of the water. The wardrobe and dressing table appeared to be fairly dry.

By eight o'clock they had all managed to gather their wits together and the whole household gravitated to the kitchen where Mrs Sprackett was brewing gallons of hot, sweet tea in an urn which had been dug out from somewhere. George went out into the back garden to survey the roof. It was as he suspected. There were slates dislodged directly over Polly's bedroom. The house had suffered a lightning strike. He should have to get on to Stripp immediately.

'You were lucky to get 'old of me, Mr Chesshyre,' said Stripp as he walked round the side of the house to inspect the damage. 'Terrible storm last night. Kept me and the missus up and the kids was 'ollerin' summat terrible. 'ate the thunder, they does. I 'ope it didn't disturb you too bad, like?'

George just about managed to remain in control. 'Ah, well, you see, Mr Stripp, I fear we had a similar experience to yourself. As you can see,' he said, pointing at the dislodged slates, 'I think the house has been struck by lightning.'

A sharp intake of breath. 'Gawd bless me it 'as an' all. Lucky the 'ole roof didn't go, I reckon. Course you know what the problem is, don't you?'

George replied that, apart from having a hole in the roof, a soaked bedroom together with associated fixtures, fittings and furniture, a hysterical maid and a traumatised family, he should be grateful if he would enlighten him.

'Well, it's yer lightnin' conductor, ain't it?'

George replied that, despite close and careful inspection, he could not discern the existence of a lightning conductor.

'Exactly, Mr Chesshyre! You ain't got one!' Stripp beamed at him triumphantly. 'I always said when they was building these 'ere 'ouses as they should've put in lightnin' conductors. It's the 'ite, see? These 'ouses stick up quite 'igh. Attract the lightnin' they do. Any lightnin' about it'll go for these 'ouses fust. Now when the lady next door moved in, Mrs Gillywilly, fust thing she said to me before I even started the decoratin', "Mr Stripp," she says, "I wants you to hinstall a lightnin' conductor. These 'ouses, bein' tall," she says, "they're venerable to lightnin' strikes," she says. Very wise lady, Mrs Willybilly.'

George replied that he was, as always, grateful for the sage advice by proxy of his esteemed next door neighbour. In the meantime, emergency repairs would have to be put under way.

'I shall 'ave to ladder it up, Mr Chesshyre, an' I'll get a tarp over it so as you won't 'ave no more rain gettin' in but I shall need to scaffold round the side and up over the chimbleys. It'd be easier if I could get at it from the back but the conser*vatory's* in the way, see?'

George apologised for having the temerity to possess a conser-*vatory* and left him to it.

Despite being prone to temporary and infrequent bouts of absentmindedness or, some might say, complete memory loss, George liked to think that he was 'pretty bloomin' well thorough' when it came to important issues. When the subject of moving from Sydenham came up he approached the campaign with military precision. The lease to 'The Limes' No 3 Scattersdale Avenue SW was full repairing and insuring. Before entering into the agreement he had instructed Messrs. Drape, Moon & Casement, Chartered Surveyors, to give the place a thorough going over. It had come back with a clean bill of health although they missed the absence of a lightning conductor. On the basis of the report he entered into the agreement but not before getting the firm's solicitor to look it over. He found it satisfactory but advised George to request a copy of the insurance policy and certificate before finally committing himself. Although he was responsible for paying the insurance premiums, the landlord arranged it in their joint names and George paid him. Looking over the policy issued by the 'Holborn Citadel Insurance Co. Ltd', he was pretty confident that the house was covered against the calamity which had just befallen them. Having satisfied himself that all would be well he telephoned their office and arranged for an assessor to come out as soon as possible.

By this time he had abandoned all thoughts of going into the office and went in search of something to eat. He had suddenly realised that the whole household had been up since well before dawn and none of them had had very much sleep. He suggested that everyone go to bed for a few hours to recover but they were having none of it. The first task was to move Polly in with Dolly temporarily. Rosalind and the girls had been busying themselves with this while he was consulting Stripp; Mrs Sprackett had set about making a substantial breakfast of sausages, bacon, eggs, fried bread, mushrooms and kidneys. Fortunately the gas supply hadn't been affected and the 'Thermoboil' was working overtime supplying endless quantities of hot water while the range was running red-hot. The teapot was retrieved from Polly's bedroom where it had been doing resolute service as a baler-out and, along with the urn which had now been converted to a coffee pot, was soon dispensing an altogether more pleasant beverage than cold rainwater. With the last of the mopping up done and a good breakfast inside them all things began to look a little more cheerful. By mid-morning Stripp was back with his lad and was lashing ladders to the wall in readiness for the temporary repairs he was confident of executing. As soon as George had got the go-ahead from 'Holborn Citadel', permanent repairs could be commenced, after which Stripp could redecorate Polly's bedroom. He couldn't see that all this would take much more than a week or so. Ten days at the outside. He was feeling quite buoyant despite lack of sleep. The weather had broken at last. The temperature was a good twenty degrees lower than the day before and the air was fresh and invigorating.

Saturday 16th September 1911

George awoke early to the sound of Stripp's tarpaulin flapping in the wind. It had broken loose again.

The insurance assessor had finally turned up on the Thursday evening. A tall, mournful looking man with a small moustache, he wore a long, straight raincoat which nearly touched the ground. He apologised for not getting out sooner but there had been a rush of work on and had George heard about the storm last Sunday night? George gritted his teeth and let this pass. He led him round the back so that he could see the extent of the damage.

A sharp intake of breath. (Whenever you encounter 'a sharp intake of breath' you know you are in for bad news; usually affecting your wallet.) 'Did you erect this scaffolding and fasten the tarpaulin up there, sir?'

George felt a tightening in the pit of his stomach. This was the sort of question he would have expected of Vicky or Alex. A ridiculously bizarre question that deserved an equally ridiculous and bizarre answer. He was on the point of saying, 'Yes, I knocked up the scaffolding with one hand and slung the tarpaulin over with the other. Only took ten minutes. I shall get it all retiled later on today after I come back from Wales with some singularly choice slate which I shall shape with my teeth.' However, being just on the right side of insanity at that moment he took a deep breath and replied that his builder, Mr Stripp, had effected temporary arrangements in order to make the building water-tight and weatherproof.

A note on his notepad. 'Have you instructed your builder further, sir?'

'No, I was waiting for you to give me the go ahead.'

A further note on the notepad. 'Have you made any payment in money or in kind to your builder, sir?'

'Not one penny, groat, shekel or bead has passed between us.'

A pause, a sideways look of deep suspicion then another note on the notepad. 'What, in your opinion, has caused the damage to the property, sir?'

'Well, it's clearly a lightning strike. Dislodged the slates. Water ingress. Collapsed ceiling. Soggy bed.'

A long note on the notepad. '...So-gg-y bed. You haven't been up on the roof yourself, sir?'

'What? Me? No jolly fear! I get vertigo on a high kerbstone!'

A pause, a suspicious sideways glance and then a note on the notepad. 'V-e-r-t-i-g-o. Can I see the interior damage now, sir?'

'Yes, of course. Follow me.' George led him up to Polly's room. He peered into the void, looked suspiciously at him again and made another note.

'Thank you, sir. That'll be all.'

'Right,' said George, rubbing his hands together expectantly.

'How long do you think it'll be before I get the go ahead to start repairs?'

'In my opinion we won't be authorising this claim, sir.'

The hand rubbing stopped abruptly.

'What? Why ever not?'

'The building doesn't appear to have a lightning conductor installed, sir. I shall have to make further enquiries but I'm fairly sure local building regulations require one to be fitted. Good day, sir. I shall be in touch.'

They say that lightning doesn't strike twice in the same place. However, at that moment, George seriously doubted the wisdom of that remark. Of course, he should have known there would be *difficulties*. There always are in these matters, especially where insurance is involved. The problem was that the situation was getting urgent. The roof had been vulnerable to the elements since Sunday evening and Stripp, decent fellow though he was, had so far not succeeded in securing the tarpaulin satisfactorily. Luckily it hadn't rained again but the wind had got up and was ballooning the tarpaulin alarmingly at times. He should have to take decisive action. If the 'Holborn Citadel' was going to drag its feet he'd have to instruct Stripp to put in hand proper repairs immediately and sort it out with Holborn later on. He spoke to Stripp first thing on Friday morning and he promised to make a start later that day or Saturday morning at the latest.

He was as good as his word and turned up at eight that morning with a wagon load of materials, his lad and two other men. They got to work immediately, the temporary tarpaulin was removed and a scaffolded and boarded shelter constructed around the chimney stack. By mid-afternoon George was feeling much happier although he wasn't looking forward to receiving the estimate Stripp had promised to draw up. More expense!

Sunday 17th September 1911

By the end of the week Stripp had made good progress and George was sleeping better not worrying that the tarpaulin was going to fly away leaving them vulnerable to another good soaking. There was the usual gibberish from Humpidge that Sunday morning. Mercifully he didn't go on too long and George formed the distinct impression that the subject of his sermon was 'Swindon Cake'.

Clementine was confined to bed with a head cold, presumably brought on by the drenching. It was a wonder they were all not down with pneumonia, thought George. However, her indisposition had not prevented her from issuing written edicts on a regular basis chiefly concerning Celandine's first piano lesson with Eugene that afternoon and her first day at 'The Laurels' the following day.

The mid-day bulletin read as follows:-

'Rosalind – Tell that young man not to tax Celandine too greatly. And I don't want her being taught any modern music. Nothing later than early Beethoven and certainly none of that French nonsense. I don't want her morals corrupted with that decadent tripe. And do try to keep George out of the way. He has a habit of meddling and he will loom over Celandine. It does frighten her so and makes her nervous. Keep the doors open so that I can hear.'

Eugene arrived promptly at four and George showed him into the music room. He explained that Celandine's mother was unwell and would not be able to supervise the lesson but that Rosalind and he would be on hand.

'I'm sorry to hear that, sir. I hope she'll be recovered very soon.'

George refrained from remarking that he hoped her decline would be rapid and terminal. 'Oh, yes, she'll be up and about again in no time,' he said. 'She's very sorry to have missed you but is eager for Celandine to get on and make progress.'

'Well, I'm glad to hear it, sir. I thought we might start with something light. A little Debussy, maybe?'

George beamed mischievously. 'Splendid!' he said. 'Just the thing!'

'*George!*'

'Yes, dear?'

'You know what Clemmie said. Nothing French.'

'Oh, is he French? I had no idea. Ah, here's Celandine now. And dressed in her new school uniform. Starts her new school tomorrow, Eugene.'

'My, well you look very smart!'

'Thank you Mr Rickenbacker.' A grave smile and her best full-moon eyes. 'I think I shall like it there.'

'Sure you will! Now I have a very pretty piece of music right here in my case that I thought of earlier and which I think will suit you very well. What do you think? Would you like to go through it with me?'

'Oh, yes please! What is it, Mr Rickenbacker?'

'It's called, *'La fille aux cheveux de lin'*. A piece from a new book of Preludes by Claude Debussy.' Sitting down on the piano stool he opened the book at the appropriate page and placed it on the stand.

Celandine studied it intently. 'It has six flats. That's G flat major. Would you play it through first, please Mr Rickenbacker?'

'Of course! Not too many black notes?'

Celandine smiled and shook her head. George was surprised. If she could read music with six flats she was further ahead than he'd thought. He couldn't imagine how Lady Disdain could be so condescending and dismissive. He still hadn't forgiven her for slapping Celandine down on the previous occasion that Eugene had played for them. He hoped her cold was getting worse.

Then George's beautiful Bechstein came to life as Eugene began to play. Soft cascades of notes echoed round the room and it seemed the whole house fell silent while the gorgeous melody progressed in Eugene's skilled hands. As the final notes died away George could see that Celandine was standing transfixed, tears in her eyes. Celandine – The sad little girl who loved Étude Op. 10, No. 3. 'Tristesse'.

'The Girl with the Flaxen Hair.'

Saturday 23rd September 1911

George had rarely experienced such a trying week. In his work, 'Little Dorrit', that eminent author, Mr Charles Dickens, relays to us, in satirical terms, a description of the existence and purpose of the 'Circumlocution Office'. Mr Dickens means, no doubt, to amuse his readers with the antics of this insufferable organisation; however, were George to meet him on the proverbial 'Clapham Omnibus', he should take great pleasure in informing him that such offices do, indeed, exist and are functioning, or not, depending on your point of view, in High Holborn and elsewhere at that present time.

Many years previously, when George was contemplating a career, he went over all the usual options available to him and we have spoken at some length concerning this earlier in this chronicle: The Army? – No. The Crimea was still fresh in people's minds and he was warned off that. The Church? – No. Interminable sermons were not new to him. He was forced to sit through them every Sunday and could not, in all conscience, inflict that kind of theological torture on captive parishioners. Besides, although for the most part a committed Tractarian, his faith waxed and waned like the moon or guttered like a candle in the wind. Finally he discovered Pascal's Wager and made that the bedrock of his belief. This was, however, a secret known only to himself. The Law? – No. All that endless wrangling in court and, 'Yes, M'Lud' and 'No, M'Lud' and defending habitual recidivists who you know are jolly well guilty. Besides, in order to get into these things it would have meant going to university though he had precious little Latin. His family weren't wealthy and they struggled to put him through a half-way decent school even though he was accepted on liberal terms. His father knew a chap who worked in the City and he suggested he try for an opening at Fysh, Fysh, Iceberg and Fysh. He'd always been pretty quick at figures and picked things up quickly. He understood equations both the 'simple and quadratical' and was very good at calculus 'differential and integral'. He took to it immediately. The thing about stockbroking, George maintained, was that everything was really quite *straightforward*. A client asks you to buy or sell some stock; you have a look round the stockjobbers who run books on that particular sector, agree a price and the deal's done: *Dictum Meum Pactum*. Of course it wasn't quite as simple as that in reality. The hours could be long, especially in the early days when you're still an oik; there was a tremendous amount of paperwork and calculating and figures flying everywhere and clients often wanted your opinion on stocks so you had to keep up with the financial news; woe betide you if you recommended a stock that smashed (He'd had some very heated exchanges over the years) but all that sort of thing came with experience. On the whole it wasn't for the faint-hearted. He was often asked: 'How can I make a small fortune on the Stock Exchange?' His answer was invariably the same – 'Start with a large one!'

The one career he never really contemplated was insurance and going by the experience of the previous week he was jolly well glad he hadn't.

In order to grasp the complexities of this potential *Jarndyce v Jarndyce* it's probably simplest if we list the *dramatis personae* of this tragicomedy:-

1) Holborn Citadel Insurance Co. Ltd.
2) Excelsior Victoria Insurance Co Ltd.
3) Ebenezer Greathead (Architects) Ltd.
4) Drape, Moon & Casement (Architects) Ltd.
5) Blinkhorn, Grist & Vobster, Estate Agents, Auctioneers & Valuers
6) City & South London Property Developers Ltd.
7) Thomas O'Hooligan (Contractors) Ltd. – In liquidation
8) Thomas O'Hooligan (Contractors) 1910 Ltd.
9) Zebrani & Stripp, General Builder and Decorator
10) London County Council
11) Metropolitan Borough of Wandsworth
12) Antiphon, Spoke, Haddock & Spoke, Solicitors

Lightning strikes generate a great deal of energy. They also generate a blizzard of correspondence, at least initially. Letters fly to and fro for a few days then everything goes ominously quiet. Finally George placed the whole issue in the hands of his solicitors which meant, he thought, that he would probably receive notice of resolution sometime around Christmas 1926. Holborn had flatly turned down the claim on the ground that there was no lightning conductor. Excelsior (through whom George had a separate contents policy) wouldn't budge until the dispute with Holborn was resolved. Greathead said they specified a lightning conductor in the original plans. O'Hooligan were suspected of cutting costs by not fitting one. The original firm had gone bankrupt and its successor denied liability. Drape didn't think one was really necessary. Blinkhorn, who let the house, couldn't find the relevant file. City & South London Properties, who own the freehold, were under the impression he wanted to buy it outright. London County Council and Metropolitan Borough of Wandsworth couldn't agree between them whether a lightning conductor was mandatory under local bye-laws.

George authorised Stripp to get on with the work, repair the roof, fit a lightning conductor, mend the ceiling in Polly's room and redecorate as necessary. If the bailiffs eventually sought entry, so be it. But they weren't having his Bechstein.

Besides, they'd never get it out of the house.

CHAPTER ELEVEN

~ Round and Round the Garden

*'When Adam delved and Eve span, who was
then the gentleman?'*

John Ball

Sunday 24th September 1911

One of the pleasures of Sunday morning is that delightful reverie in which one can luxuriate in between waking and getting out of bed. None of the week-day rush, collar stud that won't fasten, a hurried breakfast and then joining the hurly-burly; that great mass of humanity that descends from all points of the compass on the great London termini in order to once again earn an honest (or otherwise) crust.

George was drifting in and out of consciousness, not thinking of anything in particular when he became aware that Rosalind had got out of bed and was looking out of the window.

'George.'

'Yes, dear?'

'Have you seen the garden?'

George replied that he had full cognisance of its existence.

'It's very untidy.'

'Hmm.'

'It really does need a lot of attention.'

'Hmm.'

'*George!*'

'Yes, dear. A lot of attention. I'll do it later.'

'George, you know nothing about gardening.'

'In that case I won't touch it.'

'*George!*'

'Well, tell Vicky and Alex to do it. They know about flowers and things.'

'George, they're very good at flower *arranging* but they can't look after a whole garden. The back is getting very overgrown and the front looks dreadful. Clemmie mentioned it the other day.'

'Well get her to sort it out then. Give her something to do instead of complaining about everything. On second thoughts don't let her loose with a pair of secateurs. Lord knows what damage she might inflict.'

'*George!* Don't be so *absurd.* I think we should engage a gardener.'

'Oh, Lord.'

'Just part time, of course. Mrs McGillycuddy's man has some time on his hands since he laid out her ornamental Alpine rockery. It more or less looks after itself. He's been with her for over thirty years and she wouldn't allow anyone else through her gate. "His fingers are positively *verdant,* Mrs Chesshyre," she said.'

George turned over and groaned. 'But the *expense!*'

'But think of the money we'd save. Fresh vegetables and fruit from our very own kitchen garden. There's plenty of room and Mrs Sprackett wouldn't have to go to that dreadful greengrocer in the High Street any more. His prices are outrageous. You see, we'd be saving money in no time at all.'

George felt unequal to the struggle. 'Well, you'd better get him to come round, then.'

'Oh, good. I knew you'd say that! He's coming round this morning after church.'

After this *fait accompli,* George resigned himself to engaging the green man of Streatham. He supposed it made sense, really. Some decent vegetables would be welcome. The cabbage had seemed a bit stringy recently and the carrots had been tough and tasteless. The more he thought about it the more he warmed to the idea and hang the expense. He didn't suppose bailiffs could seize fresh produce still growing in the ground. They might be bankrupt but at least they wouldn't starve.

There were some excellent hymns that morning: 'He Who Would Valiant Be', sung to 'Monk's Gate'; 'For All the Saints', (Sine Nomine). Good old RVW getting a good airing and played with gusto by Eugene. George nodded off during Humpidge's sermon but awoke in time for the collection, unfortunately.

He arrived back at the house to find that, in their absence, somebody had erected a scarecrow in the back garden. When it turned round on hearing their approach the girls let out a collective shriek and rushed back into the house.

'Mr Chesshyre?' the scarecrow asked.

'The same,' replied George.

'Obadiah Stripp, sir. I has taken the liberty of castin' a eye over your garden in your absence as you might say. Mrs McGillycuddy asked me to call round. I hope you don't mind, sir?'

'No, not at all. How do you do, Mr Stripp?' George held out his hand which was shaken vigorously. 'Tell me, are you related to Stripp the builder?'

'My younger brother, sir. He was for goin' into the buildin' trade, sir, but it didn't suit me, sir. It's the ladders, you see. I prefer to keep my feet on terra cotta as you might say. And the paint, sir. Gets on my chest terrible bad, sir. No, sir. Man of the soil I am. Never 'appier than when I'm a'diggin' or a'oein' or a'rakin', sir. I remember this road when it was a field, sir. Pasture, it was, sir. Oh, it used to gladden the 'eart to see the lambs a-gambollin' in the spring, sir. Of course it's all gone now, sir. 'ouses as far as the eye can see. You won't see no lambs around 'ere again sir, except in the butcher's window Ha! Ha!'

George had never met such a garrulous scarecrow. 'Ha ha ha!' George laughed rather forcibly. 'Well, Mr Stripp,' he said gesturing with a wide sweep towards the overgrown expanse and trying to gently steer the course of the conversation back to the garden, 'what do you think you can do with this bit of pasture?'

A sharp intake of breath. (A vision of his open and empty wallet passed through George's mind.) 'Well, Mr Chesshyre. T'won't be easy. London clay, you see? Very 'eavy. It'll take some turnin'.'

'We were thinking of a vegetable garden.' George looked at him hopefully.

A further sharp intake of breath. (A bank statement decorated with much red ink.) 'Well, London clay, sir. It'll need breakin' up.

Plenty of good muck'd do it. Do you object to plenty of good muck, Mr Chesshyre?'

'If that's what's needed. I suppose it will exude an aroma?'

'Beg pardon, Mr Chesshyre?'

'Stink a bit, will it?'

'Oh, yes, sir. Best 'oss and pig manure, sir. 'oss ain't too bad but pig 'ums a bit.'

'Then carry on, by all means.' George smiled. He had a wicked feeling that this was going to get up Lady Disdain's nose in more ways than one.

Monday 25th September 1911

The weather had, at last, got back to normal. This, of course, meant a leaden sky and almost perpetual rainfall. Fortunately Stripp the Builder had the roof watertight and had told George that he would soon be in a position to start on the repairs in Polly's room. Of course, on leaving the house that morning the umbrella stand was empty. During the hot weather it was full of umbrellas of every description but now there was not one to be had, which was mystifying as he was always the first out. No matter. The rain had eased off, temporarily at least, and held at bay until he reached the office. As a precaution, he called in at Scrope's ironmongers in Moorgate at lunch time and picked up a jolly sturdy little number for five bob. He was glad of it too at five o'clock because a steady drizzle during the afternoon had turned into a sort of semi-monsoon but Scrope's special kept him dry all the way back to Scattersdale Avenue in which had appeared, during his absence, a long trench, rather haphazardly fenced off. He left the brolly open to dry in the porch and noticed, with some puzzlement, that the stand was now overflowing with umbrellas, none of which looked particularly wet.

'George, is that you dear?' came a disembodied voice from the direction of the dining room.

Rosalind did tend to have a habit of asking questions, the

answers to which were somewhat axiomatic, thought George as he took off his raincoat and stowed his brief case.

'I hope you didn't get wet, you forgot your umbrella this morning.' He was too tired to engage in semantics so just put in a brief appearance, gave Rosalind a peck on the cheek and went upstairs to change.

'Don't *stump*, George. Clemmie has a terrible headache,' came the disembodied voice.

If he'd had the energy he'd have stumped harder. On the way up he looked out over the garden to see if there was any sign of ripe 'oss or pig muck but he thought the weather must have been against Stripp the Scarecrow that day; not much seemed to have happened. He decided to have a long hot soak before going back down. He put the plug in the bath and turned on the hot tap while he changed, but on returning to the bathroom was met with a bath full of cold water. Feeling rather dispirited he put on some old trousers and a jacket and made his way back downstairs.

'There's no hot water,' he said, pecking Rosalind on the cheek for the second time. 'Don't tell me the Thermoboil's packed up.'

'I'm sorry, George,' she said, brushing his shoulders. 'The gas company has turned it off. They're doing something out in the road. They said it would be back on again tomorrow, though.'

'Did you have a cold bath, daddy?' asked Vicky.

'I most certainly did not.'

'I could never get into a cold bath,' said Alex.

'It's cold when you get into the sea, though, isn't it?' said Vicky.

'If you closed your eyes and got into a cold bath you could pretend it was the sea,' said Alex.

'You'd have to put some salt in though. And a fish,' said Vicky.

'Ugh! Suppose there was a whale!' said Alex.

'Or a jellyfish!' said Vicky.

'Would you get into a cold bath with a jellyfish, daddy?' asked Alex.

Sometimes George wondered if he was living in an asylum.

Saturday 30th September 1911

A quiet morning. George was glad the week was over. The British & Colonial Mercantile Land Trust had held an offer for sale of new shares and all his clients went for it. On top of that The Northern Alkali Company had a deeply discounted rights issue and all his clients had gone for that too. In order to pay for the new shares many clients had been offloading stock they'd held for years and consequently lost the share certificates. The accounts office would be burning the midnight oil over the following few weeks. There was talk of more rights issues before Christmas so a busy time ahead for the firm.

The gas was restored on Wednesday so he was able to luxuriate in a delayed hot bath, without, he was pleased to note, sea creatures of any description. Stripp had finished the roof. A lightning conductor had been installed and the scaffolding had come down. He was going to start on Polly's room on Monday. There was no further correspondence from any of the co-conspirators.

Celandine's school was holding an 'open afternoon' for parents and family to go in and look round. George had been looking forward to a quiet hour or two with his Bechstein but was dragooned into attending. Clementine had fully recovered and insisted that it was his duty to inspect the education establishment his niece was attending. Of course, on thinking about it, he realised that he did have a considerable financial interest; therefore it would be a good opportunity for him to see how this modern academy instilled wisdom and knowledge in its enthusiastic charges.

First impressions are very important and they were met by Miss Oswaldwhistle herself who shook hands with George most vigorously despite not having the faintest idea who he was. There was then a rather amusing comedy of errors when she was under the impression that Vicky and Alex were pupils (Not a bad idea, actually. Might give them something to do, he thought) before they were taken in charge by a senior girl who was introduced by Miss Oswaldwhistle as, so George thought, Rapunzel (but was sure he misheard – her hair wasn't long enough) and who seemed very pleasant. They were whisked round in a businesslike fashion, looked in on a neat classroom which had a globe rather precariously suspended from the ceiling; admired the well-stocked library: 'Which contains all the classics and some suitable modern literature, even Angela Brazil, of course'; and cast an approving eye over the gymnasium where some girls were putting on a display which seemed to require much arm waving and jumping up and down in the best English and Continental manner. George felt exhausted just watching. There was a bit of a throng by the time they got to the main hall, tea and cakes were being served by the girls, much to George's approval, all that exercise had made him hungry and thirsty, and he enjoyed a delicious, if rather uneven, slice of Victoria sponge. Humpidge would have had two slices.

CHAPTER TWELVE ~

~ Disharmony

———e·ɔ———

Sunday 1st October 1911

The visit to Celandine's school reminded George that he still hadn't solved the vexed question of what to do about Vicky and Alex. He had hoped that by now there would be some suitable admirers but none seemed to appear. He found it difficult to understand. They were very attractive young women; intelligent, accomplished, well-read and came from a good respectable family. A little eccentric and secretive at times, infuriating, even, but he put that down to there being the two of them. He should have thought that they would have been snapped up by now but no, not a bit of it. He resolved to talk to Rosalind about it. He was, however, diverted from his intentions by a brouhaha emanating from the dining room. Then Polly appeared in the doorway.

'They're all over the place, sir! Soon as I spies one there's another one on the table or under the sideboard. Lord bless us and save us there must be a 'undred of 'em. Look! There's another! Gawd knows where they's all come from but I'd say it's that Tarpaulin as is at the bottom of it!'

Just then, a ginger kitten ran past him in the direction of the hall. Another suddenly appeared on the breakfast table and stuck its head in the cream jug. Two more were getting into a dreadful tangle with a ball of wool. A fifth appeared to have taken a great interest in a potted palm by the door and a sixth was sat in the middle of the floor looking quizzically at Mrs Sprackett who, by now, had become very red in the face.

'Goodness! What a lot of kittens!' said Rosalind as she came through from the drawing room. 'And they're all ginger! Like miniature Tarporleys!'

'Rosalind! There are cats all over—' Clementine stopped in mid-flow as she came into the dining room to a scene of feline mayhem.

'Mummy, daddy, we've just seen—' Vicky and Alex converged on the bewhiskered menagerie.

'Auntie Rosalind, look what I found,' said Celandine, holding a ball of ginger fluff.

Mrs Sprackett was rapidly approaching the point where George feared she would explode.

'Gordon Bennett, I never seen so many kets! I won't 'ave 'em in my kitchen, mum, I don't 'old with kets in the kitchen. They'll 'ave to be drownded, all of 'em!'

'No!' Came a collective protest, although Clementine, notably, did not join in.

'We'll look after them, won't we, Vicks? Celandine?'

An insistent chorus of 'Yes!'

At that moment there was a knock at the front door. 'Daddy, it's the scarecrow!' said Alex looking out of the window.

Glad of the chance to escape George went to see what he wanted. As he opened the door, a kitten squeezed between his legs and began to play with his shoelace.

'Morning Mr Chesshyre. I see you've found 'em, then,' said Stripp, grinning and inclining his head towards George's new-found ginger friend.

'What? You know about it?'

'Yes, came across 'em yesterday in the boiler 'ouse while you were out. I jest came round to see if you had any tools, see. I 'ope you don't mind if I come round to see if you 'ad any tools, Mr Chesshyre?'

'No, of course not, although I don't suppose you found any.'

'Not so much as a rake or a 'oe, Mr Chesshyre. I've made a list of what you'll need.' He thrust a piece of paper towards him. 'But what I did find was this little ginger family all snuggled up together at the back of the boiler 'ouse wall. Oh, it was a sight to gladden the 'eart, Mr Chesshyre. Doesn't it gladden your 'eart, Mr Chesshyre? An' Mrs Chesshyre's too as I shouldn't wonder. I told Mrs Stripp when I got 'ome as 'ow I'd come across 'em by accident, as it were, an' do you know what she said, Mr Chesshyre?

She said it would've gladdened 'er 'eart to see 'em, Mr Chesshyre. We've never been blessed with animals ourselves on account of they get's on 'er chest terrible bad.'

George didn't manage to get to the bottom of how the kittens had got out or where, or indeed, who, their mother was. However, he did have a list of garden tools it was imperative to possess. More expense. It got on his bank balance terrible bad.

Things had calmed down a little by the time he'd finished with Stripp. The girls had rounded up and corralled the kittens in a box; had gone into a huddle discussing what to do with them and were no doubt thinking up unsuitable names. Mrs Sprackett had retired to the kitchen and there was, thankfully, no more talk of drownings.

There was a bumper crop of hymns again that morning: 'All Creatures of our God and King' (George thought the irony was lost on Clementine), 'Come Down, O Love Divine', 'Glorious Things of Thee are Spoken'. A fairly short drone from Humpidge. George had no idea what he was going on about although he did catch something about a hairy man and a smooth man which, if nothing else, reminded him to ask Rosalind to get him some new razor blades.

At the risk of incurring Mrs Sprackett's wrath he invited Eugene back for lunch. He'd had it in the back of his mind to do so because he'd wanted to have a bit of a chat with him about musical styles and felt sure he wouldn't be wedded to the late middle ages like some people. He hadn't mentioned it to the girls because he didn't want a repeat of the previous ablutary excesses. He was sure the 'Thermoboil' had never really recovered from that episode.

Mrs Sprackett had, despite the kitten infestation, excelled herself and produced a magnificent joint of topside of beef. The roast potatoes were particularly good and the Yorkshire puddings as light as a feather. As if this wasn't enough, an apple pie of gargantuan proportions appeared with wonderfully creamy, steaming custard. Afterwards, the afternoon being fine and warm, they went out into the conservatory for coffee. There was such an interminable babble and intermittent screeching going on between the girls that Eugene and George couldn't hear themselves think so he suggested they go to the music room where they rather startled Celandine who was seated at the Bechstein. She jumped up as soon as they entered.

'I'm sorry, Uncle George. I should have asked.'

'That's all right, Celandine,' he said. 'You don't have to ask. You have my permission to play whenever you want to.'

'Mummy says I'm not to play your piano. She says it's too good for me.'

George was rather taken aback. 'But, Celandine, the piano was always meant for you. So that you could continue your studies. And Mr Rickenbacker is an excellent teacher.'

'Mummy doesn't like Mr Rickenbacker. But I like you, Mr Rickenbacker. And I like you, too Uncle George. And Auntie Rosalind and Vicky and Alex. But mummy hates me. She blames me for daddy dying but I couldn't help it. I didn't want my daddy to die and I miss him and I wish he was here now.'

Floods of uncontrollable tears.

Before George could say anything she'd run out of the room and gone upstairs. Moments later Rosalind and Clementine came in.

'George, what's happened?' asked Rosalind. 'Why is Celandine crying like that? What on earth have you done to upset her so?'

'Have you been *looming* again George?' asked Clementine, icily. 'Just the sight of you frightens her half to death. And what have you to say for yourself, young man?' she said, turning to Eugene. 'Turning her head with more of that heathen music I suppose?'

For George that was the final straw. He snapped. 'That will DO!' he said, rounding on Clementine. 'I will not have this! And don't you DARE speak to Mr Rickenbacker like that! He is a guest in this house at my invitation, as are you, I might remind you.' George was shaken by his own ferocity. He could hear his voice but somehow it didn't sound like him. It was as though his voice was outside his body, that it was someone else speaking. His words seemed to echo round his head and he felt faint for a moment. His stomach griped as though it had been filled with a block of ice. He knew instantly as he spoke that he was crossing the Rubicon, that there was now no going back, that bridges were being burned in the most spectacular fashion and that nothing – nothing in the house would ever be the same again. But he was on the edge – on that fine point of just keeping control and in imminent and fatal danger of losing it. Events flashed through his mind rapidly as he remembered all the altercations he had had with Clementine. There had been friction ever since that day he had met them at Waterloo. It had been a battle that had ebbed and flowed ever since. The internecine struggle, trying to keep the peace, trying to be diplomatic, dealing with the infernal weather, all of this had been building up in him and now he had reached breaking point. Like a steel rod put under greater and greater stress, it will bend so far and then it will snap. But the dam had burst – and the water was now unstoppable.

'*George!*' said Rosalind, shocked.

'Oh! I've never been so insulted!' said Clementine.

'Then perhaps it's time you were,' he said, his heart thumping. 'That little girl is breaking her heart and you're too blind to see it. She's been unhappy ever since she came to live here and we've all failed to notice it. We're all to blame. She misses her father desperately and she thinks she's to blame for his death. God knows what you've been telling her, Clementine but I tell you, I will not stand by and see her upset like that.'

'You can't speak to me like that!'

'Oh yes I can. I've had enough, Clementine. Things are about to change around here and you can begin by apologising to Mr Rickenbacker. He is the most able and excellent teacher and a true gentleman. Something you seem unable to recognise.'

'Really, Mr Chesshyre, it's not nec—'

'I'm sorry, Eugene but I'm afraid it is.'

'I will NOT apologise.'

'Then you will leave my house. You're not welcome here anymore.'

'*George!*'

'I'm sorry, Rosalind, but I want this woman gone by the time I come home tomorrow night.'

'But what about Celandine?' said Rosalind clasping her hands in anguish.

'Celandine will stay here with us. I'll make her a ward of court if necessary.'

'You can't do that!' said Clementine.

'I can and I will. I shall have you declared an unfit mother.'

'Oh! Rosalind! Do something!'

'George, you can't mean it. You're not yourself. You've been working too hard. It's the sun. The heat, that dreadful summer. It's made you ill!'

'I'm perfectly well, thank you Rosalind. Now, I'm going to my study. And if you have any compassion whatsoever you will go and look after Celandine.'

He left the room and made his way past the shocked faces of Vicky, Alex, Mrs Sprackett, Polly and Dolly. As he went, he remembered Eugene. Too late. He'd apologise to him later.

Tuesday 10th October 1911

'The long hours go and come and go'

Christina Rossetti – *'The Prince's Progress'*

George's last clear memory was of having a blazing row with Clementine in the music room and telling her to get out of the house. He remembered at the time thinking that it was so unlike him to lose his temper in that way. He was feeling a mixture of anger and remorse; Celandine's outburst had taken him completely by surprise but at that moment it was almost as though the scales had dropped from his eyes. The fraught and trying relationship he had always had with Clementine had over-shadowed any understanding he should have developed for Celandine and ever since they had arrived on that hot August bank holiday she had existed in a kind of penumbra cast by her mother. Of course the last few months must have been dreadful for her; her whole world had been turned upside down. Losing her father unexpectedly and tragically would have fomented an inner trauma probably impossibly difficult to share or express bearing in mind Clementine's forceful and rigid character. Of course he didn't know what passed between them during the time of his death and their arrival at Scattersdale Avenue but he'd never heard Clementine speak to her about it or refer to it in any way. Thinking back he was amazed that she had proved so resilient in the face of what she was being asked to cope with without much support from any corner. He had dealt with her presence in a somewhat offhand and flippant way, pouring money into the problem by way of school fees and pianos as though they were instant panaceas but they couldn't replace the gaping hole that had been left in her life. She needed a father figure and he was a poor substitute. 'I like you, Uncle George,' she had said before breaking down. The poor scrap. Why should she like him? What had he done for her besides foisting a monster of a piano on her probably in a bid to assuage his own ego? 'Mummy says it's too good for me'. Of course it's not too good for you, Celandine. A thousand Bechsteins would never be too good for you. They would never replace your father.

He had gone up to his study and found himself sweating and trembling most alarmingly. What had he done? Had he been irrational? Had the Rubicon been crossed? He had steadied himself with a large Johnnie Walker Special Old Highland which he kept purely for medicinal purposes while he tried to make sense of the situation and wondered desperately whether he could salvage anything from the debris. He made his mind up that he would compose himself and then go back down in an attempt to pour some much needed oil on some very troubled waters. After a few minutes he felt no better and his heart began to race uncontrollably. His left arm suddenly became very stiff as though experiencing a bout of cramp. He remembered the glass falling to the floor and then he presumed he had blacked out.

***

Having been diagnosed as suffering a mild heart attack he was now safely tucked up in bed at St Thomas's Hospital, Lambeth. He was not allowed to do anything, which was probably quite sensible at first, but now he was feeling much better and really wished they would let him get out of bed. He was in a room of his own which was rather stark and painted in a nausea-inducing scheme of green and cream. There was a large window which let in a lot of light but was too high for him to see anything out of. There was a permanent smell of antiseptic. This was the first time he'd ever been in hospital and it was a novel and unnerving experience. He'd been barely aware of the previous few days apart from the gradual darkening at night and then the gradual lightening of the morning. He'd been sleeping a lot and felt that he'd not had much, if anything to eat, although a nurse came round regularly and insisted he drank some water. There had been other shadowy visitors and a doctor in a white coat came and looked at him occasionally.

That morning he was feeling strong enough to sit up and a rather severe nurse who bustled about from time to time proclaimed that he was, 'Looking a lot better, we'll soon have you back home'. Lying in bed not being allowed to do anything for hours at a time gives you a lot of time to think. He wasn't at all sure whether this was a good or bad thing. When he had first come round he imagined that he was in bed at home and that everything that had occurred was just a bad dream. Gradually he began to realise that he was not in his own bed and all the dreadful events were real. His blood ran cold when he thought about what he'd done. He kept going over the row he'd had with Clementine and thinking that he'd been very harsh. He'd have to make it up with her. He'd told her to get out of the house but he didn't really mean it. He'd said it in the heat of the moment and regretted it almost immediately. The poor woman had lost her husband and had been reduced to living with her sister and her cantankerous husband, not to mention the somewhat unconventional twins, a firebrand of a cook, two dotty maids and enough cats and kittens to start a cattery. He was sure they could call a truce and start again. Perhaps he could even get Eugene to explain a few things about 'modern' music and how it really wasn't so bad. In time, perhaps, she might even get to like it. And poor little Celandine. He couldn't get her out of his head. Her pale little face dissolving into tears played on his mind in a kind of nightmarish way and he couldn't get the image out of his consciousness. They must all try harder for her. Perhaps she would find some nice friends at her new school and it would stop her feeling so lonely and sad. God, they'd all been so blind. He'd had a jolly close shave. It had pulled him up short all right.

Wednesday 11th October 1911

The following morning George was feeling much better. He managed two slices of toast and marmalade for breakfast. The marmalade was surprisingly good and he wondered if he'd be able to find out its make. He was beginning to feel fed up lying in bed so he asked a breezy young nurse he'd not seen before and who was energetically bashing his pillows if he could get up for a bit.

'Holy Mother of God aren't you the keen one?' she said as his pillows were manoeuvred back into place behind his head. This very direct response rather took George aback. 'I'll see what the doctor says but you're to be patient, mind.' Direct she may have been but she gave George an understanding smile. Pillow bashing had now ceased and was being followed by some furious sheet straightening.

He assured her that, unfortunately, he was not the most patient of patients. Apparently this was uproariously funny and was seized upon with an outbreak of such robust mirth that his pillows required a further furious pummelling. 'Not the most patient of patients! Oh, it's a joker that you are, isn't that right Mr Chesshyre? A joker? Not the most patient of patients! Sure I'd never heard that before! What are we to do with you?'

Despite feeling anything but 'the joker' George was warming to this friendly soul who had no idea of the inner turmoil he was going through. Meanwhile the bustling continued.

'Now, if you're not here when I get back I shall want to know where you've been,' came the stern admonition when the pummelling had ceased and the pillows were surely dead. George was at a loss to respond to this but he didn't really get the chance because a thermometer was suddenly stuck in his mouth and his pulse was being taken. While these procedures were being carried out the doctor who'd been looking after him came in wearing a benevolent smile.

'Good morning Mr Chesshyre. How are we today?'

'We' couldn't answer him because 'our' mouth was still full of thermometer. However, George raised his eyebrows and nodded an affirmation which he hoped would be interpreted as, 'Very well, thank you, doctor'.

'Mr Chesshyre was asking whether he could be getting up for a while, doctor,' said the nurse who was apparently satisfied with the state of his pulse although his temperature was still under investigation.

'You were asking after whether you could be getting up for a while weren't you Mr Chesshyre?' she said, turning to him and smiling and nodding as if, George thought, he were a congenital idiot.

Another nod and an attempted smile.

The doctor's benevolent smile turned to a frown then back to a smile. 'Yes, if you feel up to it. Do you good. Don't overdo it, though.' With that he was gone.

'There now, what did I tell you?' said the nurse, filling in his chart at the foot of the bed. Again George was left trying to work out what it was she had told him but was immediately side-tracked by the bedclothes being pulled back and his dressing gown whirled around his shoulders in the manner of a matador, his legs swung out over the side of the bed and his feet expertly planted in his carpet slippers which just happened to be in the right place. As he assumed an upright position the thermometer was whisked away with a cursory glance and, 'Sweet Jesus, would you look at that!'; his arms were then threaded through the sleeves of his dressing gown, the cord being tied in a jiffy. He felt quite breathless but glad to be vertical again.

'Now, if you behave yourself, you can have a bath later on. Won't that be nice, now?'

George replied that the prospect filled him with deep joy.

'Is it a bath you'd be having at home, Mr Chesshyre?'

He replied that he was in possession of two but rarely had the opportunity to use them.

A look of extreme shock. 'Glory be! Why is that now? Sure if I had two baths I'd never be out of them!'

He told her that the reason was because he shared the house with eight women.

A further look of even more extreme shock. 'Holy Mother of God! Is it a priest that you are?'

For a moment George felt a faint flutter of happiness and decided to have some fun at the expense of Rome. 'I was a priest but I was defrocked by the Holy Father and excommunicated to a house of ill-repute in Streatham.'

A look of abject horror dissolved into an indulgent frown. 'Oh, go on with you! Don't joke with me! I'll put you over my knee, big as you are!'

There was a comfortable easy chair in the room and after he was settled she scuttled off with the promise of a 'cup of tea shortly'.

George was not a man given to illness. In fact he had been remarkably lucky when he thought back. Apart from the usual childhood maladies such as chicken pox and measles he seemed to have got through to his fifties remarkably unscathed. Oh, he got the odd cold now and then the same as everyone but nothing to really lay him low. Doctors and hospitals therefore were a novelty to him. He had been sitting in the chair for about twenty minutes, he supposed, when he realised that he was getting bored despite being allowed out of bed. There was nothing to read and he couldn't see out of the window; the promised cup of tea hadn't yet materialised so he thought he'd go out on a bit of a reconnoitre. He managed to get out of the chair without too much difficulty and had a look out of the window for the first time since he'd been admitted. Not a particularly pleasing prospect, he thought. Just a roof-line a few yards away and a row of chimney pots. He was, however relieved to see that a lightning conductor had been fitted. St Thomas's wouldn't have any trouble with Holborn Citadel. Dispirited by the unappealing vista, he turned his attention to the door and what lay beyond. He felt a bit like a prisoner making a break for it. He wondered whether there'd be barbed wire and sentry posts placed at strategic positions. There were. He hadn't got more than a few yards along the corridor when he was commanded to halt. '*Mr* Chesshyre! And where do you think you're going this fine morning?' He'd recognise that lovely Irish brogue anywhere. He half-turned round to face his nemesis who was armed with a cup of tea when out of the corner of his eye he spotted Rosalind advancing from the opposite direction. He was trapped. There was no way out. His two assailants bore down on him with a menacing purpose, took one arm each and escorted him back to his room. He knew when he was beaten. He was ordered back into bed and told to drink his tea, 'Like a good boy'.

'She seems very nice,' said Rosalind as the nurse left with a severe warning that there would be trouble all right if he continued to disobey orders.

'Tis a holy terror that she is,' he said when he was sure she was out of earshot.

'George, don't make fun. How are you feeling to-day?'

'Fit as a flea. Don't know what I'm doing in here.'

'You're looking much better. You've got some colour in your cheeks.'

'Well, I'm feeling quite cheerful. Molly Malone's giving me a bath later on. Won't that be nice?'

'Well, make sure she washes behind your ears and dries between your toes.'

'How are things at home? House still standing, is it?'

'Yes, of course it is.' She went over to the window and looked out, not seeing anything. Her hands clenched and unclenched. She was visibly shaking, trying to control her emotions but he could see she was losing the battle. That fleeting, rare light moment had gone. A dark cloud had descended and thrown a veil of despair over the room. When you have been married for so many years and lived intimately with a person you know instinctively when something is wrong. Something was, indeed, very wrong at that moment. 'Oh, George this is a terrible time,' she turned to him, her voice breaking. 'All this upset between you and Clemmie. I haven't been able to sleep at night worrying about it and you in here as well.'

George turned grey. The colour left his cheeks and a shiver went through him. That flame, that little light that had tried so hard to kindle over the last few minutes guttered and went out. Rosalind was the most composed of women and just the sort you'd want with you in a crisis but at that moment the façade broke and she collapsed, weeping uncontrollably. George might have been a cantankerous, peppery old bear but he would not see his family upset. In a moment he was out of bed brazenly defying the Sister of Mercy and holding Rosalind who was shaking in a manner he'd never witnessed in her before even when she got to end of her tether with him which was not infrequent. She clung to him tightly and gradually the tears subsided. He got her sat down in the chair. 'George, I'm sorry. I shouldn't be worrying you like this. You're not well.'

'Absolute rot, old girl,' he said. 'I'm perfectly all right. Probably my own fault, anyway. I shouldn't have blown my top at Clemmie. It was unforgiveable. Now it's got you upset and out of sorts. Even more unforgiveable. I wouldn't see you upset for all the tea in China. But it'll be all right. You'll see. I'll be out of here in a day or two; back home with you and the girls and I'll make things right with Clemmie. Oh, Lord, she hasn't left has she?' He remembered suddenly telling her to go.

'No George. She's still at home. She was beside herself when you were taken ill. She locked herself in her room and wouldn't come out. I could hear her crying for hours. Oh, George it was awful. I just didn't know what to do. They wouldn't let me go to the hospital with you. Poor little Celandine was in a dreadful state and wouldn't come away from Clemmie's door. But the girls were wonderful. They calmed her down. Vicky managed to coax her downstairs and Mrs Sprackett made her some cocoa. Then Alex found a kitten, Whisper, Celandine's favourite, and brought it through for her to play with. Polly and Dolly came out with some dreadful jokes. I can't think where they got them from but it seemed to cheer her a little. Oh, everyone was so kind, George. And then Alex and I went back upstairs to try to get Clemmie to open the door. Oh, George it was awful. I can't think how long we were there trying to calm her down. Then I felt faint, George and

I had to go and lie down but Alex went back to Clemmie's room after she'd made sure I was all right. I don't know how she did it but she managed to get her to open the door. Well, I heard them talking and I got up and went to Clemmie's room and she threw her arms round me and begged my forgiveness and said she was wicked and that she never meant any of it and pleaded with me not to make her go away or take Celandine from her. I told her she was being silly and that no-one was going to do anything of the kind. Then Alex brought us up some tea and that seemed to settle her a little.'

George had never felt so shocked. He had no idea that all this was going on while he was lying in a hospital bed and not able to do anything about it. Waves of guilt swept over him. Guilt that he hadn't been there. Guilt that he'd caused Rosalind so much upset. Guilt that he'd caused such calamity to fall on the household. He felt light-headed and needed all his reserves of strength to be the rock that Rosalind needed at that moment. 'Oh, lor, Ros,' he said. 'If only I'd been there. This is all my doing. I should have been more understanding. I've been perfectly beastly to Clemmie haven't I?'

'No, George, of course you haven't. You've been very accommodating. Clemmie can be very difficult. She was always known as the difficult one even when we were children. But, George, oh, it's all such a whirl in my head. What with coming up here to see you that evening and the doctors telling me you were going to be all right and then getting back home at goodness knows what hour. Eugene was a brick. He got the doctor and the ambulance and came with me in the taxi after what seemed like an age. None of us got any sleep that night. Even the storm wasn't as bad as that. I think the dawn was breaking – or it might even have been the evening – I just don't know – when Clemmie told me everything. She swore me to secrecy, George, but I have to tell you. I've never had any secrets from you, George. Oh, I still can't believe it.'

Tears again. At that moment Molly Malone came bustling in again with a face like thunder. 'Glory be, Mr Chesshyre, will you look at your poor wife now! What in Heaven's name has caused such misery? Don't take on so my little angel, sure he'll be all right. Right as ninepence in a week or two so he will.' She produced a handkerchief half the size of a bed sheet from somewhere, put her arm round Rosalind and dried her tears.

'I'm sorry, nurse,' said Rosalind, trying desperately hard to compose herself. 'I'm so grateful to you and so relieved that my husband is better. I'm afraid I've had rather a lot of shocks recently. My sister—'

'Ah, family trouble. 'tis a trial all right. And illness is troublesome to a person. Your dear sister, now, enjoying bad health is it that she is?'

'I don't know – that is – I think so, oh, I'm not sure. I need to talk to my husband about it but I don't want to worry him and he's been so ill—'

'Ros, old girl, I'm perfectly all right,' said George. 'Whatever it is that's troubling you I want you to tell me. I'm sure it can't be so bad that it can't be fixed.'

'There now, you see,' said Molly. 'You sit down here and have a nice quiet chat with your husband. I'll be off now and bring you a nice cup of tea. Won't that be nice?'

Rosalind nodded. The words wouldn't come. He'd never seen her so distressed.

George wasn't sure now, with the passage of time, how long they sat there while Rosalind gradually related the story. When everything was revealed he was shocked and surprised to the core. He had never suspected anything remotely akin to what transpired.

Celandine was not Bertie's daughter.

CHAPTER THIRTEEN ~

~ Harmonies

———— ❧ ————

'He maketh me to lie down in green pastures: he leadeth me beside the still waters. He restoreth my soul.'

Psalm 23

Friday 13th October 1911

George was discharged and allowed to go home. Rosalind went with Eugene and fetched him at ten o'clock that morning. Stripp senior had spoken to Alf and they collected George in his cab. He was a bit unsteady on his pins but it was a blessèd relief to get out of the hospital. Not that he meant that to sound unkind or critical of St Thomas's. The doctors and nurses were all excellent (especially 'Molly Malone' who helped him to get his things together and accompanied Rosalind and him out to the taxi), kind and friendly in their professional way but it was a fine feeling to see Scattersdale Avenue SW again. What he hadn't bargained on was the welcoming committee. As soon as the cab drew up there were arms being thrown round him from all directions. Alex, Vicky and Celandine would not let go and by the waterfalls of tears being shed he thought he must have died and was now a ghost haunting his old home, his family mere apparitions who would dissolve at any moment and evaporate into the ether.

Mrs Sprackett and Polly and Dolly were all in tears with their aprons up round their eyes.

'Oh, Mr Chesshyre, sir,' Mrs Sprackett went on, 'I'm so glad to see you, sir! I knew'd 'as you you'd come back to us, sir. I said all along. Didn't I say, mum? 'e'll be back before we knows it sir. But you did give us sich a fright, sir. Lord, when we see'd you a'lyin' on the floor of your sanatorium, sir, we didn't know what to do an' then Mr Bracken'opper, 'e took charge, as you might say, and 'e run along to Dr. MacAroon and 'e got the hambulance and you was whisked away to the horsepittle, sir an' we thought as 'ow we was never goin' to see you again, sir, oh, it was terrible to be'old, sir!'

After this dramatic welcome which ended in Mrs Sprackett, Polly and Dolly dissolving into tears again, George felt as though he needed a lie down. The only person he hadn't seen was Clementine. He felt some relief that she wasn't there but at the same time a sense of great uneasiness.

He must have slept for several hours. Or perhaps he just dozed. He was aware of Rosalind coming in from time to time to see how he was. The light was beginning to go when the door opened. He thought it was just her again but, to his great surprise he could just make out Clementine's silhouette in the doorway behind her. It was the first time he had seen her since he had come back home. The glimpse, however, was fleeting, and in a second she had vanished. Just for a moment he remembered the time he had seen Celandine in the doorway of his study, how she, too, had fled, wraith-like.

Two lost souls.

Saturday 14th October 1911

The next morning George woke up in his own bed for the first time in fortnight. It made him realise how hard hospital beds were and he didn't intend to try them for size again anytime soon. He was still a bit unsteady on his feet but a good night's rest had worked wonders. He went down to the dining room in his dressing gown, something he'd never done before but, despite protestations from Rosalind that he should have breakfast in bed, he wouldn't hear of it and wanted to go down to see everybody. Besides, there was the possibility of kippers, provided Tarporley hadn't got there first, and he hadn't had a home-cooked breakfast for much too long.

He was destined to be disappointed. On the dining room table was a cardboard box with a picture of a very peculiar chap with a wide grin on his face, apparently jumping over a fence. The box proclaimed, in large capitals, that it contained a commodity entitled, 'FORCE'.

'Good Lord, what's this?' he said, when he'd managed to disentangle himself from more hugs and kisses, Clementine excepted. Rosalind told him quietly that she was unwell and was confined to her room.

'That's your new breakfast, daddy,' said Alex, tucking into a sausage.

'Dr. MacAroon said it's what you have to have from now on,' said Vicky, cutting a rasher of bacon.

'But don't worry, we won't FORCE you to eat it!' said Alex.

An outbreak of giggling.

'I should bloomin' well think not!' said George, looking into the box. 'It's nothing but dry flakes of something. Can't think why he'd want me to eat that.'

'Don't be silly, daddy,' said Alex. 'You put some in a bowl and pour milk over it.'

'And you can put sugar on it if you like,' said Vicky. 'But not *too* much.'

'Well, I don't like the look of it one bit,' he said. 'I shall stick to my kippers.'

'Dr MacAroon'll be cross. He's coming to see you this morning. He said we had to keep an eye on you and make sure you don't do too much,' said Alex.

'Yes, like gardening,' said Vicky.

'Well, I shouldn't think that's very likely.'

'The scarecrow's been busy but he said he can't do much until he gets a spade,' said Alex.

'And a rake,' said Vicky.

'And a real barrow,' chimed in Celandine, only half paying attention and trying unsuccessfully to ignore the 'Force' chappie. Saucer eyes had not diminished in any way during his absence. George hoped he didn't give her nightmares. He studied her for a moment, trying not to be obvious. She looked paler than ever if that were possible. Her features were gaunt and there was a faraway look in the saucer eyes. He wondered what was going on behind the façade. Despite the happy homecoming there was deep trouble in their midst.

'Wheelbarrow, silly,' said Alex, jolting him back to the present.

'That's what I said!'

'No you didn't, you said real barrow,' said Vicky.

'I think I might like this "Force",' said Celandine (ignoring the correction) who had conquered her fear of the lurid fellow and had bravely got as far as looking into the box at the orange flakes secreted therein. 'Uncle George, why don't you try some?'

For a moment George felt relieved. It was only a small thing but the 'Force' had attracted her attention and interest. He played along with her request as cheerfully as he could even though he felt unenthusiastic at the prospect of dry flakes for breakfast. 'Oh, all right. I'm game. Perhaps I might find a pair of kippers swimming about.'

'Don't be silly, daddy!'

'Well, this chap on the box looks like he's doing well on it,' he said. 'A few bowlfuls of this and I shall be jumping fences alongside him!'

Shaking a fairly decent pile into his bowl, he poured on some milk and sprinkled a little sugar (not too much) onto the mixture. He tried a spoonful. All eyes were on him waiting for the verdict. At first the flakes were quite hard but if you left them for a few moments the milk softened them and they were easier to chew. A slightly more liberal sprinkling of sugar (to the disapproval of Vicky) made them more palatable and by the end of the bowl he was quite surprised to realise that he had rather enjoyed 'Force'. He wasn't giving up kippers altogether, though. Or sausages and bacon. It would be an insult to Mrs Sprackett and he didn't intend to offend her in any way whatsoever. Her Sunday roasts were legendary and it was the thought of one of those that kept him going during the 'Force' experiment.

Dr. MacAroon called in at about eleven. George didn't know him at all. Since they moved to Scattersdale Avenue they hadn't needed to consult a physician. Even during their time in Sydenham they very rarely needed the doctor's services. He wasn't quite prepared for the whirlwind that was about to descend on the house. Dr MacAroon was a Scot. Tall, with a military bearing and manner, he marched into the drawing room where George was 'resting' after his strenuous breakfast.

'Mr Chesshyre, good morning! How are you feeling?' Within seconds his bag was open and a stethoscope fixed round his neck. Without waiting for an answer, he carried on. 'Just open your shirt please.' In an instant the cold end of the stethoscope was prodding about George's chest. He had barely time to take a breath before it was taken away.

'Any shortness of breath?'

'Not noticeably,' he replied.

'Hmm. Dizziness? Feeling faint?'

'Only when I see the latest pile of bills,' he replied, rather pleased with his quick wit.

'Hmm. Do you smoke, Mr Chesshyre?'

'Never smoked in my life,' he replied, hoping that this was the right answer.

'You should consider taking up the pipe. Very relaxing pastime. Too much stress these days, Mr Chesshyre. Not good for us. Stress is what caused your condition. No exertion, now. A little gentle exercise, a ten minute walk each day and a large Scotch in the evening before retiring. No heavy meals at night, a light breakfast, I recommend "Force" flakes or porridge, and I'll call in and see you again on Monday. Good day Mr Chesshyre.'

The whirlwind blew itself out as quickly as it had entered.

'Well?' said Rosalind, anxiously, who had been waiting outside.

'I've got to smoke a pipe and drink more whisky,' said George with a straight face.

'George!'

'It's true! It's what he told me to do. He said smoking a pipe was relaxing and I'd not to get stressed. And I've got to take a walk each day to the pub.'

'Oh, George! You're impossible!'

'Well, I made that bit up about the pub but perhaps I could combine an evening walk with taking my medicine.'

'What medicine?'

'The whisky.'

'George, I'm going to get very cross if you don't start taking this seriously.'

'But it's true, Ros. That's exactly what he told me to do.'

'Well, I'm going to get a second opinion. When I told Mrs McGillycuddy she recommended her own physician, Dr. Ainslie-Cathcart. He's been her doctor for thirty years and she wouldn't have any other. I shall get him to call on Monday.'

'Dr MacAroon's coming again on Monday.'

'Good, perhaps Dr. Ainslie-Cathcart will give him a piece of his mind! Pipes, and whisky, for goodness sake!'

Sunday 15th October 1911

The next day, being Sunday, George was excused church. After a leisurely breakfast which consisted of a bowl of 'Force' a slice of toast and a rather illicit sausage which Vicky had left on her plate because she 'simply couldn't eat another thing', he retired to the conservatory which was comfortably warm in the early autumn sun. The house was empty apart from Polly, Dolly and Mrs Sprackett who were busy preparing the Sunday lunch and George dozed fitfully as he listened to the kitchen rattle and prattle that was going on faintly in the background. What a wonderful time of the week is Sunday morning if you don't have to go to church. You can sit in the conservatory looking out over the garden, you can hear the birds singing, there are no small boys with pea-shooters to bother you and no scarecrows to frighten you half to death. Of course it couldn't last. At half-past twelve the hurricane blew in. Suddenly the house was full of chattering, banging of doors and intermittent screeches of laughter. As if this wasn't enough something had gone wrong in the kitchen and Mrs Sprackett was scolding Polly and Dolly for some undisclosed misdemeanour. George sighed. He was just wondering how much longer he could keep out of the mayhem when the conservatory door swung open and Humpidge appeared closely followed by Eugene with Celandine trailing behind trying to be inconspicuous but failing by dint of saucer eyes giving her away immediately. As if this wasn't enough, not two minutes later Stripp senior appeared at the front of the conservatory accompanied by several kittens who immediately found it necessary to jump on George's lap, shoulder and head. So much for quiet Sunday mornings. Earnest enquiries were made concerning the state of his health. George felt like saying that he had been recuperating very nicely thank you up until a few moments ago but was in serious danger of suffering a relapse at any moment but thought better of it. Then from somewhere a cake appeared. George wasn't allowed any. Humpidge had two slices.

Monday 16th October 1911

The next morning at eleven, Dr MacAroon blew in with whirlwind force and was in the process of stethoscope exercise when Dr Ainslie-Cathcart arrived. Rosalind showed him in and George was immediately forgotten.

'Hamish! I thought that was your car outside,' said Dr A-C. 'How are you man?'

'Ah, Douglas, well, man, well. Havenae see you for a while!'

The two shook hands vigorously.

'I've been away home,' said Douglas. 'I've a younger man looking after the practice now. He's taking over completely in the new year.'

Oh dear, thought George. That's going to be very difficult for Mrs McGillycuddy.

'Are we both treating the same patient here, Hamish?' Douglas said with a grin and a nod towards George's direction. A feeling of invisibility had come over him again.

'I believe you're the second opinion, Douglas. Mr Chesshyre is a belt and braces man, isn't that so, Mr Chesshyre?'

'Well, I—'

'It was me that called Dr Ainslie-Cathcart, Dr MacAroon,' said Rosalind, slightly abashed. 'I always think it's best to get as much advice as possible, don't you agree?'

'Absolutely, dear lady,' said Dr MacAroon. 'Well, Douglas, he's all yours. I expect Mrs Chesshyre's given you the background.'

'Ah, yes. The old ticker misbehaving, eh? Well, let us have a listen.'

For the second time in ten minutes a stethoscope was produced and George was being prodded about in the upper chest area.

'Hmm,' said Dr Ainslie-Cathcart. 'Any shortness of breath?'

'Not noticeably.'

'Hmm. Dizziness? Feeling faint?'

'Only when I open my bank statement,' he replied, trying to vary things a little.

'Hmm. Do you smoke, Mr Chesshyre?'

'Never smoked in my life,' he said, wondering what was coming next.

'You should consider smoking a pipe, Mr Chesshyre. Very relaxing hobby. A lot of stress these days. Not good for us. Stress is probably what caused your condition in the first place. No exertion, now. A little gentle exercise, a ten minute walk each day and a glass of Guinness in the evening before retiring. Nothing too heavy at night, mind, a light, nutritious breakfast, something like porridge or "Force" flakes and you'll be back to normal in no time. Well, Hamish, what d'you think? Am I close?'

'Spot-on, man. It could have been me talking. Well, there you are, Mrs Chesshyre. Two minds, one opinion. Do you feel happier now, dear lady?'

For once, Rosalind was lost for words.

Tuesday 17th October 1911

George intended to follow Drs. MacAroon and Ainslie-Cathcart's advice to the letter. Everything except pipe smoking. He had never smoked and didn't intend to start now. Cigarettes gave off a vile, noxious smell, cigars invariably smelled like burning rubber and pipes exuded an odour reminiscent of old socks. Having said that George had to admit that some pipes did emit a sweetish, rather

pleasant aroma, but they, in his experience, were few and far between and he didn't intend to go to the trouble of seeking out the leaf that burned thus. Thinking back, he believed it was Sir Walter Raleigh who introduced tobacco into the country during the reign of Queen Elizabeth. He rather wondered why she didn't put a stop to it then. Her successor, James I certainly wasn't keen:-
'A custome lothsome to the eye, hatefull to the Nose, harmefull to the braine, dangerous to the Lungs, and in the blacke stinking fume thereof, nearest resembling the horrible Stigian smoke of the pit that is bottomelesse.'

Wednesday 18th October 1911

What a decent fellow that James I must have been, disapproving of smoking. The country must have smelled a lot sweeter in those days before that dreadful Raleigh had brought back his pile of leaves from the colonies. Now practically everyone smoked. There had even been a tendency for young women to take up the habit now that ready-made cigarettes were available Of course smoking wasn't allowed in the office but how long would that last? Pubs, restaurants, trains, omnibuses, theatres, they were all wreathed in blue smoke. Well, that would never happen at No. 3 'The Limes' Scattersdale Avenue. George smiled to himself. A smile of smoke-free satisfaction.

On the following Wednesday he had just finished a bowl of 'Force' and was contemplating whether he had room for a kipper when there was a knock at the front door.

'Daddy, it's the scarecrow!' said Vicky pulling the curtain to one side.

Moments later Dolly came bustling in carrying a brown paper parcel. 'Beg pardon, sir, but this just come for you.' She put the parcel down on the table. What on earth could Stripp be delivering at this time of the morning? Curious, he unwrapped it half expecting to find a pound of nutritious carrots or a turnip. Carefully packed in tissue paper was a pipe with a bent stem. Wrapped separately was a round tin, the label upon which declared that it contained 'McClelland's "Old Grenadier" Nut Brown Flake'. There was also a peculiar looking metal thing with spikes and a blade of sorts. A note fell out of the packaging. It read:-

'Abbotsford
5 Scattersdale Avenue

Dear Mr Chesshyre
I am deeply saddened to learn of your recent incapacity and trust that, if God spares you, you will soon be restored to full health and vitality. The cause of your indisposition is, doubtless, brain fag and there can be no better way of relieving it than by taking a pipe of fine Scotch tobacco. My late husband, Dugald, left several unsmoked pipes, one of which I enclose, and also the enclosed tin of tobacco. He always smoked Peterson pipes and McClelland's tobacco and would have no other. I know that as you settle down in the gloaming with these you will be reminded of the grouse moors and the heather and all the cares of daily life will disappear.

Yours sincerely
Agnes McGillycuddy (Mrs)

PS I should be obliged if you would keep your cats under control. I found one with its paw in my aquarium recently. Fortunately the fish, a close relation of the piranha, had the presence of mind to bite it. However, next time it might not be so fortunate. I wish you a full and speedy recovery.'

George was left wondering whether it was the cat or the fish that might not be so fortunate. As there seemed to be little interest in his unexpected acquisition, the talk being of some scurrilous society scandal, he wandered into the conservatory intent on trying this magical evincive of landscapes north of the border. He settled himself in a canvas chair and thus the rigmarole began. Thinking about it later, with the benefit of hindsight and experience, he felt he ought to advise anyone contemplating taking up the relaxing and stress-relieving hobby of pipe smoking that they should be under no illusion but it is a grim business. First, you have to understand that you need to be wearing a suit or jacket and trousers that have at least twenty pockets between them. Collecting together in one place the paraphernalia necessary to get the exercise underway is an undertaking in itself. Just when you think you have everything together under one roof you realise you are missing a vital item such as a box of matches. Finally, you reassure yourself that you have assembled a full manifest of accoutrements: Pipe, tobacco, matches, pipe cleaners, pipe *tool* (of which more later) ashtray, tobacco jar, pipe stand etc., etc.

For the benefit of the pipe *debutant* the following account is given, close attention to which is strongly recommended:

Step one – The opening of the tin. Of course this is impossible without a coin of some kind. You can't open it by hand alone because it is sealed at the factory by some invisible glueing method. After fishing about in your pocket for a penny (It has to be a penny. A ha'penny is too small and you can't get enough purchase on the side of the tin. Likewise a sixpence. A threepenny bit is completely useless and a florin is too thick. Of course you've never got a half-crown which, although the right circumference would, also, be too thick, akin to a florin) you eventually succeed in freeing the lid. By doing this you have started the irretrievable process of 'letting in the air'. What this means is that the tobacco will, from that moment on, start to dry out. Moisture content of tobacco is, as will be subsequently discovered, critical. Too wet and it won't light. Too dry and it burns too quickly, hot and dry. Achieving the optimal moisture content is virtually impossible. Without the aid of expensive humidors one is forced to rely on such peculiarities as segments of orange secreted in the tobacco jar; dousing the leaf with rum or whisky thus imparting a spirituous flavour; or steaming the leaf in a sieve over a *'bain marie'*, thus risking the wrath of the cook. It's at times like these that you think it would be easier just to open a packet of 'Gold Flake'. However, we must press on –

Step two – Finding the tobacco. On opening the tin you are presented with a pleated circle of thin paper which you have to fan open. Then there is a further circle of card which you have to work free from the tin and the tobacco beneath to which it has adhered. It is at this point that you finally get your first glimpse of the tobacco.

Step three – What to do next. 'McClelland's "Old Grenadier" Nut Brown Flake' is an oblong block of solid tobacco. Now it is quite obvious even to the most inexperienced novice that this is not going to fit the round hole of the pipe. You pick it up out of the tin. You agree that it is giving off a pleasant aroma. You put it back in the tin. You scratch your head. You scratch the tobacco and discover that it comes apart in a sort of series of layers. You manage to free an entire layer unbroken. This will still not fit in your pipe. You try it end on. It fits but looks rather silly. That can't be right. Surely tobacco should be in strands? The idea comes to you that you should break it up. A brave and perhaps foolhardy thing to do but you press ahead regardless. You now have a lot of untidy thick strands of varying shades of brown and black. You scratch your head again. Undaunted, you take a pinch and rub it between your thumb and forefinger Aha! Now it is beginning to look like your idea of tobacco! You take a bigger bit and do the same. Soon you have a small pile of stranded tobacco that looks as though it might fit your pipe perfectly.

Step four – Filling the pipe. The question is – how much do you put in? How tightly do you pack it? These are problems to which there are no easy solutions. Too tight and the pipe won't 'draw'. Too loose and you will find yourself sucking on hot air. You have to be brave and do what you think is right.

Step five – Lighting the pipe. Having got this far you are filled with trepidation. Rather like igniting a large rocket on Guy

Fawkes Night, you are not quite certain what is going to happen. Earlier in this history an account was given of the trials and difficulties experienced when trying to light the 'Thermoboil'. It can now be revealed that getting the 'Thermoboil' going is a pleasant, easy and agreeable pastime compared with trying to ignite 'Old Grenadier'. The first 'Swan Vesta' goes out without doing anything. As does the second. The third whimpers and dies despite some furious sucking on the mouthpiece. You manage to keep the fourth alight by sucking and moving the match around the top of the bowl. Some smoke is emitted. By this time the tobacco has somehow expanded and is falling out over the side of the pipe. Gingerly you push it back in with your forefinger which is burnt rather painfully even though you were convinced the tobacco had gone completely out. Another match is struck and moved around over the bowl. This time quite a lot of smoke is produced and you notice to your great satisfaction that you are blowing it out of your mouth. Despite the agreeable aroma of the unburnt tobacco in the tin, it doesn't smell or taste anything like that when lit. This is a grave disappointment. Still, *nil desperandum*. Another match succeeds in producing a great deal of billowing, voluminous smoke. Now you are actually beginning to enjoy yourself and the tobacco is starting to taste a little sweeter. You have conquered the beast and are sure that you look rather suave with your bent Peterson between your lips. You would stroll casually into the drawing room and impress the girls.

George was just about to get up from his chair when there was a bloodcurdling shriek and he was thoroughly drenched and practically drowned by a cascade of freezing water poured over his head. He was too shocked to say anything but on turning round beheld Polly holding a large empty saucepan, a look of horror on her face. After a moment she noticed the pipe in his hand.

'Oh, gor blimey, sir! I'm ever so sorry! I thought you was afire sir! Oh! Oh! I thought you'd gawn up in flames, sir!'

Enter Mrs Sprackett. 'Gawd bless us and save us! Whatever 'ave you gawn an' done, gel? What do you mean by pourin' a sospin a water over the master like that?'

'I thought as 'e was afire Mrs S! There was smoke everywhere an' the most terrible smell as you ever smelled!'

By this time the whole house had been alerted by the brouhaha. Rosalind and the girls had rushed out to see what all the fuss was about. The sight of George dripping wet had them reduced to howls of laughter and Polly was chased back into the kitchen by Mrs Sprackett wielding a large frying pan and threatening to tell her fortune.

A lesser man would have given up there and then. Despite having been assured that pipe smoking was a sovereign remedy for stress, the inaugural trial had proved to be precisely the opposite. However, George came from doughty stock. The household had not seen or smelled the last of 'Old Grenadier'.

Thursday 19th October 1911

A crisp autumn morning. George enjoyed a leisurely breakfast; a bowl of 'Force', which he had become quite fond of, and two slices of toast with a new type of marmalade he wasn't yet quite sure about. It didn't seem to have enough 'bits' in it. George liked his marmalade to have 'bits' in it. The girls declared them disgusting and refused to have anything to do with marmalade that had 'bits' in it.

As the house seemed to be deserted, he settled down in the conservatory with a cup of tea that Polly had made for him and the latest copy of 'The Musical Times'. There was an interesting article about Orlando Gibbons and his madrigal: 'The Silver Swanne'. George pondered on the word 'Swanne'. Why, he thought, should 'swan' be spelled with an extra 'ne'? What does it add? Pity the poor printer who has to use up an extra 'ne'. He mused on this for a while, the autumn sun quite warm through the conservatory glass. Suddenly he felt quite tired and began to doze. Swans, graceful and silver were gliding across a placid lake. A peaceful sight. A peaceful dream.

A swan gliding gracefully across a placid lake belies what is going on beneath the water line. Its feet are working hard to propel it forward but of course this is hidden from the view of the admirer standing on the bank. During the time George spent in hospital, forcibly quiet and placid, a great deal of activity was going on at Scattersdale Avenue. Clementine's breakdown and her revelations to Rosalind had, for a while, taken both sisters to the edge of insanity. Vicky and Alex, despite appearances to the contrary, demonstrated that within their breasts beat stout, kind, understanding and tender hearts and within their heads resided intelligent brains which awoke and communicated with each other, quickly deciding that they must take charge of the situation. Clementine, Rosalind and Celandine were all ministered to with equal understanding and compassion. Although the twins were not privy to the secret that Clementine had revealed, they knew from the effect it had had on their mother that what had passed between her and her sister had been shattering for both of them. Clementine for finally opening her Pandora's Box and Rosalind for accepting, without notice, the burden of having to live, for the rest of her life, with the confidence and its possible consequences.

The story, as far as George had got hold of it, was that when Clemmie and Bertie married they remained childless for several years. Whether this was by accident or design was not clear to him. Well, Bertie was away for long periods on tours of inspection. (He was in the Indian Civil Service; George wasn't sure what his duties were but he believed he was a fairly senior grade.) It seems that while he was on one of his tours Clemmie became friendly with the wife of one of Bertie's compatriots. The wife went down with one of those ghastly tropical maladies and was laid low for quite a while. Clemmie visited regularly and did what she could to look after her and make her comfortable. It was during this time that she formed an inappropriate attachment to the husband with the inevitable result and Celandine was born nine months later. The wife never regained her full health and they were repatriated on compassionate grounds a few months later. Somewhere in England Celandine's real father was living blissfully unaware that he has a daughter. Bertie never questioned it and to all intents and purposes apparently accepted her as his own. Whether he knew, Clemmie never found out. He died as Celandine's father. Since his death Clemmie had been tortured by guilt, blaming herself, blaming Celandine, blaming Bertie for dying although the poor chap could hardly have done anything about it. She was jealous of Rosalind and resented George bitterly, envious of their happy life and their two beautiful daughters. Apparently George vaguely resembled the natural father and this was another source of latent vitriol.

After all these astounding revelations George promised himself that he would be a father to Celandine. He could never replace Bertie but he had come to love that little girl as if she were his own. The poor waif needed a father figure and he would do his damnedest to be one to her. That meant no more heart attacks and no more feuding with Clemmie.

We will not dwell too long on those difficult days. It is not the business of this chronicle to delve too deeply into these delicate matters. But we will say this: Eugene was a very good friend to them all. He visited every day, enquired discreetly of Vicky and Alex how they all were; asked if there was anything he could do; played some quiet Chopin Nocturnes for them and, with the permission of Vicky and Alex, asked Humpidge to call. Which he did. We have made fun of Humpidge and will probably do so again. However, in concluding by drawing a discreet veil over this passage, we can confirm that Humpidge was a man of great experience and understanding; of sage advice and soothing balm. And he was very fond of swans.

CHAPTER FOURTEEN ~

~ Legacies

———❧❧———

'The poplars are felled, farewell to the shade,
And the whispering sound of the cool colonnade.'

William Cowper

Friday 20th October 1911

George was a man with no medical training whatsoever and would make an absolute hash of tying the most simple bandage or treating a moderately minor cut or bruise; however, he felt fairly sure that most qualified members of the medical profession would agree with him when he said that, in his opinion, anyone who had experienced a mild to moderate heart attack and was in the first stages of recuperation should not be subjected to any untoward frights or shocks.

He had just finished a most agreeable breakfast which consisted of a bowl of 'Force', a grilled sausage and a grilled rasher of best smoked back bacon ('Force' alone was not enough – he got rather hungry by eleven o'clock and was apt to hunt about a bit for the biscuit barrel) when Alex and Vicky announced that it was time for his daily walk. He'd been let off this up to now on account of the girls insisting on accompanying him in case he keeled over but, up to that day, they had always been 'too busy'. Of course it took them an hour and a half to get ready, disappearing into their bedrooms and reappearing looking exactly the same as when they went up, which gave him an opportunity to spend some time with the Bechstein. It really was the most beautiful instrument and was settling down nicely. It would soon be due for its first service and check-up and he made a mental note to arrange it with the supplier. A Chopin étude was up on the music stand and he ran through a few bars *'piano'*. He hoped it wasn't too 'modern' for Clementine.

Just as they were about to leave there was a knock on the front door. Being nearest George opened it to reveal a seven foot brown bear, its arms outstretched and mouth open showing a set of fearsome looking teeth. There was a shriek in perfect unison and Vicky and Alex fled leaving him to deal with the ursine leviathan. It hardly needs saying that to be confronted with such an evil looking monster was not the sort of thing you expected on a Friday morning in Streatham SW. To say that he was taken severely aback is something of an understatement and his first instinct was to whack it with an umbrella. Of course the stand was empty. His heart was thumping in a manner that would not have been approved of by Drs MacAroon and Ainslie-Cathcart. He was about to slam the door when a head popped out from behind the animal. 'Mr Cheesewire? Bear. Sign here.'

A piece of paper was thrust into George's hand and he scribbled something where the man was pointing. 'I thenkeyow. Oh, and there's this as well.' A smaller parcel was produced and dumped into his outstretched arms. Before he knew it he had gone, accompanied by another man who had presumably assisted him in delivering the bear to the door. George's initial shock now subsiding somewhat, he slowly came to the realisation that the bear was, in fact, not dangerous in that it had been thoroughly subjected to the art of the taxidermist. He was, by now, aware that there was an audience behind him, curious regarding the animal and more curious, no doubt, to see what he was going to do next.

'George, what on earth is that?' said Rosalind.

'Daddy, why have you bought a bear?' asked Vicky.

'Perhaps there's a man inside. Is there a man inside daddy?' Alex's contribution.

'Gawd bless us and save us if it ain't a bloomin bear! As if we ain't got enough animals in the 'ouse with kets a-runnin' all over the place,' from Mrs Sprackett, who had come up from the kitchen, rolling pin in hand.

'Oh, my life! I shall never be able to sleep with that monster in the 'ouse! 'orrible it is!' from Dolly.

'Cor! Look at 'is eyes! Pierce you right through they does!' from Polly.

George was sure that there was a perfectly reasonable explanation for its appearance although he couldn't for the life of him think of one at that moment but he intended to get to the bottom of it as soon as possible. The first thing to do was to get the thing off the doorstep and into the house despite the previous protestations. Polly and Dolly had disappeared, closely followed by Mrs Sprackett, but Vicky and Alex showed remarkable bravery and, taking an arm each, manoeuvred it into the hallway.

'It's quite light, actually,' said Alex.

'I don't think there's a man inside it daddy,' said Vicky.

Once inside George was able to take a good look at the animal. There was nothing pinned to it to give a clue as to where it had come from. Then he remembered the other smaller parcel that had been delivered with it. Inside was a box tied with string. There was an envelope on top addressed to him in longhand. On opening it he read:-

'Chipping Grange
Chipping Loosely
Stroud
Glos
15th Oct '11

Dear Mr Chesshyre
Forgive me for not getting in touch before but I've had rather a lot of trouble with Samuel's will. However, it is all sorted out now and I am sending herewith two items which he left to you. As you see, we are still here in Chipping Grange but hope to return to Tulse Hill soon. When we do we will arrange to call on you when convenient. Morgana and Guinevere send their regards.

Yours sincerely
Caroline Fitzpatrick (Mrs)'

'George, who is this Fitzpatrick woman?' asked Rosalind reading over his shoulder.

'She's Sam's sister. You remember I told you about her when I came back from the funeral.'

'You did no such thing!'

'Yes I did. You probably don't remember. As I recall you were too caught up in arranging Celandine's education to take much notice of me.'

'Well I don't remember. What's she like?'

'Oh, I don't know. Ordinary.'

'What a wonderfully descriptive vocabulary you have George. Now I can picture her as though she was here in the room with us.'

'Well, I don't know. I didn't take much notice. She was wearing a black dress thing.'

'How surprising, seeing as she was attending a funeral. What was her husband like? Ordinary, I suppose.'

'Oh, he's dead. She's a widow.'

'Really?'

With that she flounced off.

Women were a mystery to George.

Saturday 21st October 1911

After much to-ing and fro-ing, by the next day the bear had been installed in the hallway and George had to admit he'd taken quite a liking to the fellow. He didn't look quite as fierce if you viewed him at a sort of three quarters angle and his fur was very soft. The girls had taken to giving him a stroke every time they passed although Polly and Dolly had so far refused to go anywhere near him. Of course he had to have a name. He should have thought that he would have been christened 'Bruin' or 'Bruno' or something suitable but, no – the girls had unilaterally decided to call him 'King George the Second'. They steadfastly refused to offer an explanation although he had a strong suspicion that it was some mischievous attempt at making fun of him. Of course Mrs Sprackett was outraged.

'I can't think what those gels is thinkin' of callin' that 'orrible monster after our gracious majesty. Blasphemy, that's what it is an' no mistake. Gawd knows what the old queen'd've made of it an 'er only ten years in 'er grave. I don't know what the country's comin' to. Bears in the 'allways and kets a-runnin' all over the 'ouse. Rack'n ruin this country's goin' to. Rack'n ruin. I can't bear it no longer, I shall 'ave to go an' 'ave a lie down. Polly, you come an' wake me, gel, when it's time to put the sprouts on.'

Whilst King George the Second was purely decorative (of sorts) the item contained in the smaller of the two legacies was rather more useful. Such was the commotion surrounding the bear and its unexpected arrival George had not given it much attention. However, on opening the box a rather battered violin case was revealed. The catch was broken and fastened with a piece of string but once opened a rather fine looking violin was enclosed. It had strings attached but there was no bow. George knew nothing of violins except that the best were made by Antonio Stradivari. Close inspection not surprisingly revealed no signature resembling that name so he didn't imagine it was particularly valuable. As Eugene was due to give Celandine a piano lesson in the afternoon he would ask him what he thought.

Sunday 22nd October 1911

No church again for George. After breakfast (a particularly fine grilled kipper which went down very well, a voracious and envious Tarporley watching every mouthful with an intensity most unseemly in a well-brought-up cat) he spent a very pleasant and peaceful morning in the conservatory with 'The Sunday Times', Messrs Peterson and McClelland, after warning the kitchen that he was liable to be seen emitting smoke from time to time, he was *not* 'afire' and did not require extinguishing. During the interval following the soaking he had discovered what the little metal implement was for. It rather ingeniously combined several useful tools, a bit like a *couteau suisse*. There was a flat round 'tamper' on top for pushing the tobacco into the bowl without burning your fingers; a 'spike' for pricking the tobacco if it became clogged and the pipe refused to 'draw'; a 'reamer' which was used to scrape the bowl when necessary and also to clear the ash or 'dottle' from the bottom of it. He had not, so far, discovered a suitable appendage for removing stones from horses' hooves. Lest the reader should think that he had become an expert too quickly, it must be admitted that much of this knowledge had been gleaned from Eugene who, to George's surprise, revealed himself as a pipe smoker during his lesson with Celandine the previous day.

He'd managed to square things with him since the frightful scene with Clementine. He'd apologised and thanked him profusely for everything he did during those difficult days. Of course he became the hero who could do no wrong amongst the girls and Clemmie had softened her attitude considerably. He'd even heard them discussing Ravel recently. Things were looking up.

Eugene took the violin to have it appraised by the string experts at the Royal College of Music. He admitted to playing 'a little' and promised a demonstration when it was returned.

Monday 23rd October 1911

Monday dawned – A bright, crisp, autumn morning. George only realised that it was Monday after breakfast when he saw Celandine in her school uniform. He had not been in to the office for over three weeks and he had to admit that he had not really missed it. There were chaps that he knew who couldn't wait to get back to business after holidays or being indisposed and he could remember a time when he felt like that but at that moment he shouldn't care if he never saw the office again. Secretly he knew he'd had a narrow escape although the doctors and Rosalind wouldn't admit it openly to him. He'd known chaps who'd been as right as ninepence one moment, felt a bit odd, then keeled over stone dead without so much as a 'by your leave'. He didn't want that to happen to him. Despite the tribulations with Clementine he'd really actually quite enjoyed being home and spending time with Rosalind and the girls. Perhaps it was time he thought of retiring or at least taking up something different. Something where he wasn't forced to travel into the City every day on those bally slow trains to and from suburbia. It had been getting busier by the year and there was so much hustle and bustle now. He was convinced people were getting ruder, too. Goodness knows what it was going to be like in ten years time with all the building going on everywhere and motor traffic growing by the day. The old days were slipping past. They shouldn't see their like again.

Clementine had taken to her bed again with another head cold. It's odd that nobody else ever seemed to catch it. George supposed there would be a succession of edicts during the course of the day which he resolved to tear up and feed to the 'Thermoboil'. That should keep the water hot! Rosalind said she'd walk with Celandine to school and he said he'd tag along too, it being a pleasant morning for a stroll. Alex and Vicky said they *would* have come but it would take them until lunchtime to get ready. He really needed to talk to Rosalind about those two.

Celandine seemed to have settled into school well. George thought it had taken her mind off things and given her lots of other interests. He hoped it would be the beginning of a new chapter for her. As they approached the gates she was greeted enthusiastically by a gaggle of girls and they all went in happily chatting with a final wave at the door for Rosalind and him. She was obviously a popular girl. On the way back he noticed that the field at the end of Scribblesdale Avenue was being marked out by some men with sticks and theodolites. A row of mature poplars was being cut down. Probably been standing there for a hundred years, minding their own business, not doing any harm to anyone. Now gone in a morning to make way for villas like his. He felt a pang of guilt. Had there been a row of poplars where No 3 Scattersdale Avenue now stood? More building. Where would it end? Mr E. M. Forster described it as a 'red rust' of suburbia, creeping ever outwards into Surrey, Middlesex and Kent. Why could the poplars not be allowed to live? Surely the building plans could accommodate them?

There was nothing much in the post. A letter from Antiphon, Spoke, Haddock & Spoke begging to inform him that things were progressing well in the lightning conductor case. They hoped to have it wrapped up by the new year (a bit optimistic, George thought, and they didn't actually state *which* new year) and would he kindly furnish them with a cheque for £25 / 0s / 0d on account? More expense. At this rate he'd never be able to retire. Perhaps the violin would turn out to be by Antonio Stradivari.

Saturday 28th October 1911

The violin was not by Antonio Stradivari. Eugene brought the dispiriting news when he came on Saturday afternoon for Celandine's piano lesson.

'I'm sorry to disappoint you, Mr Chesshyre,' he said, taking it out of its case. 'I had the head of strings look at it and he thinks it was made in Bohemia about 1870 or 1880. It's not valuable but it's well enough made and plays quite nicely. I have a bow with me this time. Would you like me to play something for you?'

'Please do, Eugene,' said George enthusiastically. 'I'm keen to hear what my inheritance sounds like.'

'Better than a big old bear roar huh?' said Eugene with a grin. Celandine, who was sitting on the Bechstein's stool, thought this very witty and gave him an admiring smile. 'Just need to tune up a little. Celandine, honey, could you play for me the 'G' below middle 'C'?'

George was not sure that it was appropriate to call Celandine 'honey' but let it pass.

'Sure, Eugene,' said Celandine. Good grief, she was picking up the American dialect. He hoped Clementine didn't hear her. All hell would break loose.

The violin was soon tuned to Eugene's satisfaction. 'Well, here we go,' he said. 'You'll have to forgive me, I'm a little rusty. Haven't played for a while, it not being my first instrument and all.'

There followed what George could only describe as a virtuoso performance of a piece by J. S. Bach the title of which he never did actually discover. The violin might have only been a mediocre piece from central Europe but in Eugene's hands it came alive. The tone was really quite bright and sweet and he really would challenge any non-expert to tell the difference in sound between this and a much more valuable instrument. Like bees round a honey-pot, by this time the room had filled with an admiring audience. Even Polly and Dolly were impressed and joined in the clapping enthusiastically.

'Ooh, 'e do play luvly, don't 'e Poll? Don't 'e play luvly Mrs S.?'

'I love a good fiddle, me. I never knew 'e could play the fiddle. An' 'e's good on the Joanna too! Makes you want to get up an' dance, don't it Doll?'

'Ooh, yes! Dance all night, I could to that. Luvly! Mind you, it is a bit 'eyebrow' as you might say.'

'Well, if that's 'eyebrow', I don't mind I'm sure. Make me dance all around the 'ouse it would!'

'I'll dance you gels back to the kitchen if you don't mind out.' Mrs Sprackett's ire was roused. 'Fiddlin's all right for those as likes it but it ain't for the likes of you two, now get orf with you and get them spuds peeled or there won't never be any dinner!'

Exit Polly and Dolly, arm in arm and dancing all the way to the kitchen.

'Oh, I wish I could play like that!' said Celandine.

'Aren't you taking lessons?' asked Eugene.

'Yes, at school. But I've only just started.'

'Well, I'd be happy to teach you a little more at home if your mother agrees.'

'Oh, yes please! May I, Uncle George?'

'Well, it's not really up to me, but I'll see if I can persuade your mother.'

'I'm sure that won't be difficult, George,' said Rosalind.

'I think we've got the makings of a trio!' he said. 'Eugene, have you got a violin?'

'Yes, sir. I do.'

'Splendid! Then Celandine can play my newly acquired 'Stradivarius' and perhaps I can accompany you both on the – er – 'Joanna'!'

Sunday 29th October 1911

The next day being Sunday, George felt well enough to go along to the morning service but immediately there wished he hadn't bothered. Humpidge was obviously intent on giving a marathon sermon which wailed and droned for hours. George swore it was longer than the 'Ring Cycle'. Unfortunately it seemed the organ was out of action, Eugene was away and the only other instrument in the church was a superannuated 'Joanna' which looked as though it had served for many years in the public bar of the 'Dog and Duck'. It was painfully out of tune and to make matters worse was 'played' by an old fossil of a woman who could have been Humpidge's mother. It put George in a sour temper which was only sweetened by the smell of roast beef as he came in through the front door. Tarporley had taken to sitting for hours in front of 'King George the Second', staring up at him. It was a mystery as to what he found so fascinating. Still, George supposed, a cat could look at a king as the old saying went.

Since coming back from hospital he had taken to having a bit of a nap after lunch. He was sure some people might have thought this the act of a lazy man but he didn't care. He'd had it on the authority of two eminent doctors that he had been suffering from stress, not to mention brain fag and, although not officially prescribed, come to the conclusion that forty winks after a substantial roast dinner was beneficial especially on a Sunday. He was given to understand that in the Mediterranean countries they indulged in this practice, calling it, he believed, the 'siesta'. Very civilised if you asked him. There was far too much rushing about hither and thither these days and he was convinced the world was speeding up. It wouldn't have surprised him if astronomers discovered that the world was spinning out of control and that at some not too distant date in the future centrifugal force would overcome gravity and they would all be flung off into the void of outer darkness. There was a subject for a sermon! He'd tell Humpidge next time he saw him.

Usually his 'siesta' took the form of a doze sitting in an easy chair in the drawing room, or the conservatory if there was too much noise going on, but that day he felt wearier than usual so decided to have a proper lie down on the bed. He must have dropped off into a deeper sleep than he had intended because he woke with a start and noticed to his surprise that it was gone three. As he came to he was aware that there was a lot of noise coming from somewhere downstairs. Shrieks of laughter were echoing round the house. Rather odd for a Sunday afternoon. Curious, he made himself presentable and went downstairs intent on finding the source of the raucous commotion.

In the previous month George had suffered a heart attack, been unexpectedly drenched with a saucepan of cold water and then, if this wasn't enough, greatly alarmed by the appearance of a stuffed bear at his front door. Men of stronger mettle had been brought low by far less. However, on opening the drawing room door he was to experience another shock to the system, many more of which, he was convinced, he would not survive.

Sitting around the room drinking tea and eating cake were; Rosalind, Alex, Vicky, Clementine, (who had apparently made a remarkable recovery) Celandine, Caroline Fitzpatrick, Morgana and Guinevere. Polly, Dolly and Mrs Sprackett were busy with teapots, sandwiches and cake stands. All eyes turned on him as he entered the room and the racket that had caused him to come downstairs in the first place abruptly ceased. His first instinct was to make a hasty retreat. After all, you can have too much of a good thing. However, he decided that would be unchivalrous and sent a surprised beam around the room.

'Oh, George, there you are!' said Rosalind as the racket started up again as quickly as it had died. 'Look, we have visitors. Isn't that nice?'

He made a tentative step into the room wringing his hands and bowing in a slightly obsequious manner. 'Splendid! Splendid!' he said with a forced grin. 'How wonderful to see you again Mrs Fitzpatrick.' The grin remained as he spoke, rather after the fashion of a ventriloquist's dummy.

'Oh, Caroline, please!'

'And Morgana!'

'I'm Guinevere.'

'Of course, Guinevere. How do you do?'

'*I'm* Morgana.'

'Of course you are! How could I forget?' Had doctors MacAroon and Ainslie-Cathcart been present they would have consulted over a diagnosis of *Risus Sardonicus.*

'Daddy was in his study doing important work, weren't you daddy?' said Vicky.

'Was I? Oh, yes, of course. Ha ha! Important work, you know.'

'Really?' said Caroline. I hope we haven't disturbed you. We've been rather noisy, I'm afraid.'

'Oh, no. Not at all. Don't hear a thing when I'm concentrating on important work. Ha ha!'

'What important work was it you were doing today, daddy?' asked Alex.

'Yes, do tell,' said Caroline. 'I'm fascinated.'

Just then he noticed Tarporley looking in through the window. 'Well, it's very important work regarding the study of the relationship between cats and bears. For the Natural History Museum,' he added desperately.

'Fascinating!' said Morgana. 'I didn't know you were a naturalist Mr Chesshyre.'

'No, daddy. You always told us you were a socialist,' said Vicky.

'Well I—'

'Perhaps you're a suffragist, Mr Chesshyre?' said Guinevere.

'Well, I do tend to suffer rather a lot, you know. Ha ha!'

'Oh, don't! You're all being very cruel to Uncle George!' said Celandine as she handed him a cup of tea. He accepted it gratefully. What a kind and thoughtful girl Celandine was. 'Uncle George hasn't been at all well and has to rest after lunch, don't you Uncle George?'

'Come and sit down, George,' said Rosalind, making room on the settee. 'We're making dreadful fun of you. Come on. Have a piece of cake. It's Mrs Sprackett's Victoria sponge.' Mrs Sprackett who had been supervising the distribution of the cake swelled visibly. 'Caroline, Morgana and Guinevere just looked in on the off chance as they were in the area. They've been telling us about

Chipping Grange and how you've been so helpful to them over Sam's affairs.'

'Well, I haven't really done anything,' he said feeling a bit more relaxed.

'You've enabled me to get rid of that dreadful bear,' said Caroline.

'He's very talented you know,' he said. 'I'm teaching him to play the violin.'

Peals of laughter.

'Of course he's only picked up the 'bear' essentials so far!'

More roars of merriment.

'And of course he 'Bruins' the tone!'

Uncontrolled screeches.

'Do you know that he has taken to smoking a pipe?'

'Oh, George don't be so ridiculous!'

'I swear it's true! And he smokes "St Bruno" tobacco!'

Handkerchiefs to mouths and gripping of furniture. Silent screaming. George swore they'd all been at the sherry bottle.

CHAPTER FIFTEEN

~ Decisions

Monday 30th October 1911

The following day George spent a quiet morning getting over Sunday's shenanigans. Celandine was on 'half-term' so no stroll to the school until the following week.

'I suppose this 'half-term' is deducted from the fees?' he said to Rosalind as he stirred his second cup of tea, 'half-term' being a concept unfamiliar to him.

'Don't be silly, George. Of course not.'

'Well, if they have a week off in the middle of the term it's not a full term is it? I never had half-terms when I was at school.'

Rosalind sighed. 'Yes, of course, George, we all know you were at Dotheboys Hall with Wackford Squeers. Education is more enlightened these days. And in any case, Celandine has some homework to do before she goes back.'

George was not convinced. 'Sounds pretty slack to me. I'm pretty sure they don't have half-terms at Rugby.'

'No, George. They beat the boys until they bleed then send them to bed without any gruel.'

'Something of a 'gruel school', eh?' George was pleased with this brilliant witticism.

'Oh George, don't start those dreadful jokes again.'

'You thought they were pretty funny yesterday. Even Lady Disdain was laughing.'

'George, please don't call her that. I've told you a thousand times. It's very disrespectful.'

'Well, she doesn't respect me.' He'd forgotten, momentarily, that they'd tacitly called an uneasy truce and buried the hatchet. Since his heart attack and subsequent return home there had been a subtle but distinct and profound change in his relationship with Clementine. The story was out. He knew it and she knew that he knew it. It was as though the pressure had been released, relieved and they both saw each other in a different light. Once or twice when he had stolen a few solitary moments with his beloved Bechstein he found himself wondering whether there was more to the story of Clementine and Celandine's biological father. Was it really as Rosalind had relayed to him? Was there a possibility that she had been *forced*? Would that explain the strict and rather cold attitude she had towards Celandine at times? Of course he hadn't mentioned this to Rosalind but he wondered whether he ought. Had she thought it too? Had Clementine told her more than she had told him? Perhaps the truth would come out eventually. Perhaps. But then ...

'Actually she's very fond of you.' Rosalind went on. 'She told me she's very touched by how kind you are to Celandine.'

'Hmm.' George reflected. 'Well, you know how I feel about her. She seems much happier than she was when she first came here. Couldn't get a word out of her.'

Rosalind smiled. 'She loves her school and she's made lots of friends. In fact I suggested that she could invite a few here one afternoon this week for tea.'

He pulled a face. 'Oh, right. I'll keep out of the way, then.'

'There's no need to do that, George. Unless you want to continue your "cat and bear studies".'

Another 'face'. 'Very funny. Not my idea of a relaxing afternoon being surrounded by a lot of screeching schoolgirls.'

'They don't *screech*, George. They're all very well-behaved, grown-up young ladies.'

'Ha! Like Vicky and Alex, you mean? They're supposed to be grown-up but they can still screech when it suits them.'

'They're going to help with the tea-party. We can have a little sing-song after tea. I thought of asking Eugene if he would play the piano.'

George was horror-struck. 'Oh, Lord! He'll never get out alive once they get their claws into him. Do you know he calls Celandine "Honey"?'

Rosalind was nonplussed at this outrage. 'Yes, George. I heard him the other day. It's just his way. It's probably normal in America. It doesn't mean anything.'

'I wouldn't be so sure.'

'Oh, don't be ridiculous, George, she's much too young for that sort of thing.'

'Just now they were grown-up young ladies.'

'George, you know very well what I mean. Don't be so *difficult*. Anyway, I'm sure he'd be delighted to come along. I'll drop him a note to-day.'

'Hmm. All right.' He stretched in his chair and suppressed a yawn. 'I could do with a bit of male company. I tell you I got the shock of my life yesterday when I walked in and saw all you women sat there staring at me.'

'Oh, what nonsense.' Rosalind cast him a look of mock derision. 'You love it really. You know you really are very lucky having so many girls to look after you. Caroline was telling me that poor Sam had nobody. He lived in that great big barn of a place on his own apart from a daily who came in and did a bit of cooking when it suited her. Just think, he had no one to talk to, no one to make fun of or to have a joke with. No one to look after him when he wasn't well. She was quite upset when she was telling me about it. She didn't see Sam often, certainly not since he moved out to Strood and she'd rather lost touch with him. It was quite a shock to her when she realised how he'd been living.'

George winced. "Stroud", he said, very deliberately.

'What? I'm sorry George. I thought that's what I said.'

He sighed. At that moment he had neither the energy nor inclination to relate yet again the story of his being sent on a tour of the great London railway termini on the day before the funeral. 'It seems like you two got on very well,' he said, forcing his mind back to the Fitzpatrick coterie.

'Well, we're quite alike, really,' Rosalind went on enthusiastically. 'We've both got two daughters about the same age. Of course she lost her husband some time ago and finds herself in a similar position to Clemmie in some ways. She was very apologetic about calling unannounced and was very anxious that they might be *de trop*, but she seemed so pleasant that I really couldn't turn her away could I? And her girls are delightful. They hit it off with Alex and Vicky straight away and they made a fuss of Celandine and Tarporley when he came in to see what was going on. You really should have told me more about them when you came back from the funeral, George. I'd have invited them round sooner.'

Another sigh of resigned exasperation. 'Rosalind, my dearest, sweetest one, as I recall, you didn't really want to know much about it. You were more interested in Celandine's school at the time as I told you before.'

'You could have told me afterwards.'

'I'd forgotten all about it by then. If you remember we had that bally lightning strike. Sam went completely out of my mind.'

Rosalind reflected. 'Oh, yes, of course, George! I'm sorry. That was awful, wasn't it? But it's all dealt with now. There's a nice new lightning conductor on the roof and we won't get hit again.'

He grinned impishly. 'Yes, I shall get Polly and Dolly to take it in turns to go up on the roof and polish it regularly.'

'*George!* You do come out with the most outrageous things.'

'All right. They can take it in turns with Vicky and Alex. Give 'em something to do.'

'George. If you say any more I shall leave you and take the girls with me. It'll just be you and Clementine here on your own. You can polish the lightning conductor and Clemmie can hold the ladder steady for you. Won't that be nice?'

'Ha! Oh, all right. I give in. Bloomin' business is still in the hands of Haddock, though. I wouldn't be surprised if there's something fishy going on. Lord knows how it's going to turn out. And it's costing me a fortune in the meantime. I've just had Stripp's bill.'

'Oh, goodness, George! Is it very much?'

'Not far short of four hundred pounds. And we still haven't replaced the bed in Polly's room. That'll add another twenty or so. I think we'll be lucky if we recoup fifty percent of the costs. Insurers never like paying out you know, especially in controversial cases like this one. I shall have to sell some more stock. Perhaps I should let the Bechstein go.'

Rosalind was horrified at this suggestion. 'No, George! It's your pride and joy! I know you were rather forced into it but you love it so much. Even Clemmie was impressed although she didn't let on. And Celandine adores it. So do the girls. And Eugene.'

George got up, walked over to the window and looked out, not really seeing very much, his mind occupied with thoughts of the future. 'Ah, I don't know, old girl. This heart scare's really left me pretty whacked, you know. I don't seem to have the energy I used to have. I'm not sure when I'm going to be able to go back to the office if at all. Perhaps I'd better think about retiring for good. Annuity rates are quite favourable at the moment. I might as well enjoy what little time is left to me.' He returned to his chair, sank down wearily and stared into space.

Rosalind was troubled but tried to put a brave face on things. 'Oh, George, don't be so maudlin! You've years left in you. And blow the office. You've served them well over the years. Look at how you've built the business up. It was only a small firm when you joined wasn't it and now it's one of the biggest broking houses in the City. They owe you a lot, George.'

'It's the *travelling* every day, Ros. It's getting busier and busier and I hardly ever get a seat in the morning now you know. These young coves have got no manners and they sprawl all over the seats and smoke their filthy pipes. Young City clerks most of them. I tell you the City's going downhill fast. Heaven knows what it will be like in five years' time. And all the new houses being put up. They're building behind Scribblesdale Avenue now. That'll be filled with oiks all scrambling to get on the morning trains.'

She put her hand on his. 'Oh, George it sounds awful. I had no idea it had got so bad. You really must give it up. You have every good reason and I'm sure Doctor MacAroon would agree. After all, Sam retired on health grounds didn't he? Just think what a nicer life you'd have than him.'

'Yes, poor old Sam. I hadn't realised what it was like for him out there all on his own. I'll look into it. Of course being a senior partner my share's become pretty valuable. If I could get another partner in and buy me out I should think it would be worth a fair bit.'

Rosalind brightened visibly. 'George that's an excellent idea. Would it take long do you think?'

He reflected for a moment. 'Well, we've got a couple of good chaps who are in line for partnerships. I don't know whether they'd be able to raise the capital, though. I'll write to the other partners and sound the idea out. You never know, I might end up better off than I am now in the long run. And I wouldn't have to pay for that bally extortionate season ticket. Goes up every year and the trains get more unreliable and more crowded. D'you know, I feel better already.'

CHAPTER SIXTEEN

~ Very Modern

Wednesday 1st November 1911

A beautiful autumn morning. The first frost of the season and after the early morning mist had cleared the sun broke through with some surprising warmth. How much more pleasant was this than the relentless tropical heat they were forced to endure just a few weeks ago? Today was the day of the tea-party which meant much hustling and bustling about in the dining room and the kitchen. As luck would have it, that morning the piano tuner was due to call for the Bechstein's first service so George was able to make his excuses, retire gracefully from the party preparations and disappear in to the music room to supervise operations there. Of course there was not much he could do; the tuner was a taciturn fellow who didn't let on much except to say, 'It's settled in nicely, Mr Chesshyre'. That was all he got out of him apart from a bill but he supposed 'It's settled in nicely' was all that was really required.

By the time the tuner had finished, the dining room and kitchen were still out of bounds so he made his way to the conservatory and had a go at some 'Old Grenadier', this time keeping a wary eye out for any saucepans of cold water that might be coming in his direction. Luckily none did although a cup of coffee and a trio of Bath Olivers arrived at about half past eleven. Stripp Senior was in the garden doing some weeding and piling up material for a bonfire. He didn't notice George so he was spared the inevitable plea for some new tool or other that it was absolutely imperative that he should have.

Lunch consisted of a cold collation seeing as they were going to have a 'big tea'. George was curious to know what constituted a 'big tea', the term hitherto unknown to him.

Earlier in this chronicle we have given a brief description of the game 'musical chairs'. George was, for a moment, fearful that they were to be subjected to this somewhat raucous interlude, however it occurred to him that 'young ladies' of Celandine's age and disposition would probably be beyond that stage, if indeed they had ever gone through it in the first place. His supposition proved to be correct when the guests began to arrive just before three. There was: Miss Helen Twelvetrees, Miss Alison Fortesque-ffrench, Miss Beatrice Finlayson and Miss Hermione Spottiswoode. Each was introduced to him by Celandine and each gravely shook his hand with a: 'How do you do, Mr Chesshyre?', and a barely imperceptible curtsey.

'Big tea' was a solemn and serious affair. Eugene was delayed and so wasn't able to join them until later; however, when he did arrive, the atmosphere changed immediately. There were entreaties to hear him play and, seeing resistance was in vain, after asking George's permission which was duly given, he led them into the music room. Being thenceforward ignored, he went back out to the conservatory and had another go at some 'Old Grenadier'. He must have dropped off because when he came to the house was quiet and the sun had gone below the horizon. It was getting chilly so he went in search of something to warm him up. He was just settling down in the music room with a large Johnnie Walker when there was a commotion outside, the front door banged and the music room door was flung open wide. A gaggle of excited, flushed, chattering girls swarmed in followed by Eugene whose cheeks were equally ruddy.

'We've been playing baseball!' said Celandine. 'It's like rounders only much better!'

'Yeth!' said Miss Twelvetrees. 'I thcored a home run!'

'I was the pitcher,' declared Miss Fortesque-ffrench. 'I'm a jolly good pitcher aren't I Eugene?'

'I was the catcher!' said Miss Finlayson. Hermione wanted to be but I was better, wasn't I Eugene?'

'Oh, it was such a scream, daddy! Wasn't it Vicks?' said Alex.

'I thought it was a bit silly, actually,' said Vicky, pouting.

'That's just because she dropped a catch, isn't it Eugene?' said Celandine. 'You're such a butterfingers sometimes Vicks! Will you play something for us, Eugene, *pleeease?*'

'Oh, yes! Do play something for us!' in virtual unison.

It's singularly curious how a man can feel a stranger in his own house.

'Well, now,' said Eugene, slowly edging backwards towards the piano (a nervous and unconvincing smile on his face) and removing a manuscript from his music case. 'Let's see if you like this. Who wants to turn the pages for me?'

George thought this a rather rash move.

A clamour of *'Me! Me! Me!'* ('Grown-up' young ladies.) In the end Celandine won and stood proudly by the Bechstein ready to turn the pages at Eugene's command. What followed George could only describe as the most peculiar music he had ever heard. It seemed to bounce along at a very strange time and involved the left hand moving left and right almost continuously. The girls' faces were struck with awe and several jaws dropped open; even Miss Twelvetrees' braces were revealed. Glances were exchanged which said emphatically, 'This is extraordinary!' Eugene finished the piece to awed silence followed by enthusiastic clapping and jumping up and down on the spot.

'Hooray! Hooray!'

'Play it again, Eugene! Encore! *Encore!'*

'What's it called Eugene?'

'It's called "Maple Leaf Rag",' revealed Eugene. 'It's by a composer called Scott Joplin.'

'Hooray! Play it again! *Please!'*

'All right. Here goes—'

Again the strange tune filled the music room. This time George was beginning to get used to the odd rhythm and the tune began to make some sense. By the *third* time of playing it he was, to his astonishment, tapping his foot. He'd never done that before. He concluded that he must be very *modern*.

By then it was six o'clock and one by one the girls left as their parents collected them. George half expected a barrage of complaints to rain down the next day when they learned of their offspring's adventures with baseball and being exposed to music that was bound to corrupt them.

Of course the bally tune was going round in his head all evening and he could still hear it when he went to bed.

Thursday 2nd November 1911

George woke with 'that blasted tune' still going round in his head. He should have to speak to Eugene. He was sure it couldn't be natural. An awful thought occurred to him; what if one of the girls was heard humming it? What would their parents say? They would demand to know where they had picked up such tunes. Then, of course, the inevitable happened – the tune went out of his head and he spent all morning trying to remember how it went. Just when he thought he'd got it – it went again.

Saturday 4th November 1911

The tune was now but a faint memory and he had been exorcised of its influence; however that afternoon Celandine had her piano lesson and she was bound to ask Eugene to play it again.

Sunday 5th November 1911

It was back. As he feared, it was played three times the previous afternoon. He resolved to be resigned to it. Late in the day he realised that it was Guy Fawkes Night; however, as it was Sunday, a peaceful evening passed. It had been quiet the night before too. Perhaps that part of Streatham didn't go in for pyrotechnics. Of course it might just have meant that they were living in a Catholic enclave.

Monday 6th November 1911

If the English never have anything to talk about they can always fall back on the weather as a suitable subject for passing the time of day. You never quite know what you are going to be faced with when you wake up in the morning. There might be brilliant sunshine streaming through your bedroom window (always depending, of course, on which side of the house your bedroom faces); there might be a howling gale outside, with or without rain lashing down in unmerciful sheets making the forthcoming journey to work a very unappealing prospect; it might be dull and overcast; it might be warm or chilly, regardless generally of the time of year and, of course, it might be dark or light. 'Of course', people say; 'It's what makes living in England interesting. I shouldn't care to live in a country where you know that the weather is going to be the same, day after day, whatever the time of year.' George had to admit he had a certain sympathy for this line of argument. What he liked about England was the change in the seasons. Back in July they were existing in a sort of natural crucible, all living things wilting in the incessant heat. Yet they knew that in a few short months they would be coming into autumn and then winter. They knew the weather would change. The heat wouldn't last forever and they looked forward to crisp autumn mornings and to seeing the first frosts on the trees and hedgerows. This morning was one such.

'George.'

'Hmm.'

'Are you awake?'

'Hmm.'

A prod. 'George!'

'Hmm.'

'*George!* Are you awake?'

Another prod. As we have intimated before in this chronicle at moments such as these George knew it was futile to protest that he was, in fact, sound asleep.

'It's freezing in here. I think there's been a sharp frost. Go and have a look out of the window.'

'It's too cold.'

'Put your dressing gown and slippers on.'

'It's too dark.'

'Switch the light on then.'

'It's too cold.'

'*George!*'

'I don't know which is worse, too hot or too cold,' he grumbled as he pulled on his dressing gown and drew back the curtain to examine the state of the world. He couldn't see much because there was frost on the inside. He scraped his finger down the pane. 'Yes, I think we can safely assume there is a severe frost,' he said as he watched a small pool of melted water form on the windowsill below.

'Has Polly got any fires going?'

He replied that no fires had been kindled within his purview and that this was not an unusual conclusion seeing as he had just got out of bed and had not, as yet that morning, had the opportunity of touring the house to inspect all the fireplaces.

'Well, we need to do something, George. I'm sure this house is colder than Sydenham. I never really felt cold there.'

'Sydenham was smaller, and it was semi-detached. It was much easier to heat than this great pile,' he said, getting back into bed.

'Mrs McGillycuddy was telling me she's had radiators fitted in all the rooms. "It's *transformed* the house," she said. "I wouldn't go back to coal fires," she said. "Radiators are so simple and convenient. You just turn a knob and they heat the room almost instantly."'

'Well, we're stuck with coal fires, I'm afraid.'

'Doesn't that boiler thing heat the house as well?'

'No, just the water.'

'Do you think Mr Stripp could make it heat the house?'

'Why don't we just install Mrs McGillycuddy? She talks enough hot air to heat the whole bloomin' avenue.'

'Don't be such a *grump*, George. Ask Mr Stripp to come round and have a look at it.'

'Rosalind, have you any idea what it would cost to have radiators put in? We can't afford it. We've still got the insurance claim outstanding and in any case we'd have to get permission from the house agent.'

'But it would be an *investment*, George. Just think how warm and cosy it would be and you know you need to keep warm after your illness. Mrs McGillycuddy says that exposure to cold can be fatal. One winter her cousin, Angus, froze to death at home. His body was found in a bothy. "Stiff as a board, he was. Sitting on a bench in the kitchen, holding his staff erect, his eyes staring wildly and an unearthly grimace on his face, his faithful dog, Murdo, sitting beside him, his tongue lolling, stiff as a board like a Staffordshire ornament." You wouldn't want that to happen to you, would you, George? Or to me or the girls or Clemmie?'

'It's a pity McGillycuddy wasn't there. She could have breathed on 'em and thawed 'em out.'

'*George!*'

Wednesday 8th November 1911

Stripp the younger was inspecting the 'Thermoboil'. The procedure started, as always, with a sharp intake of breath. 'You see the thing is, Mr Chesshyre, what you've got 'ere is a "Thermoboil No 3". Good boiler. Good boiler, don't get me wrong. A perisher to light, mind you. D'you 'ave trouble lightin' it Mr Chesshyre? Once you've got it goin', mind, it'll 'eat your water a treat. Trouble is, there's no taps, see? You can't run a send off for radiators. And there's no return. You can't run radiators if there's no return. No, what you need is a "Thermoboil No 5A" but you can't get 'em; you can't get 'em, Mr Chesshyre, not for love nor money. It's a bloomin' pity because they've got just the right taps for radiators. Still a perisher to light, mind you. D'you 'ave trouble lightin' this un Mr Chesshyre? No, what I reckon would suit you is the "Vulcan 8". Lovely boiler. Give you plenty of 'ot water an' 'eat all your radiators too. I put one in for Mrs Gillywilly next door. Swears by it, she does. "Mr Stripp," she says, "I don't know where I'd be without my 'Vulcan 8', warm as toast in the winter, I am," she says. Course, it won't be cheap.'

'Course, it won't be cheap'. Of course it wouldn't. Nothing ever was. George had been threatened with nothing less than outright revolution unless the house was heated satisfactorily. Apparently the fires wouldn't 'draw'. 'I'm sorry, mum, but there don't seem t'be no draught,' they were informed by Dolly. 'The coal's wet an' it's all slack anyway. I stuck me 'ead up all the chimbleys an' Polly did too, didn't you Poll? But we couldn't feel no draught. I reckon as there's summat stuck up the chimbleys. Seagulls, that's what it'll be, mum. I 'ears 'em screechin' fit ta bust I does. Nests on the chimbley pots. I reckon as 'ow they need sweepin'.'

'Dolly's right, mum,' Polly chipped in. 'I stuck me 'ead up the chimbley too but there ain't no draught. I said to Doll, didn't I Doll, as 'ow in my ma an' pa's 'ouse in 'oxton there's a luvly draught? Nearly sucked me pa's carpet slippers orf one night it did. Didn't I say, Doll?'

'D'you know, mum,' went on Dolly who by this time was warming to the seagull theory, 'seagulls is a terrible menace. One Sunday when I was visitin' me ma an' pa in 'ackney, we was jest sittin' down to our tea when there was the most terrible commotion as you ever 'eard. Ma was jest butterin' a piece of bread as she 'ad cut the crust orf. She cuts the crusts orf on account of 'er 'avin' no teeth, least, none as she can say as is 'er own. Anyway she was jest about to take a bite when this seagull came down the chimbley a-squawkin' fit ta bust 'e was an' covered in soot because me pa 'adn't 'ad the chimbley swept like me ma 'ad told 'im to an' she went on at 'im but 'e said the chimbley-sweep was too dear an' 'e'd do it 'imself but 'e never got round to it, anyway the seagull, once 'e knew where 'e was, 'e spied ma's piece of bread an' 'e swooped, mum, you never saw anythin' like it, 'e swooped across the table and took the piece of bread right out of ma's 'and and ate it up as quick as you like an' then 'e spied the cat, mum, an' the cat was froze to the spot, 'e's not a very brave cat, mum an' 'e's scared of mice but 'e likes chasin' butterflies, mum, course, that's only in the summer although 'e did catch a moth once wot was' 'overin' around the light one night but 'e fell orf the table an' 'e didn't take to chasin' 'em much after that anyway like I said the seagull, 'e spies the cat an'—'

Unfortunately George and Rosalind never did get to hear the conclusion of Dolly's seagull adventure because at the critical moment Mrs Sprackett came looking for her and Polly and they were ushered out with promises of a tongue lashing when they got back into the kitchen.

Thursday 9th November 1911

A temporary reprieve. The day dawned mild and overcast, the wind in the west. There was more good news in the post. A letter from Mr Septimus Haddock, partner at Antiphon, Spoke, Haddock & Spoke, Solicitors, begged to advise George that the lightning conductor dispute had been satisfactorily resolved and he was pleased to enclose a cheque in the sum of £296 / 14s / 9½d from Holborn Citadel. Negotiations with Excelsior Victoria were at an advanced stage and he was hopeful of a settlement from them regarding the interior damage very shortly. His joy was tempered somewhat, however, by Haddock's request for £15 from him, 'on account'.

George had dug his heels in over the heating issue. He thought Polly and Dolly may well be right and that the chimneys did need sweeping. If they could get the fires going with some decent coal it would be a darn sight cheaper than installing a 'Vulcan 8' with all its accompanying paraphernalia. Besides, he wasn't at all sure that the landlord would agree to it. He'd written to the house agents at the insistence of Rosalind but thought it might be a fruitless exercise. He was surprised that Lady Disdain had not complained about the cold but she had been remarkably quiet on the subject. Hopefully she had acclimatised slowly over the past few months.

The urgent matter for the moment was to find a reliable chimney sweep. They had a good one in Sydenham but he wouldn't work out as far as Streatham. Stripp the elder was in the garden that morning so George sauntered out on the pretext of asking him if he could recommend anyone. Of course, he should have guessed what the answer was going to be before he even asked the question.

'Oh, 'e's a champion sweep, Mr Chesshyre. Does a luvly job, 'e does. Don't make no mess an' 'e don't leave no soot all over the furniture. 'e'll 'ave those chimneys swept as clean as a whistle before you can say "Jack Robinson". I love a nice coal fire, me. Gladdens the 'eart to see it, I reckon. I was only sayin' to Mrs Stripp the other evenin' as we was sittin' round the fire in the kitchen, Nellie, I says ('er proper name's Ellen but I calls 'er Nellie when we're on our own), don't it gladden your 'eart to see a nice coal fire a-blazin' of a winter night? "Yus," she says, "I can't think of anythin' that gladdens the 'eart more than a good roarin' fire a-blazin' in the grate of a winter night." She's got the chilblains y'see, Mr Chesshyre. Suffers from 'em terrible bad she does on account of 'er doin' a lot of washin' an' scrubbin'. Of course she rubs 'em with mutton fat when she can get 'old of some an' it stops the smartin' a treat it do but she can't keep 'old of spuds an' carrits when she's a-peelin' of 'em and they shoot all over the kitchen sometimes. Many's the time a King Hedward's flew past me ear, Mr Chesshyre, which is a surprise to a person when 'e ain't expectin it an' lookin' forrard to a mutton chop an' is dozin' in front of a fire of an evenin' after a-labourin' out in the wind an' the rain. Are you partial to a mutton chop, Mr Chesshyre?'

George replied that he did, indeed relish a chop on occasion and made a mental note to enquire of Rosalind as to whether mutton fat was employed in the kitchen to salve chilblains and, if it was, to warn her of the potentially alarming prospect of flying vegetables and to wear suitable protective headgear before venturing in during the course of vegetable prep.

(*Post Script* – George asked Rosalind about this (she gave him a very odd look) but she assured him that all the girls, including Polly, Dolly and Mrs Sprackett used *Vaseline* to prevent chilblains and chapping. George was most relieved.)

Friday 10th November 1911

The weather remained mild. Stripp the younger appeared with his chimney-sweep equipment. George had been trying to make a mental count of the number of fireplaces in the house and made it about ten give or take a flue. Of course Stripp lived up to his reputation (as George had no doubt he would) and moved from room to room with professional speed and efficiency. All furniture was covered in white dust sheets before sweeping began but it seemed hardly necessary because they came off again as clean as they went on. A lot of soot was brought down (and a lot of seagulls disturbed) which was surprising as the house was only about three years old, and stored in hessian bags in the tool shed. 'If you don't mind, Mr Chesshyre, I'll leave them for my brother. 'e'll use it on your garden. Very good for the soil is soot. You can clean your teeth with it too. I'll put some in a pot for you and the family to clean their teeth with if you like, Mr Chesshyre. Make 'em sparkle it do. That's a strange thing now ain't it Mr Chesshyre, as 'ow something so black can make something so white?'

George thanked him for this generous offer but said that, on the whole, he preferred to use 'Calox Dentifrice Powder', but he would mention it to the girls, who, he was sure, would be outwardly intrigued and privately disgusted.

Saturday 11th November 1911

George was expecting a delivery of 'best trebles'. After Stripp had finished up the previous day he asked him what kind of coal he had been using. He told him that he hadn't ordered any yet and was just using up what was in the cellar. They went down to have a look. A sharp intake of breath. 'Oh, no, Mr Chesshyre. That's no good. Look, it's all slack. No. No good at all. No wonder the fires wouldn't draw. What you want is best Kent trebles and doubles for the bedrooms. Burn luvly, they do. Order a ton of each an' the 'ouse'll be as warm as toast in no time. In fact, if you leave it with me I'll order it from the yard on me way 'ome. Course, it won't be cheap.'

Of course it won't.

Sunday 12th November 1911

There were now two tons of best Kent trebles and doubles in the cellar and a large bill in George's wallet. Tarporley was keeping guard after staying at a safe distance as the coal was delivered but, curious to know what was going on, crept down the cellar steps as soon as the dust had settled, King George the Second having been forgotten, for the time being at least. Polly and Dolly were kept busy all the previous afternoon and by the evening the house was tolerably warm. The weather had turned cold again, the wind in the east. Of course the bathrooms were cold, there being no fires in them. George was beginning to feel the cold more and more now, a combination of age and 'brain fag' no doubt. He was wondering whether the 'Vulcan 8' idea might have some merit after all. He'd have to wait and see what the house agent said.

Monday 13th November 1911

'Maple Leaf Rag' was going round in George's head again. It was there when he got up that morning and wouldn't leave him alone. Of course it had to be played about five times on Saturday afternoon, three times by Eugene and twice, somewhat haltingly, by Celandine, so it was not surprising it was nagging at him again. Celandine had told him that this Joplin fellow had written 'lots more rags' and that Eugene was going to introduce her to them. George couldn't get the measure of it. Eugene said it was 'syncopation' and it was the 'coming thing', 'all the rage' in America. He was sure he would understand it in time. Vicky and Alex called him an old fogey but he'd show them!

'Force' had reappeared on the breakfast table and George had a large bowl that morning. He had got to rather like it and had been disappointed by its temporary absence which was due, apparently, to it being so successful that the manufacturers couldn't keep up with demand. He had taken to spreading 'Marmite' on toast as an alternative to marmalade which was now apparently frowned upon. Luckily he was the only person in the house who would eat 'Marmite', everyone else declaring it to be the most disgusting thing they had ever tasted and: 'How could he eat that stuff?'

After breakfast Rosalind was wearing her 'I'm going to badger George' face. She thought he didn't notice this but, living in a houseful of women, one would have to be a particularly thick-skinned numbskull to be unaware of its peculiar *modus operandi* and not be aware when it was approaching, invariably accompanied by unusually excessive attention to one's personal needs and comfort:

'George.'

'Hmm?'

'George!'

'Hmm?'

'*George!* We need to discuss Christmas.'

'Oh, Lord, must we?'

'Yes, it's just over a month away and we need to decide what we're going to do.'

'I'm going to stay in bed.'

'*George!* Please be serious!'

'I am being serious. Lot of fuss.'

'Well, I shan't get you a present, then.'

'Well, I shan't get you one, then. More expense.'

'George, it will be the first Christmas in our new house and we shall have Clemmie and Celandine with us. We have to make an effort. What about your mother?'

'What about her?'

'Are we going to invite her?'

'Oh, Lor, do we have to? She's as deaf as a post. I shout myself hoarse trying to make her hear and she refuses to use the ear trumpet I got for her.'

'But we can't leave her on her own and she hasn't even seen the new house yet. You said you were going to invite her over ages ago.'

'It's too far.'

'It's only Maidenhead. You could fetch her on the train.'

'That means trawling through London with her in tow. You know she got lost at Paddington once.'

'She went to the ladies' room.'

'Yes, but when she came out and I finally spotted her she was about to get on a train to Penzance. I only just managed to rescue her. Got a funny look from the guard, too.'

'Well, the girls can go and fetch her then.'

'Good God, no. Heaven knows where they'd end up. I'll get Alf to meet us at Paddington. At least we won't have to negotiate our way across to London Bridge.'

'Good, that's settled then. And I thought we could invite Caroline and the girls.'

'Good grief woman! We shall be bursting at the seams. I shan't be able to hear myself think!'

'Oh, it'll be lovely. Don't be such a *Scrooge*, George! There's a carol service at the church and at Celandine's school, too. You know you like carols, George.'

God Rest Ye Dismal Gentlemen.

CHAPTER SEVENTEEN ~

~ The Best in the World

—⚬⚬—

Tuesday 14th November 1911

Lady Disdain, who prided herself on 'minding her own business' and 'wouldn't for the world interfere in the smooth running of the household' announced at breakfast that she had, by the by, just happened to notice, as she had been looking out of the drawing room window, that they had new neighbours at No 1. It had been empty for several weeks although it wasn't really notice-able. The previous occupants, an elderly couple, were hardly ever there; when they were they kept themselves to themselves and George had never got further than passing the time of day with them very occasionally. George thought he was a retired navy officer and the gospel according to St McGillycuddy was that they'd gone to live in Esher with the wife's daughter and her husband.

One thing that appealed to George about Scattersdale Avenue was that all the houses were slightly different. The architect had taken the trouble to design each one individually so that the avenue didn't have the appearance of a regimented row of identical buildings. No 3 had provision for a motor house at the side although one wasn't built at the time of construction. No 1, however had; built of the same type of brick and with the same architectural decorations. A sort of villa in miniature for a motor car. Navy type didn't possess a motor car so the doors were always closed when George passed; however, that morning when he went out for his constitutional, the doors were open and in the driveway stood an immense silver monster. One side of the bonnet was up and two figures were bent over examining the nether regions of the works. Just as he passed, one of the figures straightened up and he recognised it as Alf. A grin appeared on his oily face when he saw him. 'Morning Mr Chesshyre.'

'Good morning,' said George. 'Having trouble with your new cab?'

'Ha ha! Very good, Mr Chesshyre. I'll need to take a bloomin' lot of fares before I could 'ave one of these beauties. Luvly, ain't she?'

'Very imposing,' George agreed. At that moment mechanic number two stood up to see who Alf was talking to.

If the motor car was imposing its owner almost stole its limelight. A very large gentleman of about George's age, red in the face with whiskers to match and wearing a loud Norfolk jacket and plus fours. He was, as he found out later, getting his first glimpse of his new neighbour: Brigadier The Honourable Archibald Campbell-Bristow, KSA. Appearances can be deceptive and George had to admit that at first sight he was sure the man would have a voice to match his appearance. Loud and bullying. But not a bit of it. Seeing Alf recognise him he wiped his hands in a piece of rag and walked over to where they were standing admiring the glittering behemoth. 'Bit of trouble with the mag,' he said. George had no idea what a 'mag' was but nodded sagely. 'Sorted out now. Bristow. How do you do?' He held out a tolerably clean hand.

'Chesshyre, next door, No 3. How do you do?'

'Ah, yes, Alf mentioned you. We've just moved in here. Lived here long?'

'Since July.'

'Ah, bit of a warm one wasn't it? Still, we had some good runs out in the Ghost.'

'Ghost?'

'Yes,' he said nodding in the direction of the motor car. 'Silver Ghost. Rolls-Royce, you know.'

'Ah, I see.'

'Do you drive, Chesshyre?'

'Alas, no. I leave that sort of thing to Alf, here.'

'Probably very sensible. Bit of an indulgence for me really. Still, the wife enjoys a spin out. And the grandchildren, of course. Do you have grandchildren, Chesshyre?'

'Not yet. Two daughters. Can't get them married off.'

'Oh, they will, old boy. Before you know it.'

'I wish I shared your optimism!'

'Ha! Well, I must get on. Have to meet the wife at the station. Won't do if I'm late. Be put on a fizzer. Hell to pay eh? What?' He grinned.

Alf had closed the bonnet and a swing of the starting handle had the Ghost whispering into life. George watched as they pulled away and understood immediately how it got its name. He wondered how difficult it would be to learn to drive.

Wednesday 15th November 1911

George had threatened to ban 'Maple Leaf Rag'. Celandine was practising it that morning before school and now even Mrs Sprackett was humming it. 'Oh, I *do* like that tune, mum. Makes me want to dance round the kitchen it do. And that Miss Celandine, she plays it luvly. Got it orf to a T, she 'as. Not as luvly as Mr Knickerbocker of course but that's to be hexpected, 'im bein' a professional as you might say. Course, My late 'usband, Sprackett, 'e was a beautiful piano player. 'e used to know all the latest music 'all songs, not the vulgar ones of course. 'e 'ad a luvly singin' voice, too, did my Sprackett. What you might call a *barrow*tone. Oh, I loved to 'ear 'im sing. "Come into the Garden Maud" was one of 'is favourites, only 'e used ta sing "Come into the Garden Dais" – Daisy bein' my Christian name as you might say. Course, I couldn't come into the garden because we didn't 'ave one but we used ta pretend. Dolly 'ave you got them spuds peeled yet? They should be boilin' by now. I'll 'ave your 'ide, you see if I don't!'

The best Kent trebles and doubles seemed to have done the job and, now that the chimneys had been swept, the house had warmed up very nicely. George thought he might have solved the problem of the cold bathrooms too because, on mentioning it to Stripp, he suggested he had free-standing heaters installed and promised George he'd get some details.

Meanwhile, George had been trying to ignore the subject of Christmas.

Saturday 18th November 1911

It was useless to try to ignore Christmas. The kitchen had become a madhouse. There was a heated argument that morning which concerned, apparently, the correct proportions of dried fruit required in a Christmas pudding. The making of the pudding was an annual ritual which George would never understand. It seemed that everyone must 'have a stir' and a battle royal then ensued over who was allowed to 'lick the spoon'. Then there was 'making a wish'. If that was not enough, exactly the same battles were fought over the Christmas cake. Of course George was completely superfluous to these goings on except when, 'Daddy, we need sixpences!' He then became mysteriously visible again in a manner that would have surely been approved of by Mr H. G. Wells.

Eugene came that afternoon as usual for Celandine's piano lesson. To George's everlasting relief, 'Maple Leaf Rag' did not feature in the tutorial. Not that he had anything against 'syncopation', it was just that it was very infectious and the very devil to shake off. Instead they had some more Debussy – 'Arabesque No 1', a beautiful piece unfamiliar to George which Eugene played with his usual brilliant professionalism. George had a feeling that even Clementine was beginning to thaw. Surely she couldn't be unmoved by *'la belle France'*? The Saturday afternoon lessons were becoming more like concerts. The whole household seemed to gravitate to the music room when Eugene played and you could have heard a pin drop. The Bechstein shimmered. George wondered if it would still shimmer, a hundred years on.

Sunday 19th November 1911

A brilliant frosty morning. 'Force' had given way to porridge and an argument developed over the correct way to prepare it.

'You have to make it with milk,' said Vicky.

'I couldn't eat it if it wasn't made with milk,' said Alex.

'And sprinkle sugar on it,' added Celandine.

'Well, I think it should be made with water,' said George. (He didn't really think it should be made with water. He was just feeling mischievous.)

Pained and contorted expressions all round. (The plan was working.)

'And sprinkled with salt.' he added for extra dramatic effect.

'Don't be silly, daddy. It would be inedible,' said Vicky.

'Well, Mrs McGillycuddy eats it like that,' he said with casual authority. 'And she's Scottish so she ought to know. In fact, I happen to know that she eats it for breakfast, lunch and dinner every day of the year except Christmas Day.'

'*Does* she Uncle George?' Celandine looked at him; saucer-eyes had become dinner plates.

'Oh, yes,' he said. 'And on Christmas Day, as a special treat, she has roast capercaillie with porridge stuffing and porridge gravy followed by porridge pudding and Marmite.'

'*Does* she Auntie Rosalind?' Dinner plates sought a higher authority.

'No, of course she doesn't. George, don't be so ridiculous,' said Rosalind.

'The man's an idiot,' said Clementine.

'Where does porridge come from, daddy?' asked Vicky, ignoring the protestations.

George, determined to have a bit of fun, leaned back in his chair, his hands clasped behind his head. 'Right up in the Scottish Highlands, near Drumnadrochit,' he said. 'A wild, remote place called Bog o' Porridge. It's a dangerous business digging it out. Many brave men have died in the process, sinking up to their sporrans in it. Of course, if they're lucky, their kilts fan out and prevent them from sinking to a dreadful death. Sometimes, if you're walking in the gloaming, you might hear the mournful skirl of a lone piper signifying that another brave Highlander has sunk to a watery, salty death, winning porridge for the likes of us. Robbie Burns wrote a poem about it: "Tae a Porridge, Laddie", and Harry Lauder sings a song about it: "I Love My Porridge, my Salty, Salty Porridge".'

'George, I've never heard such rubbish,' said Rosalind.

'I don't know how you put up with it,' said Clementine.

***

Despite the fortification of the salty, salty porridge, George's spirits were depressed as he sat and endured yet more drivel from Humpidge. The church was very cold that morning and George thought that he should get Stripp to persuade the parish to invest in a 'Vulcan 8'.

The brigadier was tinkering with the Silver Ghost as they returned. General introductions all round. The Silver Ghost was the only topic of conversation at lunch.

'Daddy, we think you should get a motor car, a Silver Ghost like Mr Toad's next door,' said Alex.

'Mr Toad?' said George. 'Why on earth do you call him that?'

'It's in Celandine's book, isn't it Celandine?' said Vicky.

'Yes, "The Wind in the Willows", said Celandine. 'Mr Toad is mad on motor cars and he looks just like the man next door.'

'If we had a Silver Ghost we could go to the seaside in it,' said Vicky.

'If we go to the seaside we'll go on the train like everybody else,' said George.

'But we haven't been to the seaside for *ages*. Can we go, daddy, please?' said Alex.

'It's the middle of November!' he said. 'We'd be frozen stiff.'

'Well, next summer, then. Will we have a Silver Ghost by then?' asked Vicky.

'And what, pray, do you think I shall use for money? Perhaps the garage will allow me to exchange an apparition of five pound notes for an apparition of a motor car.'

'I don't understand that, daddy,' said Vicky.

'He's just being silly as usual,' said Alex. 'Don't be silly, daddy.'

'I'm being ghostly serious,' he said. 'Have you any idea how much a motor car like that costs?'

Silence.

'Well, I'll tell you. A great deal of money, that's how much,' he said rather lamely. 'Anyway, I can't drive.'

'But Mr Toad could teach you,' said Vicky, determined not to give up. 'I shouldn't think it's that hard.'

'Well, then, why don't you ask him to teach you if it's so easy?' he said, trying to divert the argument.

'Perhaps I shall. And he can teach Alex too.'

'Oo, yes! Then we can take it in turns to drive to the seaside!' said Alex.

'And you could drive me to school in the mornings and bring me home in the afternoons!' chimed in Celandine.

'Don't be silly, Celandine. Whoever heard of children being taken to school in motor cars?' chided Vicky.

God help us if they ever get the vote, thought George.

Monday 20th November 1911

The bright frosty weather continued. No Silver Ghost appeared to spirit Celandine away to school so she was forced to walk as usual. George was still not sure about the fires. The house was so big and it took Polly and Dolly so long in the morning to get them going it was getting on for noon before the whole house had really warmed up. It was the early mornings that concerned him. Since his heart attack he'd noticed the cold more and more and Rosalind had mentioned it too. Even Lady Disdain had started to grumble about how cold it was, especially first thing. The fire-places in the bedrooms were quite inadequate and, of course, were only lit in the evenings. By morning they had gone out and the rooms were deathly cold, as were the bathrooms. By coincidence a letter arrived in the post that morning from the house agents, Blinkhorn, Grist & Vobster. Apparently they had had several complaints about 'Thermoboils' and were looking into replacing them. There would be no cost to leaseholders which was a good thing because George couldn't afford it anyway. The agent proposed to come round the next morning to look at the matter further. George would get Stripp to attend as well as he knew far more about these things than he did.

Tuesday 21st November 1911

Mrs Sprackett was not used to having men poking about in her kitchen and was most put about when Stripp, the house agent, representatives from The Gas Light and Coke Company and Messrs. Potterton & Co of Balham SW descended on her just as she was frying a large kipper for George's breakfast. If this wasn't bad enough Tarporley, having tired of keeping sentry over King George the Second and also guarding the Kent best doubles and trebles, decided more interesting things were going on in the kitchen and jumped up on to the top of a kitchen cabinet to survey the scene where he (or she, it had still not been definitively determined) was joined by three kittens, each of which had designs on the kipper. Mrs Sprackett, it all being too much for her, had an attack of the vapours and 'had to go and have a lie down' leaving the kipper in the charge of Polly and Dolly who didn't mind in the least having two smart young gentlemen (Stripp and the house agent being excluded from this description) to eye up while the kipper finished off. To their disappointment, however, the entourage, with effusive apologies, spent scant time examining the plumbing and passed quickly out through the back door and into the boiler room where they remained for some minutes. Their hopes were dashed even further when it became apparent that no return through the kitchen was likely and the group disappeared round the side of the house.

About an hour later a meeting was convened in George's *sanctum sanctorum*. They were to have a 'Potterton Victor Easilite 6' boiler, with radiators in every room including the bathrooms and servants' quarters. Apparently it was very *modern* and would knock McGillycuddy's Vulcan 8 into a cocked hat. Stripp would tender for the contract and they should hear within the week if he had been successful. George was a bit concerned about being without heating and water of any kind while the works were going on but Stripp had all the answers.

'I'll fit all the radiators fust, Mr Chesshyre, an' as much pipework as I can; you'll still 'ave your old boiler workin' for 'ot water and cookin', then, when everythin's in place I'll whip out the

'Thermoboil' and put the 'Victor' in. You'll still 'ave your coal fires. It won't affect them.'

'How long d'you think it will take to do the whole job?' George asked.

'Week should do it. Ten days at the outside an' I won't turn the gas off unless it's absolutely necessary.'

Wednesday 22nd November 1911

George spent a fitful night with a lot of things on his mind He still hadn't resolved the office quandary. He remained on Dr MacAroon's panel and he was not at all keen on him returning to the City. For now the status quo remained but he should have to make a decision before too long. Then there was this bally heating business. For all his confidence he wasn't convinced that Stripp could pull this off without a great deal of inconvenience, even assuming he got the contract. He didn't mind for himself, he could rough it along with the best for a bit but he really didn't want Rosalind, Clemmie and the girls to be upset. He could foresee endless grumbles from Mrs Sprackett, Polly and Dolly as well. And, of course it had all come at the wrong time of the year. If they had decided to do it back in the summer at least there wouldn't have been the risk of being cold. But during the winter was a different story. It had turned relatively mild again but that could change at any time. He needed to think hard about this.

Thursday 23rd November 1911

> 'No warmth, no cheerfulness, no healthful ease,
> No comfortable feel in any member-
> No shade, no shine, no butterflies, no bees,
> No fruits, no flowers, no leaves, no birds,
> November!'

Thomas Hood

Fog. A gloom had descended on Scattersdale Avenue. The postman was delayed but turned up eventually with a large parcel addressed to George.

'What on earth is that, George?' asked Rosalind as she poured them both a second cup of tea.

'I haven't the foggiest,' he said.

Groans from around the table.

'Aha!' he said as he managed to unravel about ten yards of brown paper. 'It's Sam's papers. Caroline said she was going to send them on to me to look over. I'd almost forgotten all about them.' There was a letter enclosed. 'It's from Caroline,' he said. He read it out loud.

'Joyous Gard
24 Windermere Road
Tulse Hill
SE

Wednesday

Dear George, Rosalind & family

It was lovely to meet you all recently. George, I am enclosing all of Sam's papers as arranged. I'm sorry it's taken so long to get them over to you but so much going on with solicitors etc. etc. Shd be plsd if you cd look over them but don't worry if it's too much. Dreadful fog coming down. Must get this to the PO quickly. Can you all come over for tea Sunday? Shd love to see you all.
Do come.

Caro. M & G send love. X'

CHAPTER EIGHTEEN

~ Snap Decision

Friday 24th November 1911

The fog had lifted and had been replaced by wind and rain. George wasn't sure which was worse. Rosalind had sent a post card to Caroline accepting her kind invitation, however George wasn't sure how they we're going to get there. They might just all squeeze into Alf's cab if Celandine sat on Rosalind's lap.

He spent the rest of the day going through Sam's papers. It was pretty dry stuff and he was getting rather bored with it and about to call it a day when he came across a sealed foolscap envelope marked 'Chipping Grange. Deeds'. Intrigued, he opened it and withdrew the contents. It consisted of the title deeds to Chipping Grange. Mystified, he scrutinised them more closely. It was George's understanding that Sam had a long lease on the property which would probably have expired on his death. However, what he now held in his hands were the deeds to the property, title transferred, in fee simple absolute and without encumbrances or entail, to Samuel Ezekiel Kitcat, 'dated this third day of October 1907'.

Saturday 25th November 1911

The fog was back; a real 'particular'. There had been quite a hard frost during the night. You never know what you're going to be met with when you wake up each morning in this country, thought George. Never mind. A good breakfast; scrambled eggs with a couple of very decent rashers. Tea tasted better that morning as well. He felt sure the water varied in quality. Had an odd colour to it sometimes when he ran the tap for a shave.

Usually cleared itself if he let it run a bit though. He'd ask Stripp about it. He was bound to know.

George was with Rosalind in the drawing room glancing through 'The Times' and thinking it was about time for morning coffee when there was a soft knock on the door and Polly, closely followed by Dolly entered. He thought this was a bit odd. Dolly was carrying the tray with the coffee as she normally did; why Polly had got involved he wasn't sure. They both fussed around nervously, the coffee was poured and the fire was poked with somewhat unnecessary zeal. 'Thank you Polly, Dolly,' said Rosalind, standing to pour the milk as she always did. At this point there was usually some chirpy comment about the weather or what sort of mood Mrs Sprackett was in and how it might impinge on what was intended for lunch; however this morning there was an awkward silence and rather than bustle out of the room in the usual way they remained near the door and faced Rosalind. 'Polly? Dolly? What is it?' asked Rosalind quizzically.

Nervous shuffling and looking at feet.

'Well, mum,' said Polly after being nudged in the ribs by Dolly. 'We've come to say as 'ow we're givin' in our notice.' George didn't know who was the more shocked, Rosalind or him.

'Giving notice?' repeated Rosalind, deeply concerned. 'What, both of you?'

'That's right mum,' said Polly.

'But why? Aren't you happy here?'

'Oh, yes, mum. Very happy.' Dolly found her voice.

'Then I don't understand—'

'It's the alligators, mum,' Polly's turn.

'Alligators?'

George put down his paper. This was bizarre, even for No 3 Scattersdale Avenue.

'Yes, mum. Alligators. Mrs Sprackett 'eard from Mr Stripp as 'ow there's goin' to be alligators and that you're 'avin' them all over the 'ouse. Didn't she say, Doll?'

'Ooh, yes. Alligators. Beggin' your pardon, mum, but we don't think it's right 'avin' alligators all over the 'ouse, I mean, I never saw one meself but Doll saw one at the zoo didn't you Doll?'

'Ooh, yes. 'orrible it were! Crawlin' about in its cage an' when it opened its mouth, well, you never saw such teeth, mum. 'undreds of 'em there was. Fair made my flesh creep it did. Didn't I say, Poll?'

'Couldn't sleep for days after, could you Doll?'

'Gave me the nightmares somethin' terrible it did, mum. An' I read in a book as Miss Celandine left in the drawin' room that one night in India a alligator crept into this man's bedroom at night while 'e was asleep an' bit 'is legs orf an' swallowed 'em 'ole, boots an' all, an' when 'e woke up in the mornin' 'e didn't 'ave no legs, Didn't I say, Poll?'

'I should 'ate to wake up in the mornin' with no legs!'

'So if it's all the same to you, mum, an' with the greatest respect, we couldn't live in a 'ouse where there's alligators a-roamin' about everywhere.'

Neither Rosalind nor George quite knew how to respond to this extraordinary duologue, however, at that moment Mrs Sprackett entered the room. Hopefully she might be able to shed some light on the peculiar performance. 'Beggin' your pardon, mum, but I was jest lookin' for these two. Come on, I need you back in the kitchen. There's spuds to be peeled an' carrits to scrape. If you don't get a move on there'll be no dinner and then where shall we be?'

'Mrs Sprackett, would you wait a moment, please?' said Rosalind. 'Polly and Dolly have just told me they're handing in their notice. Did you know about this?'

'What?! I most certainly did not know, mum. It's the first I've 'eard of it. What d'you mean by givin' notice without so much as a bye your leave?' She turned to Polly and Dolly with a look of thunder on her face.

'We're ever so sorry Mrs S.' said Polly, wringing her hands, 'but we know about the alligators an' we don't think it's right to 'ave alligators a-roamin' about the 'ouse a-bitin' everybody's legs orf like in Miss Celandine's book an' we wouldn't get no sleep knowin' they was a-roamin' about at night an' in the kitchen as well an' jes' think of poor Tarpaulin an' all the kittens as 'ow they'd gobble 'em up 'ole. Oh, it's too 'orrible to think of Mrs S!'

Mrs Sprackett with a great deal of effort recovered her composure and turned back to Rosalind. 'I'm sorry, mum, but these gels 'as clearly took leave of their senses.'

'But Mrs S,' protested Dolly, 'we 'eard Mr Stripp tellin' you as 'ow there was goin' to be alligators in all the rooms what would be 'eatin'!'

'You daft gel!' said Mrs Sprackett. ''e didn't say "alligators", 'e said rallidators, wot 'eats the rooms up to make 'em warm instead of the coal fires. Gawd bless us an' save us wot notions you gels get in your 'eads. You see wot 'appens when you listen in to things as you ain't supposed to listen in to? You gets the wrong end of the stick and then you comes in 'ere a-worryin' the mistress an' the master! I never 'eard of such a thing! Oh, I'm ever so sorry, mum. Come on you two, you get back into the kitchen; I'm goin' to give you such a piece of my mind …'

Ashen faced, Polly and Dolly were ushered out of the room before Rosalind or George could get a word in. With the passage of time, he wasn't sure who laughed longest or loudest, all he knew was that his sides ached for hours afterwards.

Sunday 26th November 1911

George was really rather glad that the heating system was to be upgraded because he didn't think the poor old 'Thermoboil' could stand much more abuse. It had been going full blast from six o'clock and it had been impossible to get anywhere near the bathrooms. Of course all this frantic washing and bathing and doing and undoing of hair was due to their appointment with the Fitzpatricks that afternoon. Church attendance was cancelled for everyone apart from Clementine, who was very pious and wouldn't dream of missing a Sunday. George's own view was that she had eyes for Humpidge. He wasn't sure who he felt most sorry for. Lunch was ordered to be 'light' because there was the distinct possibility of them being presented with a 'big tea'.

George had managed to get hold of Alf in the meantime and he had assured him that everyone could pile into his cab. 'Be a bit of a squeeze, mind.' 'A bit of a squeeze' turned out to be something of an understatement. Indoor young ladies (and not so young ladies) tended, by their very nature, to be slight of build. Not all, but those residing at 3 Scattersdale Avenue were. Outdoor young ladies (and not so young ladies) tended, especially during the winter, to expand alarmingly due to the wearing of voluminous coats, scarves, muffs and hats, etc., etc. When further burdened with sundry bags of divers descriptions, umbrellas, sunshades or parasols ('it might rain'; 'the sun might come out'), a potted begonia, two kittens in a basket ('for Morgana and Guinevere'), a large, round cake tin containing, presumably, a cake; that which would probably have fitted during the summer months would not do so on a cold November afternoon.

Concerning 'two kittens in a basket' reminds us that earlier in this chronicle the reader may recall that we found it advisable, when relating the details of the melodramatic farce surrounding the lightning conductor debacle, to list the *dramatis personae* intimately involved, lest there should be any confusion as to who was who and what was what.

The reader may also recall the dramatic occasion when the family were suddenly and unexpectedly overrun with 'kets all over the 'ouse!' Since then not much has been spoken of or heard about them and so it is probably advisable at this point to allocate identities to the little creatures. Despite Mrs Sprackett's avowed intention to "ave 'em all drownded', we are sure the reader will be relieved and delighted to learn that no kitten suffered such a cruel fate and that they had, in the meantime, been running round freely and enjoying themselves, driving Mrs Sprackett to distraction, and sleeping in George's carpet slippers, blissfully ignorant of the ominous and imminent prospect of 'alligators in every room'.

As the kittens had permanently set up home in No 3 Scattersdale Avenue and Tarporley (whether 'he' was the father or the mother, they never did find out although he/she seemed to regard them all with an aloofness bordering on the negligent) had transferred his/her allegiance to King George the Second, it fell upon the girls to appoint themselves *defensores feles*. This, of course, meant that they all had to be given names. A description has already been given as to the peculiar method and reasoning concerning how Tarporley came by his/her name, an appreciation of which will prepare the reader for the perfectly apposite and appropriate names conferred upon the litter, viz:-

Crewe
Pru
Middlewich
Sandwich
Nantwich
Whisper
Hector Crisper-Bacon

The reader will forgive us for making no further comment. However, we must turn our attention back to the Tulse Hill tea party expedition. Unbeknown to George, but observing this pantomime with some astonishment, was the brigadier who had been working on the Silver Ghost next door. He sauntered over and tapped George on the shoulder as he was trying to persuade Celandine that it was not a good idea to present Morgana and Guinevere with two unexpected kittens which had been identified as being none other than Crewe and Sandwich. (How she could tell them apart was a mystery, they all looked the same to George.) 'Having a spot of bother, Chesshyre?'

George turned round. 'Eh? Oh, yes. Quarts into pint pots, you know, ha ha!'

'Where are you off to?'

'Oh, only Tulse Hill. Been invited out for tea.'

'You could do with an extra vehicle, I should say.'

'We could indeed, but, alas, this is all we have.'

'Well, can't have the ladies squashed in like that. Come on, I'm going up that way myself. I can take four.'

If Vicky and Alex got out of bed in the mornings as quickly as they got out of Alf's cab George would be very happy. In a flash they were ensconced in the back seat of the Rolls Royce. A split second later Celandine was sitting in between them. That left Rosalind and Clementine. 'You go, Clemmie,' Rosalind said. 'Keep an eye on them. George and I'll go in the cab.'

'Very good of you, old man,' said George to the brigadier. 'Are you sure you don't mind?'

'Well, we'll have a riot on our hands if I retreat now. Rather face a battalion of Boers, eh? What!?'

And so they set off, Alf's Unic followed by the brigadier's stately Silver Ghost. After circling round Tulse Hill for a few minutes (despite Alf's assurance that he knew exactly where he was going) they pulled up outside 'Joyous Gard', 24 Windermere Road. The girls were eventually persuaded to alight and, while they thanked the brigadier profusely with much fluttering of eyelashes and barely suppressed titters (despite Clementine's icy glare), George arranged for Alf to return with a colleague and two cabs at six.

Before Alf and the brigadier had chance to depart they were engulfed with more effusive femininity. Caroline, Morgana and Guinevere had been looking out for them and swept down the steps, arms outstretched and so began a period of hugging and kissing somewhat after the continental style, from which Alf and the brigadier were not excluded, much to their embarrassment, although apparently not to Caroline who all but invited them in to join the party. Eventually they extricated themselves and beat a hasty retreat, almost getting into the wrong cars by mistake.

Once inside they were ushered into the drawing room where portraits of medieval knights hung all round the walls. George settled himself into a very cosy armchair, exchanged a few pleasantries and then let them all get on with it. There was little point in trying to keep up with eight chattering females especially when you hadn't a clue as to what they were going on about. He was beginning to get a bit hungry and was looking forward to 'big tea'. Eventually they were led into the dining room and he could see immediately that he wasn't going to be disappointed. There were plates of cold meats; ham, beef, chicken, corned beef; pickles and sauces; salads of all descriptions; cold potatoes, bread, butter; an enormous iced cake; stands with fancies and decanters of port and sherry. George didn't think a tea could be bigger. The chatter continued remorselessly throughout and, try as he might, he was not able to bring up the subject of Chipping Grange with Caroline. Eventually the clock was striking six and Alf was due with the two cabs. Leaving was a mirror image of arriving but George noticed that Alf and his colleague very wisely remained in their cabs. He resigned himself to discussing the matter of Chipping Grange with Caroline in a more suitable and quiet environment.

We have to report that Crewe and Sandwich returned with them. They had been declared 'adorable' but it was felt that they wouldn't get on with Tulse Hill cat; a large, malign male tabby called Uther Pendragon.

George didn't ask. We feel this was wise.

CHAPTER NINETEEN ~

~ A Woman of Property

Wednesday 29th November 1911

There was a letter in the first post from Messrs. Blinkhorn Grist & Vobster confirming that Stripp had been awarded the contract to fit the new heating system and that work was to commence as soon as it was convenient to all parties. This threw George into a bit of a spin. He didn't want the girls staying there while all that was going on. Despite Stripp's assurance that they would be hardly aware of his presence, George was convinced there would be *difficulties*. However, he was diverted from the problem temporarily by the arrival of Caroline *sans* offspring. He'd asked her to call in on the pretext of discussing Sam's papers and in particular the Chipping Grange mystery.

After the usual effusive greetings of the English and continental varieties, they settled down in the drawing room to go through things. 'Most of these papers are routine stuff. Not of much interest,' said George as Rosalind poured the coffee. 'But there is something here I really think you ought to have a look at.' He withdrew the title deeds to Chipping Grange from their envelope and handed them to a puzzled Caroline. 'As you can see,' he said, leaning across and pointing out the relevant details, 'it appears that Sam owned Chipping Grange outright. He bought it, apparently, back in 1907.'

'But, I – I don't understand,' Caroline frowned. 'I always understood that he leased it from the local landowner, The Duke of something or other; there was no mention of it in his will. I brought a copy with me.' She reached into her handbag and handed George an envelope.

He scanned through it. 'This will's dated 1904,' he said. 'Three years before he bought the Grange. There isn't any possibility that there's a later will?'

Caroline pursed her lips. 'Well, I've certainly not come across one and the solicitors haven't mentioned one.'

'Hmm.' George continued to survey the document. 'The solicitor that drew up this will is not the same one that carried out the conveyancing for Chipping Grange,' he said. 'He's used a local firm for that which is a bit odd considering the magnitude of the transaction, although I suppose being local, they knew the property well. Presumably his usual firm wasn't aware that Sam had bought the Grange, otherwise there's no doubt they would have strongly advised drawing up a new will to include it. I'm sure Sam would have got round to it in time but perhaps events rather overtook him, poor chap.'

Caroline was stunned. 'I can't take all this all in,' she said, sitting back in her chair. 'So what – what happens to the Grange now?'

'Well, the will states quite clearly that all Sam's property, real and personal, passes, excluding a few small bequests, such as a stuffed bear,' (he cast her a look of mock disapproval) 'to you on his death. The deeds to the Grange appear to state that Sam held the property in fee simple absolute; that means the freehold, with no entail or onerous encumbrances apart from one or two restrictive covenants regarding wayleaves and easements which are nothing really to worry about.' He continued to peruse the document. 'Look,' he said, collecting all the papers up and knocking them square on the table, 'I think it's best if we let Sam's original solicitor have a look at it all but, on the face of it, you are the new owner of Chipping Grange.' He grinned.

Caroline, meanwhile, had turned quite pale. 'Good heavens! This is such a shock. I had no idea. What on earth am I going to do with it?' She turned round and cast a pleading look towards Rosalind who was just as perplexed and no help at all.

'We'll you could sell it,' said George. 'I should think it would fetch a tidy sum. According to the plans there's quite a bit of land attached.'

'Great Heavens!' said Caroline, fanning herself and refusing an offer of sal volatile from Rosalind. 'Let's not get ahead of ourselves. I shall wait to hear what the solicitor has to say. Perhaps when this becomes known the will might be contested.'

'It's possible, of course,' said George, 'but I should think it's unlikely. Sam was unmarried and you're his nearest living relative. Can't see that anyone else would have any claim. But you're right; let's wait until the solicitor's seen it. There could still be inheritance tax implications especially after the budget last year.'

Just then they were interrupted by Dolly. 'Beggin' your pardon, mum, but I need to mend the fire. If I leave it too long it goes out an' it won't draw. Won't be a minute.' There followed a great deal of vigorous poking, banging, scraping, shovelling, sweeping, sparking and smoking. 'There we are, mum, best I can do. I shall be glad when we gets them new alli – rallidators. Save me an' Poll a lot of work as I shouldn't wonder accordin' to Mrs S. Not that we minds 'ard work, mind. I was jest sayin' to Poll as 'ow—'

'Thank you Dolly, you can leave it now,' said Rosalind tactfully.

'Right you are, mum. I'll come an' 'ave another look presently. Only it gets terrible cold in 'ere, don't it mum what with the frost an' everythin'? I was jest sayin' to Mrs S. as 'ow—'

'Yes, *thank* you Dolly!' Hint taken, she finally tripped off.

'She seems a willing, pleasant girl,' said Caroline.

'Oh, yes.' Rosalind smiled. 'She's been with us for longer than I can remember. We're very lucky with our staff. When I hear some of the stories and problems that some people have I'm very grateful for Polly and Dolly and Mrs Sprackett. They'd be very hard to replace, I'm sure.'

'I hope you don't mind me asking,' said Caroline, looking puzzled, 'but what did she mean by 'rallidators'?'

Rosalind looked at George and they both burst out laughing again.

'Radiators,' said George, when he'd recovered his composure. 'We're having radiators put in all through the house and a new boiler for heating.' Caroline was clearly more confused and wondering why such a dull domestic subject as heating the rooms should cause such merriment. George tried, to the best of his ability, to explain to her that the rumour had got abroad that they were going to fill the house with alligators and that it had caused such panic and alarm that Polly and Dolly had decided to leave.

George thought Caroline was more tickled by this story than

Rosalind and him and she roared with laughter which, of course, set Rosalind and George off again. 'Gosh, How modern!' she said when the gales of merriment had died down sufficiently to enable her to regain her composure. 'But won't that mean an awful lot of disruption?'

'I'm afraid it will,' said George. 'I'm still trying to work out the best way of managing it.'

'George doesn't want us to stay here while the work's going on,' said Rosalind.

'Good gracious, I should think not! What will you do?'

'I'm thinking of renting a place temporarily, just for the duration,' he said. In fact he hadn't, but it was the first thing that came into his head.

'I've got a better idea,' said Caroline, a smile spreading across her face. 'Why don't you stop at the Grange? As it appears to be mine I shouldn't think anyone would object. Besides, you could keep an eye on it for me while things are being sorted out.'

'That's very kind of you Caroline,' said Rosalind hesitantly, 'but we couldn't poss—'

But Caroline was having none of it. Her mind was made up. 'Nonsense! That's settled. You can all have a lovely holiday in the country while all that ghastly banging and clanging is going on.'

'Well!' said George. 'If you're absolutely sure. I think this calls for a celebration. Shall we get the girls in?'

'Oh, yes,' said Rosalind, immediately warming to the whole idea. 'I'm sure they'll be thrilled!' She went out into the hallway and called to them. 'Girls, come in here a moment. We have something to tell you.'

There was a momentary pause, then a thundering of footsteps on the stairs. Vicky and Alex burst in, curl papers flailing behind them.

'What? Oh, hello Caroline!'

'What is it? Caroline, hello!'

Celandine appeared from the music room where 'Maple Leaf Rag' had just commenced but was mercifully truncated and fell to earth prematurely. 'Yes Auntie Rosalind? Oh, good morning Mrs Fitzpatrick.' (Celandine was such a *polite* girl, thought George. He wished Vicky and Alex would take a leaf out of her book, but preferably not of the Maple variety.)

The momentous news was conveyed to them which resulted in much hugging and kissing of cheeks in both the English and continental fashion.

'Right,' said George, when the effusiveness had died down. 'Sherry for everyone, I think.' Celandine you can have a little drop with some seltzer. Don't tell your mother. Where is she, by the way?'

'Oh, she's having a lie down. She's got a head cold coming on.'

'Oh, dear,' he said, unsuccessfully hiding a smile. 'Well, you can tell her the good news later on. I'm sure some fresh country air will do her the world of good. In fact I think it will do us all the world of good!

Cheers!'

Saturday 2nd December 1911

The day dawned frosty and bright. George had arranged with Stripp that he could start work a week on Monday, the 11th. If all went well they should be back in the house by the beginning of the following week or soon after. Of course there were *difficulties*. The first of these concerned Celandine. Going down to Chipping Grange *en famille* would mean her missing school. An *exeat* on the ground of an impromptu holiday was unlikely to be granted. Celandine herself wanted to go but would miss her schoolfriends. Lady Disdain was implacably against her going but could not come up with a solution as to what to do with her if she stayed at home. George could see both points of view but could not disregard the fact that he was paying the school fees and there was no chance of a refund for non-attendance even for the most plausible of reasons. In the end a compromise was reached. They would ask the school to set Celandine some work to do while she was away. Everyone seemed happy with this arrangement.

They would all travel down on Monday morning and, after making sure they were settled in, George would return to oversee the work. Of course it would have been more sensible to go down on Saturday in order to put some clear blue water between them and the commencement of the works but Lady Disdain didn't think she'll be up to it by then; Celandine had a piano lesson on Saturday afternoon which she simply *couldn't* miss; packing could not possibly be accomplished in the short time available and Mrs Sprackett steadfastly refused to travel on a Sunday. George booked himself in to the 'George and Dragon' for the duration and would be able to keep an eye on things from there. When he was satisfied that everything was running properly and as it should be he'd go back down to Chipping Grange to collect them all.

CHAPTER TWENTY ~

~ When Icicles Hang by the Wall

———⟳⟳———

Sunday 10th December 1911

George had seldom spent a more trying week. Moving house from Sydenham to Streatham was simplicity itself compared with 'packing to go on holiday'. The number and volume of trunks and cases amassed throughout the house in the previous few days was beyond the imagination of the average man. He had kept out of the way as much as possible and confined his efforts to administering the arrangements for conveying the equipage and its attendants to and from Chipping Grange. At one point he was seriously of the opinion that it would be necessary to request that the Great Western Railway attach an extra luggage van to its train; however, on enquiry, he was assured that everything could be accommodated in its normal parcels van. By Wednesday it was apparent that most of the trunks would have to go on ahead, space in the fleet of cabs arranged with Alf being, of necessity, finite. The GWR van duly arrived on Friday morning and departed for Paddington, its springs groaning under the weight. Delivery at Chipping Grange was organised for Monday morning, 'The Lady at the Post Office' being entrusted with a key and would be in attendance when the van arrived.

Monday 11th December 1911

The day started well. It then went rapidly downhill. The cabs had been booked for ten o'clock so they were able to enjoy a reasonably relaxed breakfast. At a quarter to nine Stripp's van drew up closely followed by another. 'We won't get in your way, Mr Chesshyre, but I thought we'd make an early start. We'll jest start bringin' some materials in if that's all right with you Mr

Chesshyre? We won't do no bangin' and 'ammerin' until you've gone if that's all right?'

'Carry on,' said George. 'We'll be away at ten so you'll have the place to yourselves.' There then commenced a series of bangs, crashes, and peculiar noises like bells being rung as a seemingly endless stream of pipes and associated ironwork were unloaded from the vans and either stacked up outside the front door or lodged in the hallway narrowly missing King George the Second.

At a quarter to ten a horse and cart drew up outside the main gateway. 'Daddy, it's the scarecrow!' came the cry in unison from Vicky and Alex.

Stripp senior appeared at the front door. 'Ah, Mr Chesshyre, I'm glad I've caught you before you've gone, I got a load of muck for the back garden as I told you about.' Before George could say anything the cart had been unhitched, backed into the driveway and was being unloaded by two burly gentlemen he felt it would be unwise to challenge. Within a minute or two a large steaming pile of 'ripe 'oss muck' had been deposited by the side gate. Meanwhile assorted pipes were advancing from an alternate direction. Even as the pile of manure was growing ever higher, three cabs drew up on the other side of the road, their own side being full of horses and vans. George decided that it was time to take firm, decisive action, round everyone up and get going as soon as possible. He could, when necessary, be highly demonstrative and so, within ten minutes, he had ushered Polly, Dolly and Mrs Sprackett into the leading cab, Rosalind, Clemmie and Celandine into the second, leaving Vicky, Alex and himself to climb aboard the last. Having ensured that 'everyone had got everything' and instructing Stripp senior to secure the house when he had finished for the day, they set off for Paddington.

The train was already in the platform when they arrived and, having ensconced Polly, Dolly and Mrs Sprackett safely in a ladies only carriage, found their two empty compartments, one of which was commandeered for Rosalind, LD and Alex, the other reserved for Vicky, Celandine and himself. The two porters he had engaged were very helpful and stowed the hand luggage (all 'wanted on voyage') neatly and efficiently. George was quite proud of these arrangements, chiefly because it kept him and Lady Disdain separate. Things were looking up again.

They bowled along at a fair old clip and, not having to change at Swindon, drew into Stroud station just over two hours later. The journey was remarkably incident free except for when Mrs Sprackett, on waking from a doze, saw an engine called 'The Great Bear' and had a 'bad turn' which necessitated a 'medicinal' nip of brandy. Vicky felt ill at the sight of the 'sticky brown' carriages but made a remarkable recovery as soon as they got going. Luckily 'Lady Disdain' did not seem to be out and about that day.

Cabs on the station forecourt were engaged in the same formation as had left Streatham and soon they were making the slow, tortuous climb to Chipping Loosely. As they did so it started to snow. Not heavily, just a flake or two at first but by the time they had reached the Grange it was coming down quite thick and fast. George had an ominous feeling that things were starting to go 'downhill' again. The 'Lady at the Post Office' had been keeping an eye out for them and greeted them as they extricated themselves and their luggage from the taxis. Handing George the key she said that the GWR van had only just left and that all their trunks were stacked in the hallway as he had asked. This was something of a relief to George as he had, on the way down, pondered the grisly possibility that it might have been misdirected to Strood. By now the light was beginning to fade and the snow was coming down faster.

Houses that are not regularly occupied can quickly get damp and can feel colder than the grave even in clement weather. Chipping Grange was certainly cold but didn't feel particularly damp. None of the fires had been lit recently and so the first job for Polly and Dolly was to get as many going as possible in order to warm the place through. Unlike Scattersdale Avenue, the Grange still relied on gas for lighting so the drawing room, kitchen and hallway were soon bathed in a soft gaslight accompanied by the familiar hiss. Vicky, Alex and Celandine were willing and able assistants to Polly and Dolly and soon fires were sparking into life throughout the Grange, the chimneys of which seemed thankfully free of seagulls, much to Dolly's relief. Mrs

Sprackett busied herself organising things in the kitchen and Rosalind and Clemmie began the marathon task of unpacking after bedrooms had been allocated, this latter task, much to George's surprise, being achieved with remarkably little fuss, there being no long-drawn out discourse regarding the position of the sun, the moon, the stars and other heavenly or celestial bodies likely to have an influence over the sleeping arrangements of those sensitive to such matters.

By half past six things were looking ship-shape. The fires had all got up, there was a warmth spreading through the house, the boiler had been lit with little trouble (it was not a 'Thermoboil') and hot water was beginning to course through the pipework. With a bit of luck they should all be able to have a hot bath before bed time. Transferring from kindling duties, Polly and Dolly were now assisting Mrs Sprackett in the kitchen and soon the aroma of frying bacon, sausages and eggs began to permeate through the house. Tired, but well-fed, warm and happy at the way things had gone so smoothly, Rosalind and George went to bed at eleven. He should be able to go back to Streatham in the morning secure in the knowledge that everything at Chipping Grange was in hand and under control.

Tuesday 12th December 1911

> *'In the bleak midwinter, frosty wind made moan,*
> *Earth stood hard as iron, water like a stone.'*

Christina Rossetti

By borrowing Celandine's school ruler George had been able to ascertain that approximately seven inches of snow had fallen in the night. Chipping Loosely had been transformed into a sparkling Arctic vista which would, no doubt, make a charming and appropriate Christmas card but had, at a stroke, thrown his plans out completely. He should certainly not be able to get down into the town that day. Of course any difficulties he might have been experiencing were completely overshadowed by the wondrous awe in which the white visitation was held by Vicky, Alex and Celandine. A prolonged and extremely dangerous (to George) snowball fight raged for most of the morning followed after lunch by the building of a gargantuan snowman which was topped off with the requisite coal eyes, carrot nose, George's cap and, to his extreme annoyance, his Peterson pipe.

He had taken his life into his hands avoiding the icy missiles in order to fight his way to the Post Office. He needed to make a telephone call to Stripp to let him know that he wouldn't be coming back that day. Of course there were *difficulties*. On arriving at the Post Office he realised that he didn't know his telephone number and so had to retrace his steps and face a further bombardment while he searched for his diary in which he had noted it. Returning to the Post Office the 'Lady' informed him most pleasantly that she would be pleased to assist him but she would have to 'book' his call as it was of the 'trunked' variety and not immediately executable. A long and complicated conversation took place between her and a disembodied voice at the telephone exchange at the conclusion of which she informed him that the call had been 'booked' for four o'clock that afternoon. Another trudge back through the battlefield.

By four, hostilities had ceased, the combatants having retired to their respective billets, and so he was able to return to the Post Office, retrieving his pipe on the way, and await the call from the exchange. By half-past four no connection had been made and so he was obliged to send a wire explaining the situation and also asking Stripp to inform the George and Dragon. (Another hostelry he would have to apologise to.) When he returned for the last time (he hoped) that day, the Grange appeared to be full of steaming outercoats, scarves, gloves, boots and shoes drying in front of numerous coal fires heroically kept going by Polly and Dolly.

While the battle of Chipping Grange was being fought and Signals Division was trying to communicate with the outside world, the Catering Corps in the form of Rosalind and Mrs Sprackett had managed to get through (almost unscathed by frozen flying shrapnel) to the village butcher and baker in the hope of being able to order enough food to keep them all going for the duration. Good news was forthcoming in that they could expect a delivery later on in the day. True to their word, a beef-faced butcher's boy turned up towards evening and the baker's lad materialised not long after with the promise of a further delivery first thing in the morning. They might be snowed in but at least they wouldn't starve.

Wednesday 13th December 1911

A hard frost in the night and the snow heavily encrusted underfoot. The novelty apparently having worn off already and, no doubt still exhausted from the previous day's exertions, the Arctic warriors did not appear until mid-morning. A wire from Stripp in the afternoon to say that the work was progressing well but he'd had to move the piano. 'If there's so much as a finger-mark on it I'll sue the hide off him,' said George to Rosalind.

Thursday 14th December 1911

A thaw had set in; water dripping everywhere and rivulets mean-dering down the pathways and off the roof gables and hips. A thunderous roar about mid-day when an avalanche of melting snow slid off the steeply-gabled roof of the east wing. The snowman had shrunk, was looking forlorn and had lost his carrot. A frost set in after dark and two foot stalactites were hanging from the porch roof.

George had a long and very serious discussion with Celandine concerning 'Country Life'. Her English teacher had, on the instruction of Miss Oswaldwhistle, set her an essay to write on that bucolic subject. Eventually he persuaded her that it was probably not a good idea to find a farmer and ask him to let her milk a cow; he similarly convinced her that hay-making really *was* over and that organising a nature ramble to pick wild flowers at that time of the year could only lead to disappointment.

Friday 15th December 1911

Rain. Heavy, driving rain. George wondered if this was typical of the weather in that part of the world. He thought the summer in London was bad but he was beginning to think that they had it easier in the suburbs than up on those exposed moorlands. Their fifth day there and no two had been the same. Perhaps that's what had attracted Sam, he liked the variety, not knowing from one day to the next what he was going to face when he got up in the morning. But now it felt damp. The rain was relentless and the wind was penetrating the very fabric of the building. The odd figure battled by, bent against the monsoon and mistral; the persiennes rattled against the frames. The mood had become restless, the initial excitement having worn off everyone now just wanted to get back to Scattersdale Avenue. Perhaps this had not been such a good idea, especially at that time of the year. A rain-sodden postcard arrived by the second post. From Caroline. Hoping that they were enjoying themselves and looking forward to seeing them on their return. Yes, they were enjoying themselves in the way that you do when you look back when the bad memories have faded and you have just fixed the good parts, like the snowball battle and the snowman, in your memory.

Despite the general restlessness a good fire in the drawing room cheered them all up a little. In between snowball fights Celandine had been diligently working at the tasks set by the school. However she had come a little unstuck with an arithmetic assignment. George was consulted and came down with a bad headache after trying to remember the difference between numerators and denominators, highest common factors and lowest common multiples. A glass of milk and a biscuit arrived half way through this tripos and the junior wrangler's mind wandered off onto things agricultural. The senior wrangler went to bed that night wondering how difficult it might be to find a farmer willing to let them milk a cow.

Saturday 16th December 1911

The day dawned bright. The rain had blown through and the sky had cleared to a brilliant, but cold, blue. There was a lot of snow still lying but patchy, with oases of dark green showing through in places. The village roads were generally passable with care and one or two carts were out and about. George had given up trying to telephone Stripp and had sent another wire that morning enquiring after progress.

After a long and rather silly discussion, he managed to convince Vicky and Alex that vulgar fractions were not 'rude'.

Geography and history were on the curriculum that morning and after being pressed as to an estimate of the total annual tonnage of coffee produced by Brazil, thought it unlikely that Mary, Queen of Scots had ever stayed at Chipping Grange and that her headless ghost was not haunting the bedrooms at night.

Monday 18th December 1911

A wire from Stripp that afternoon. He had worked all through the weekend and the new system was fully installed and running well. They could return at their convenience. George wasted no time in ordering the GWR van and wiring Stripp to say they would return on Wednesday and to arrange for Alf to meet them at Paddington with three cabs.

A history tutorial had been pencilled in for that morning during which George was forced to admit, to much disappointment, that he did not possess a copy of the Domesday Book and that it was unlikely that Streatham Library would have one. He was unable to express a reliable opinion as to the acreage of Chipping Grange to the nearest rod, pole or perch, and was adamant that the inhabitants of Chipping Loosely should not be referred to as 'villeins'.

CHAPTER TWENTY ONE

~ Advent of Modern Life

Wednesday 20th December 1911

They were back! Everyone was exhausted but happy. The 'Victor' was purring nicely and there were warm radiators in every room. Hot water gushed from every tap. Stripp had done an excellent job. There was no mess, no manure heaps in the front and not the slightest hint that the Bechstein has been moved.

George was pleased and relieved to note that the whole house was free from alligators, crocodiles, caymans, lizards or other exotic tropical fauna of any description whatsoever.

Thursday 21st December 1911

Chipping Grange was rapidly becoming a distant memory. Of course the whole exercise was unwise from the beginning, thought George. He should have delayed having the heating work done until the following summer when a week in the country would probably have been far more enjoyable but, anyhow, it was over and done with and the house was as warm as toast with no smoky coal fires and freezing bathrooms. He had no idea that morning what the weather was doing outside as he lay in a soporific reverie contemplating a leisurely breakfast. What cared he if the wind howled and the rain lashed; the blizzard blew and the fog loomed? He had the 'Victor Easilite 6'. What luxury it was to live in the modern, go-ahead twentieth century. Of course it didn't last. A prod in the back.

'George.'

'Hmm?'

'Do you realise that it's Christmas on Monday?'

'Hmm.'

A sharper prod in the back.

'*George.*'

'Hmm?'

'It's Christmas day in five days.'

'Hmm.'

'There's an awful lot to do.'

'Hmm'

'*George!*'

'Yes, dear. Christmas. I'm staying here.'

'*George!*'

'Well, it'll soon be over. Turkey and a balloon. Don't know what all the fuss is about. Same thing every year.'

'But George. We haven't done any shopping. There's presents to buy and wrapping paper and cards. Cards! We haven't done any cards! I shall have to go into town.'

'Well don't expect me to come. You know I can't stand crowds. Besides, I need to go into the office.'

'Oh, why?'

'Letter in the post yesterday. Partners' meeting. Need to discuss how to proceed.'

'Oh, George, can't it wait until after Christmas?'

'I'm afraid not. I've left it too long as it is and there's the distinct possibility of transferring my partnership. In any case it'll have to be decided by the New Year.'

George had to admit here to a little subterfuge. It was true, he had received a letter from the firm but the matter of the partnership was not as urgent as he had made out. He'd do anything to get out of having anything to do with Christmas. The truly terrifying and rapid depletion of his bank account was contribution enough.

'The best laid plans of mice and men gang aft agley', according to Robert Burns, although what ganging aft agley actually means had always remained a mystery to George. He'd ask the McGillycuddy woman but would probably get a three hour lecture on the Bard of Ayrshire. He was just enjoying a rather succulent kipper which Tarporley also had his eyes on when they who must be obeyed bounded into the room.

'Daddy, we haven't got a tree.' Alex opened the gambit.

'We always have a tree,' came the echo from Vicky.

'You can't have Christmas without a tree,' Celandine reinforced the argument.

'Sorry, no trees this year,' said George, defending his kipper from Tarporley. 'The new king has banned them.'

'Don't be silly, daddy,' in twin unison.

'Has he *really* banned them?' From Celandine, dinner plates in sparkling form.

'Of course not. Daddy's just being a Scrooge. Stop being such a Scrooge, daddy!'

'Christmas is a lot of humbug,' he said buttering a piece of toast. Just then there was a knock on the front door.

'Daddy, it's the scarecrow! D'you think he could get us a tree?'

'I'm sure if you ask him nicely and call him Mr Stripp he'll find you a bloomin' giant redwood between now and Christmas Eve,' he said, opening a jar of marmalade of a type hitherto unknown to him.

'Daddy, you're hopeless. Come on you two. Let's go and ask him,' came the parting shot from Vicky. There followed a lot of excited chatter from the direction of the hallway after which several pairs of feet rapidly ascended the stairs. Finishing a cup of tea George went out to see Stripp.

'Mornin' Mr Chesshyre. I jest thought as I'd call round seein' as 'ow you're back from 'oliday and I 'opes as you 'ad a pleasant break. An' Mrs Chesshyre as well an' the 'ole family. It gladdens my 'eart to see you back Mr Chesshyre. I said to Mrs Stripp last night it gladdens my 'eart to know that you're all back safe an' sound, an' you know what she said to me Mr Chesshyre? She said it gladdened 'er 'eart to know that you was back with us again from the country. Of course we never was ones for 'olidays, not Mrs Stripp an' me on account of the country air don't agree with 'er. It gets on 'er chest terrible bad. Mind you, we do like to go down to the seaside once in a while. Very particlar to the seaside is Mrs Stripp an' me. Last August Bank 'oliday we went down to Brighton by hexcursion train an' we sat on the beach eatin' jellied eels. Very partial to jellied eels is Mrs Stripp. It gladdens 'er 'eart to 'ave a tray of jellied eels sat on the beach at Brighton, but jest as she'd finished 'em the cheeky young deckchair attendant come along an' 'e said to 'er, "Beggin' yer pardon, missus, but would you mind a-movin' because the tide's waitin' ta come in?" Well, the missus was fair put out as you might say at the heffrontery of that young shaver, an' before you could say "Jack Robinson" she'd got up and took 'im by the scruff an' pushed 'im over into the water flat on 'is fizzog. "There," she said. "I apologise most 'umbly for hinconveniencin' the tide but as you're so hintimate with it you can hinform it with my compliments that it can come in now as quick as it likes and with my blessin' too." And d'you know, Mr Chesshyre, Mrs Stripp was the 'ero of the 'our, the 'ole crowd what 'ad gathered round ta see the sport clapped an' cheered an' declared that Mrs Stripp was the 'ero of the hour an' that the young shaver was a cheeky young cur and no better than 'e ought ta be an' that 'e'd got what 'e deserved. Mind you, we went orf Brighton a bit after that.'

By this time George had rather lost the thread of the original conversation but attempted to turn it back to the subject of the holiday. 'Thank you,' he said. 'Actually the weather was very bad while we were away and we're all really glad to be back home, especially now your brother has made such a good job of installing the new heating system.'

'A magician with the pipes and the gas, Mr Chesshyre. Course I prefers the feel of the soil on my 'ands as you might say. I got most of the muck dug in while you were away apart from one day when we 'ad a 'ard frost. Gets on me lungs does a frost but it does the sprouts a world o' good. Jest right for Christmas dinner. You need a good, 'ard frost in sprouts to put a bit o' flavour in 'em. Don't do carrits no good mind if you can't get 'em out o' the ground. Jest think, Mr Chesshyre, this time next year you'll 'ave sprouts an' carrits an' spuds an' broccoli all out o' your own garden. Nothin' like fresh veg out your own garden I say. Now that I come to think of it, I've got plenty o' veg in my garden Mr Chesshyre. I'll fill a trug an' bring it round Christmas Eve if that'd suit you an' Mrs Chesshyre.'

'Very kind of you, Stripp,' said George, who was struggling to keep up with the pace of the conversation, his mind still pondering on Mrs Stripp's altercation with the deck chair boy.

'I'm sure we shall enjoy some fresh vegetables on Christmas Day. As long as you don't leave yourself and Mrs Stripp short. We wouldn't want that would we?'

'Now don't you worry about us, Mr Chesshyre. I've got enough veg to stock a greengrocer's an' much better quality as some as is sold round 'ere I can tell you. Ashamed to put it on display, I'd be. Mrs Stripp was only sayin' to me the other evenin', "Stripp," she says, "d'you know I've jest seen Moulder's in the 'igh Street sellin' carrits at 2d a pound! And they was stale. Mouldy carrits I calls 'em." Likes 'er veg fresh does Mrs Strpp.'

Interesting as this vegetable discourse was, George was anxious to get on. He thought he'd better mention the Christmas tree. 'I hope my girls haven't been troubling you too much about Christmas trees,' he said. This proved to be a grave error of judgement.

'D'you know, Mr Chesshyre, I'm sure I don't know when I met such lovely girls as yourn. The sight of them three girls gladdens my 'eart, Mr Chesshyre. Lifts my spirits a tonic they does of a mornin'. I often mention 'em to Mrs Stripp as 'ow they's such lovely girls and d'you know what she says, Mr Chesshyre? She says it gladdens 'er 'eart to think of it. Of course we was never blessed with children, Mrs Stripp and me, on account of 'er sister's babbies a-wailin' an' a-'ollerin' give 'er the 'eadaches most terrible bad.'

George made some suitable sympathetic and appreciative comment and attempted to steer the monologue once more in the direction of Christmas trees, this time with a little more success.

'Now don't you worry, Mr Chesshyre. I knows where I can lay my 'ands on the most beautiful Christmas tree as you ever did see. Direct from Spitalfields, fresh as a daisy. I'll bring it round tomorrow mornin' directly if that suits you Mr Chesshyre.'

'Very good of you, Stripp. The girls will look forward to it.'

At that point he was overwhelmed by a cohort of chattering women sweeping through the hallway on their way out to do some Christmas shopping. As they seemed to gather up Stripp on their way out and he receded rather like jetsam on an ebb tide he took the opportunity to escape to the music room for a bit of peace and quiet in the company of Messrs Bechstein and McClelland.

Friday 22nd December 1911

It is a curious fact, not, to George's certain knowledge, widely recognised, that the girth and height of the annual Christmas tree increases by some exponential logarithmic equation at the same rate, and in line with, the size and number of the family offspring it is intended to delight and entertain. When the girls were small a dainty little tree adorned the drawing room. You know where you are with a small tree. It is manageable, you can lift it with one hand, carry it around under your arm if needs be, decorate it without resorting to a stepladder in order to stick an angel on top, dispose of it after twelfth night with the minimum of fuss. At ten o'clock that morning he began to regret his sarcastic comment regarding giant redwoods.

It might be recalled the difficulty and anxiety experienced when the Bechstein was delivered; the shock and alarm which rippled through the house when King George the Second appeared, uninvited, at the front door. The current morning's events easily equalled those two now latterly mentioned. What could only be termed an evergreen battering ram proceeded ominously over the driveway towards the porch supported at each end by Stripp in the vanguard and one of his muck shovellers in the rear. Its approach was accompanied by shrieks of delight as the girls thundered down the stairs and flew out of the door in order to escort the tree through the entrance and into the drawing room where, apparently, it had been decided to place it. Having been leaned carefully against the wall temporarily, a monstrous flower pot was next brought in together with a sack of, as George was to find out, soil in which to 'plant' the tree. When everything was in place the tree was 'unleashed'. Its roots firmly embedded in the soil, the string bands holding its branches together were cut and the tree allowed to spread itself, engulfing half of the drawing room as it did so, in all its spiny glory. Of course this is one of the most annoying things about Christmas trees. The moment you bring them into the house the needles begin to drop. It doesn't matter what small corner the tree is confined to, the needles get everywhere. George was convinced that Christmas trees grow legs in the night and wander round the house dropping their sharp little calling cards wherever they felt like it so that, should you be unwise enough to be padding about the bedroom without your carpet slippers sometime in early August the following year, you inevitably stepped on some of the annoying and painful little pins which had been lurking in readiness for the unwary since the previous December.

The drawing room was, thought George, about thirteen feet high from floor to ceiling and this monster had very little headroom so that, when the time came to stick the angel on top (a task always delegated to him because no-one else would venture that far up a stepladder) she'd better keep her wings folded otherwise they'd get a liberal coating of distemper.

The house was, by degrees, disappearing under a welter of paper chains, lines of twirly coloured paper, crepe streamers, balloons, paper lanterns, sprigs of holly, bunches of mistletoe (he avoided these with great care) and strings of Christmas cards, more of which appeared with every post, draped across any convenient fireplace or wall. A mountain of oddly shaped parcels, each wrapped with varying degrees of expertise, was growing daily underneath the commodious branches of the tree. Polly and Dolly had taken to wearing peculiar green conical hats much to the annoyance of Mrs Sprackett and even Tarporley had, at times, been 'decorated' with a sparkly necklace. George made himself useful by writing out a Christmas drinks order and taking it to Oglethorpe's, the wine and spirit merchant in the High Street. He had taken care to order some Johnnie Walker Special Old Highland. He'd need it in January when the bills started to roll in.

Saturday 23rd December 1911

The days immediately leading up to Christmas are usually fairly grisly, full of rush and panic. On the morning of Saturday 23rd George escaped the mayhem of Scattersdale Avenue only to exchange it for the rush and bustle of the crowds of travellers and shoppers as he made his way across London and on to Maidenhead to collect his aged mother who always spent Christmas with them. Each year it became more of a trial for him and more especially for her. She'd been deaf for years and it was getting progressively worse. Of course she denied it. 'People don't speak clearly! Why don't they speak clearly?' in a voice that would shame the most bellowing and stentorian of drill Sergeant-Majors. Two or three years previously George had given her a long and highly flared ear trumpet but she refused to use it. 'I'm not deaf, George. People don't speak clearly!' He had arranged for Alf to meet them at Paddington and was back in Scattersdale Avenue in time for lunch.

'Why have we come here, George? This isn't Sydenham.'

'No, mother, this is our new house. In Streatham. You remember I told you we'd moved.'

'You did nothing of the sort. Why have you moved? Nobody told me you'd moved. Does Rosalind know you've moved?'

'Yes, of course. She's inside. And the girls.'

'Pearls? She's got some new pearls? Rather extravagant, George.'

'No, mother. The girls. Vicky and Alex. They're here with Rosalind. And there's Clementine and Celandine. They're living with us now.'

'The cook and her girl?'

'No, mother. Rosalind's sister and her daughter.'

'Rosalind's sister is your cook? Is that wise, George? Why wasn't I told?'

'No, mother. Mrs *Sprackett* is the cook.'

'A bracket and a hook? Why do you need a bracket and a hook? Honestly George I don't understand why you talk such nonsense. And this isn't Sydenham. I can't think why you've brought me here. And look at that fellow over there. Looks like a criminal if you ask me. Look he's stealing that motor car. George, call the police at once.'

'Mother, that's our next-door neighbour Mr Campbell-Bristow. And the car belongs to him. He's not stealing it.' Archibald gave them a cheery wave as he drove off. 'Come on, let's get you inside. It's very cold standing out here.'

'Well, I don't remember this. And what's that smell? Smells like horse manure. Why does your garden smell of horse manure, George?'

'It's for the roses, mother.'

'Moses? What's he got to do with it? I hope you're not being profane, George. I've told you before about being profane.'

By now Alf had driven off with a knowing and pitying look to George. They had progressed as far as the front porch and he'd managed to get the door open. He was hoping for some sort of reception but there was no-one to be seen except King George the Second on whose outstretched arm a handbag was immediately hung as though it was a perfectly normal and convenient hat or coat hook. He steered her into the drawing room, took her coat, got her comfortably seated and was just thinking about offering her a drink when the door flew open and Vicky, Alex and Celandine, closely flowed by Rosalind and Lady Disdain, flooded into the room with effusive welcomes, squeals of delight and kisses and hugs of the English and continental variety. He gave all this a wide berth and went over to the sideboard to sort out some drinks. Oglethorpe's had delivered in his absence and he busied himself unpacking the crates which had been stacked just inside the door. After a few minutes, when the effusiveness had died down, he deemed it safe to venture back in and take some orders.

'Mother, what would you like to drink?'

'Mink? I'm not wearing a mink.'

'No, DRINK, mother. What would you like to drink?'

'Drink? Why didn't you say so? You must speak up George. I'll have a sherry. Is it dry?'

'Medium sweet, mother.'

'Well, I'll suppose it'll have to do.'

'Clemmie?'

'Port and lemon, please.'

'Any port in a storm, eh Clemmie? Ha ha!'

'Don't be so vulgar, George. Rosalind, I don't know how you put up with it.'

'Oh, it's just George's little joke. I'll have the same, please George.'

'Two ports and lemon coming up.'

'What about you girls?'

'Port and lemon, please!' in perfect three-part harmony.

'You can have the lemon but there won't be much port in it.'

'Oh!' Three faces fell, crestfallen.

'I think I'll join you ladies in a port. An excellent one I think you'll find. Dow's twelve year old ruby.'

'Which one is Ruby?' beamed the aged P. 'Is it you dear?' The girls were surveyed with a regal smile, eventually settling on Celandine.

'No, mother, this is Celandine. Clementine's daughter. She's your great niece.'

'Your father took me there once. I remember it was very hot.'

'Where, mother?'

'Nice. It's in France, I believe. I don't care for France. It's too bohemian.'

This was the cue for LD to pipe up.

'George *will* insist on playing French music. It's corrupting Celandine. Of course it's all that young American's fault. I don't care for Americans. They're always so loud.' Anglo-American relations were in danger of relapse. He'd have to nip this in the bud.

'Eugene's not loud, Clemmie.' he came to his defence in as diplomatic a way as he was able, anxious not to start another war.

'Well of course you wouldn't think so. And Eugene is the exception to the rule, I will grant you. But I know it to be true speaking generally.'

Just then they were rescued by Polly announcing lunch. Of course there was a palaver. 'Mrs Sprackett asked me to mention in particlar, mum, as 'ow she 'opes Mrs Chesshyre senior is particlar to tomato soup seein' as 'ow it's easy to digest an' she begs pardon but she 'opes as she ain't put too much salt in it only she forgot as 'ow she put some in an' then 'ad to shoo Tarpaulin away an' she might 'ave forgot an' put another lot in but then she thought to put a potato in it so as to soak up some of the salt an' she 'opes as 'ow there ain't no potato left in it as she strained it most particlar.'

George poured himself another very large port and just the tiniest spot of lemon.

Sunday 24th December 1911

On Sunday, being Christmas Eve, there was an air of expectancy about the house. A hard frost had set in overnight and the grass, trees and hedges sparkled silver in the morning sun. There wasn't much sign of snow, so a white Christmas was not realistically on the cards except the greetings variety with which the house was festooned. After much discussion, debate and argument at cabinet level, it was decided that Vicky would move in with Alex and share her room while George's mother stayed. (More 'musical bedrooms'.) Of course there were *difficulties*. Vicky felt she was being turned out, Alex felt invaded and the Aged Parent didn't think much of either: Room, bed, view, furniture, curtains or wallpaper. Disapproval was also vented regarding the bathroom: Bath (taps at wrong end), radiators (not natural), blinds (too French), electric light (too dangerous), and washbasin (too high).

George was looking forward to a leisurely breakfast but his hopes were dashed when there were heated exchanges between the Aged P and Lady Disdain about the suitability of Marmite for the breakfast table:

'I've forbidden Celandine to eat it.'

'Nonsense, I've eaten it for fifty years.'

'Marmalade is proper for breakfast.'

'Nonsense, I've eaten it for fifty years.'

Then there was an argument about morning church.

'I don't care for modern churches. George, take me to Westminster Abbey.'

'I doubt they'd let us in, mother. Besides it's too far.'

'Oh, well, I suppose we'll have to make do with what we can get. Is it low or high?'

'High.'

'I don't care for high.'

'Low.'

'I don't care for low.'

'I'm sure you'll enjoy it. There's a carol service this morning.'

'Mourning? Why should I be in mourning. Your father's been dead twelve years. Passed on before the old queen, God rest her soul. I don't care for that Edward fellow. Too familiar with the French.'

'He's dead, mother.'

'Dead? When? Why wasn't I told?'

'He died last year. We've got a new king now. George the Fifth.'

'Yes, of course. Quite right too. I don't care for that Edward fellow. I remember now, I saw him in Maidenhead last week getting off a 'bus. They come from Windsor, you know. And they punt on the Thames . . .'

***

The church, high, low or somewhere in between, had been got up very nicely for the Christmas festivities. There was a nativity scene and a splendid tree, which, judging by the size, was another of Stripp's, 'direct from Spitalfields'. Of course the trouble with having Sunday followed immediately by Christmas Day is that you get rather too much of a good thing. It's all very well pulling all the stops out on Sunday morning and having a carol service but you've got to follow it in the evening with something and presumably if you have a tendency towards the 'high' end you might even feel obliged to have a midnight mass. Then on Christmas morning itself you have to do the same thing all over again. Presumably the clergy are used to this sort of thing and take it in their stride but for the (un)faithful congregation it can seem a bit of a trial having to trudge back and forth several times over two consecutive days just when you're trying to get to grips with all the stuff Christmas throws at you at home and the whole thing needs a bit of thinking about. In the end George decided he would ration his attendance to Sunday carols and Christmas Day whatever it was in the morning. He refused to turn out in the middle of the night. Besides, Rosalind always insisted on seeing the New Year in so that would be a late night and more than enough for him. Being Scottish on her father's side she made a lot of Hogmanay which George didn't mind at all as long as the McGillycuddy woman kept her nose out.

Anyhow, there was a good turnout for the carol service. A choir appeared from somewhere, one not normally in evidence, and helped things along with a pretty vigorous gusto, some attractive descants chiming in at appropriate places. Eugene had got the organ cranked up nicely and they rattled through a lot of the old favourites: 'Hark the Herald Angels Sing', 'The First Noel', 'God Rest Ye Merry Gentlemen' and 'While Shepherds Watched Their Flocks by Night' (or 'Washed Their Socks by Night' as George remembered singing at school) among others. Fortunately Humpidge's sermon was mercifully short and consisted of a somewhat eerie echo the meaning of which was apparently not entirely lost on the congregation, the Aged P remarking to George afterwards, 'What a wonderful sermon. I could understand every word he said. Why can't you speak clearly like that, George?'

Opening the front door when they returned he almost tripped over a hundredweight of Brussels sprouts that had been left lying in the porch. Before he had time to warn the others, Stripp senior appeared from the direction of the kitchen. 'Ah, I'm glad I've seen you Mr Chesshyre. I've brought the vegetables around as I told you about. I've just got to take these sprouts in to Mrs Sprackett who's wantin' 'em most particlar because she knows 'ow fond you are of sprouts. I likes a sprout myself, Mr Chesshyre. Very partial to a sprout, I am especially at Christmas. Are you partial to a sprout, Mr Chesshyre? Mrs Stripp always makes sure she's got plenty o' sprouts in at Christmas although she don't eat 'em 'erself on account of they gives 'er the wind most terrible bad.'

'I'm pained to hear it,' George replied. 'I hope she's able to eat other vegetables without ill effect?'

'Oh, yes. Carrits an' spuds an' turnips. Peas an' the bro*ccoli*. But not cabbage on account of its havin' the same effect as sprouts although she might try a bit of Savoy once in a while. I give Mrs Sprackett a lovely Savoy as I 'opes you will enjoy Mr Chesshyre. An' plenty of veg of all variety as I said as I'd bring round it bein' Christmas Eve.'

George beamed. 'I'm very grateful to you Stripp. You must let me have your account as soon as possible. Don't forget the tree as well. Magnificent specimen.'

'I won't think of it, Mr Chesshyre. It gladdens my 'eart to be of service. I told Mrs Stripp about the Christmas tree, as 'ow beautiful your girls 'ad decorated it and do you know what she said Mr Chesshyre? She said it would gladden 'er 'eart to see it, Mr Chesshyre.'

George's beam immediately widened. 'Then see it she shall, Mr Stripp. Bring her round this afternoon. No, in fact bring her round tomorrow. Both of you. Come and join us for Christmas dinner!'

'But Mr Chesshyre! We couldn' t … I mean …'

'Nonsense! We've got more than enough here thanks to your very generous bounty. The more the merrier, I say! But no sprouts for Mrs Stripp, eh? Ha! ha!'

George was aware of the consternation he was creating but he was feeling expansive and in the Christmas spirit after the carols. Anyhow, it was the season of goodwill. He had been known to show some at times. Besides, he was painfully aware that as the only male in the house he was going to be in a very small minority and felt that he needed a bit of support.

Stripp had just left when there was a knock on the door. Vicky got there first. 'Daddy, its Eugene. He's carrying a handbag!'

This intelligence had everyone rushing to see Eugene with his unusual accessory. 'I'm sorry to interrupt you,' he said after the usual effusive greetings from the girls, 'but I believe Mrs Chesshyre left this at the church.' He held the bag out.

The Aged P, who had been eying him suspiciously, pointed to the bag and said, 'Young man, I have a bag the very same. Where did you get it?'

'Ma'am, this is your bag. You left it in the church.'

'Left in the lurch? Why on earth have you been left in the lurch?'

'No, ma'am, this is your bag. Your name is on the label.'

'What is the boy gibbering about? My name's not Mabel!'

Celandine, who George swore was brighter than all of them, was scribbling something on a piece of paper. Gently touching her great aunt's arm she showed her what she had written.

'My bag? Left in the church? Well why didn't the boy say so? Thank you Ruby, dear. You're a very kind girl. Young man,' she said, turning again to Eugene, 'as you have found my bag you shall have a reward. George, tell the boy he must come to Christmas dinner.'

Of course George jumped on this idea immediately before anyone had any time to object. 'Capital idea,' he said. 'Do come, Eugene, you would be very welcome!'

Eugene cast a worried look around him. 'Well, sir, it's very kind of you but the Reverend Humpidge has invited me for Christmas dinner.'

George waved this objection away airily. 'Oh, bring him along as well. He can say grace!'

'Well, if you're sure …'

'Yes, absolutely. What's two more? The more the merrier I say.' George's beam was at its most benevolent brightest.

***

By that evening George was feeling very pleased with himself. He stretched out in his easy chair in the drawing room, his hands behind his head, his Peterson drawing sweetly with a fresh fill of 'Old Grenadier' and a glass of Johnnie Walker Special Old Highland next to him on the occasional table. 'A good day's work, I should say, old girl,' he said to Rosalind who was looking pensive.

'Mrs Sprackett's not happy,' she said. 'When I told her about all the extra guests you'd invited she turned quite pale and then quite puce.'

'Oh, she'll manage,' he said dismissively. 'Besides, she's got Polly and Dolly and Caroline's two girls are coming to help as well aren't they? And they're all having a slap-up dinner in the kitchen after aren't they?'

'Yes, George. You will remember to go in and thank them all won't you?'

'Of course. And they'll all get an extra Christmas box by way of a thank you.'

George always said, Christmas is the most wonderful time of the year!

CHAPTER TWENTY-TWO

~ Rise and Fall

—e·э—

Christmas Dinner at No 3 'The Limes' Scattersdale Avenue
Streatham London SW, Monday 25th December 1911

Those attending:-

Mr George Hector Chesshyre (Head)
Mrs Rosalind Victoria Chesshyre (His wife)
Miss Victoria Beatrice Chesshyre (Their daughter)
Miss Alexandra Florence Chesshyre (ditto)
Mrs Adele Christina Chesshyre (Head's mother)
Mrs Clementine Poppy Greenstreet (Head's sister-in-law)
Miss Celandine Lavender Greenstreet (Her daughter)
Mrs Caroline Adelaide Fitzpatrick (Family friend)
Miss Guinevere Linette Fitzpatrick (Her daughter)
Miss Morgana Linesse Fitzpatrick (ditto)
The Reverend Algernon Euphrates Humpidge
(Vicar of this parish)
Mr Eugene Washington Rickenbacker
(Family friend and music teacher)
Mr Obadiah Nathaniel Stripp (Gardener)
Mrs Nellie Stripp (His wife)

We give the above list as a memorial to the reader lest he or she forget or confuse the principal players in this merry yuletide festival. George felt that he needed to confess to a certain exuberance relative to his actions in encouraging the attendance of the entire company. He was now convinced that a certain rashness on his part was brought to bear by his own hand and he only had himself to blame for such a numerous and disparate congregation of revellers. On reflection he realised that he got carried away distributing largesse and invitations the previous day but would have to live with the consequences. Of course he had known for some time that Rosalind had invited the Fitzpatricks and the Aged P was permanently fixed on the invitation list. What was worrying him was that he was going to be surrounded by a lot of squawking women from whom Christmas provides no escape; in fact you are more securely trapped at Christmas than at any other time of the year. The opportunity to invite Stripp presented itself as a way of tipping the scales a little in the right direction although of course this was immediately cancelled out by the prospective presence of Mrs Stripp. When the Aged P took it upon herself to invite Eugene and Humpidge entered the equation simultaneously he rather breathed a sigh of relief. Of course it was only later that he realised that the sum total of invitees had risen to seven, making a total of fourteen when added to the Chesshyres and the Greenstreets.

On Christmas morning itself he awoke with a bit of a headache. Rosalind was not sympathetic. 'It serves you right, George. I told you last night to go easy on the whisky but would you listen? Of course not. Clemmie was appalled and goodness knows what your mother thought.'

'Oh, come on Ros,' George protested. 'They practically got through a bottle of port between them and that bottle of Bristol Cream you were hogging ended up considerably lighter than when it started the evening.'

'I only had one glass! Well, perhaps two. Mrs Sprackett had some for the sherry trifle.'

'Ha! That's what she says. I'll bet she was knocking it back in the kitchen. You mark my words, There won't be much cream of the Bristol variety in that trifle.'

George was just on his way to the dining room looking forward to a leisurely breakfast when there was a furious knocking on the front door. As he was nearest and nobody else seemed to be about he opened it with some trepidation in case there was some monstrous ursine creature without bent on wishing him a merry Christmas. Stood on the doorstep were two girls of about twenty. 'Merry Christmas, sir!' came in unison. 'Mrs Fitzpatrick sent us. I'm Aggie and she's Maggie. We're hexpected.'

Before he knew it they had divested themselves of their overcoats, hats, scarves and gloves, dumped them on him and were disappearing through to the kitchen without so much as a 'by your leave'.

'George, why are you wandering around with those coats?' asked Rosalind as she came down the stairs. 'Who was that at the door?'

'Aggie and Maggie,' he replied, struggling under the load and attempting to hang the coats, etc. on pegs. 'They're Caroline's girls come to help in the kitchen.'

'Oh, good.' She swept past him. 'I'd better go and make sure they're all right. Mrs Sprackett's been very testy recently. I don't want them getting the sharp edge of her tongue as soon as they arrive.'

Of course leisurely breakfasts are almost impossible to attain on Christmas Day. There is so much frantic hustle and bustle, kitchen noises, bangs, clangs and intermittent screams not to mention the occasional oath-giving. George sometimes wondered whether it was all worth the trouble. He was pretty sure there wasn't much turkey about in Bethlehem not to mention sprouts and Christmas pudding. He didn't suppose there was the spectre of bills mounting up either or sisters in law draining bottles of port as though it might go out of fashion at any moment. Still, he didn't want to sound like a Scrooge. He'd got as far as a second piece of toast when he was unceremoniously shooed out of the dining room on the pretext of 'getting things ready for lunch'. He resorted to the drawing room but was immediately surrounded by Polly, Dolly, Aggie and Maggie removing any chair suitable for use at the dining table. Even the conservatory was not immune. Various bits of furniture were being lifted or shoved or turned round or shunted to and fro amid shrieks and grunts and groans. There was almost a disaster when Sandwich and Hector Crisper-Bacon got themselves entangled in the Christmas tree and nearly brought it down. Tarporley was sat on King George the Second's head observing the proceedings with detached calmness.

By mid-morning it was fairly clear that any idea of attending the Christmas morning church service had been abandoned as hopelessly optimistic. The 'Victor' had been working overtime since very early in the day and both bathrooms were perpetually occupied. Taps appeared to be running permanently and great clouds of steam ballooned voluminously out onto the landings each time a door was opened. By mid-day ablutions had largely ceased and shimmering apparitions dressed in their best finery were appearing at regular intervals throughout the house. George had put on a soft collar and linen jacket. He refused to wear a wing collar, Christmas or not. Of course there were murmurs of disapproval, 'Your father always wore a wing collar at Christmas. Standards, George. You must not let standards slip.' He was somewhat gratified when Eugene arrived wearing a soft collar. He felt it, however, not wise to call attention to this act of sartorial vandalism lest it be denounced as 'Loud' or 'American' or 'Decadent' or 'French' or even 'Bohemian'. Humpidge appeared next and was settled in the drawing room after being introduced to the Aged P; both were plied with a sherry and, in Humpidge's case, a slice of cake; the Aged P refusing the offer of such a confec- tion on account of it would 'spoil her lunch'. Still, at least it wasn't 'decadent'. A conversation of sorts was conducted between them although as they were both as a deaf as a post it was interesting to speculate on the nature of the discourse.

The Fitzpatricks arrived in a blizzard of coats, hats, gloves, parcels, hugs, kisses and greetings (of the English and continental variety) and swept into the drawing room accompanied by Vicky, Alex and Celandine much to the consternation of Humpidge and the Aged P. Eugene was greeted with equal effusiveness and for a moment or two George feared for his safety and was on the point of going in and rescuing him from this avalanche of femininity.

The last to arrive was Stripp and Mrs Stripp. Nellie Stripp was an enormous woman who quite dwarfed her husband. Unable to sink into an armchair she perched on a dining chair that was hurriedly retrieved from the dining room and made short work of a port and lemon. 'Oh, I does like a port and lemon of a Christmas, Mr Chesshyre. I only said to Stripp on the way over, I do 'ope 'as 'ow Mr Chesshyre 'as got some port an' lemon. It gladdens my 'eart, it does – but only at Christmas, of course.' This rider was hastily added in case George should get the impression that she was very familiar with port and lemon throughout the rest of the year, although, judging by her complexion, he imagined that this might not have been far from the truth.

The English might be known for their reserve but there was precious little on show that morning. George was sure a mathematician could plot a graph showing the relationship between loss of inhibition and quantity of alcohol consumed. For a good hour and a half he was kept busy topping up glasses, 'Just a *small* one, then,' and 'I don't mind if I *do*,' and, 'Oh, George, I shall get squiffy!' The volume of the chattering going on rose exponentially with the relentless drop in the level of the bottles on the sideboard. On two occasions at least when he was occupied elsewhere filling Lady Disdain's sherry glass, Nellie Stripp heaved herself off her chair and helped herself to a very large port and a very small lemon. Vicky, Alex, Morgana, Guinevere and Celandine had secreted themselves into a corner and looked suspiciously as though they were plotting something dastardly although the nature of this was not immediately obvious; He did, however, notice that of the half dozen bottles of Italian vermouth he had laid out on the sideboard the previous evening, only four remained which was curious as no-one to his knowledge had requested one.

After much discussion with Mrs Sprackett, Rosalind had agreed on half past one as a suitable and convenient time for lunch to be served. However, half past one came and went and there was no sign that lunch was imminent. George was not immediately alarmed and continued to fill glasses as necessary. Christmas lunch for fourteen was no mean task and a few minutes here and there made no difference. At two o'clock an agitated Polly appeared at the doorway. 'Psst! Excuse me mum,' she caught Rosalind's eye. 'Beggin' your pardon, mum but there's been a hincident in the kitchen.'

'What sort of incident, Polly?' asked Rosalind.

'It's Mrs Sprackett, mum.'

'Yes? What about her?'

'She's drunk, mum!'

'I don't believe it!'

'Oh, it's terrible, mum. She got 'old of the sherry bottle and she's on the ram-page, mum!'

'George, you'd better come with me and see what this is all about.'

'I'll let Eugene know,' he said. 'He can look after everyone for a minute or two.'

They followed Polly to the kitchen where Mrs Sprackett truly was on the ram-page. She held a sherry bottle in one hand and a carving knife in the other. Dolly, Aggie and Maggie were cowering, terrified in the corner. George placed himself between them and Mrs Sprackett. 'You girls go out through the back entrance and into the garden. You too Ros. You'll be quite safe out there.' They didn't need to be told twice and rushed immediately towards the back door. He hadn't taken his eye off Mrs Sprackett during the evacuation and now squared up to her. 'Now then, Mrs Sprackett, what's all this about?' he said in his most authoritarian voice. George could be very authoritarian when he wanted to be even if Vicky and Alex thought it uproariously funny and did impressions of him when they thought he wasn't listening.

'Oh! Oh! I can't live without 'im Mr C. but 'e don't love me. I'm spurned, Mr C. *Spurned!*'

George thought he'd better try to elicit the identity of the object of her affections. 'Who is it, Mrs Sprackett? Who is it that's spurned you?'

'Oh! Oh! Obadiah! He don't want me even though 'e brings me carrits an' sprouts!'

'Do you mean Stripp? The gardener?'

'Yes! Sob. Obadiah. I made sure 'e was makin' a play for my affections with 'is sprouts an' I makes 'im cheese sammidges an' all an' 'e sits in 'ere of a mornin' and I makes 'im a cup of tea with the top orf the milk particlar an' hextra sugar but 'e don't love me. 'e told me as 'is affections was for another! Oh! Oh! Sob!'

'Mrs Sprackett,' said George advancing towards her with as much stealth as he could muster, 'shall we put the knife down? Just let me put the knife somewhere safe.' He reached out slowly and taking hold of her arm managed to prise the knife from her grip which wasn't particularly strong. In fact he was sure she wasn't even aware that she was holding it by that stage. The 'rampage' had largely blown itself out and she sank down on a chair, her head in her hands, quietly sobbing all the while. He thought this would be an opportune moment to bring Rosalind back in, the danger, if there ever had been any, now clearly passed. He went out into the garden to find them all huddled round the entrance, ashen-faced but obviously dying to know what was happening. 'It's all right. You can come back in now,' he said adopting a soothing voice. 'Mrs Sprackett's had quite a shock and needs to go and lie down to recover.'

'*She's* 'ad a shock! Stone the crows she gave *us* a shock an' no mistake!' said Maggie.

'We thought we was goin' ta be stabbded! An us not even in our own kitchen, too!' added Aggie.

'Fine bloomin' Christmas this is! Cooks a-rampagin' about wavin' carvin' knives at us!' Came back Maggie.

'I thought there was somethin' funny goin' on,' chimed in Dolly. 'Didn't I say, Poll? She ain't right, I said. Didn't I say, Poll?'

'It's the sherry wot done it,' said Polly. 'Cor! She didn't 'alf sink a few after the turkey was put in. Swiggin' it straight out the bottle she was! I never saw nothin' like it on this earth not even when me pa 'ad a bust up with me ma when she went orf with me Uncle Fred. She come back eventually, though.'

George took the opportunity of letting this little storm of disapproval blow itself out naturally and took Rosalind aside to explain to her what had happened and the origin of this most uncharacteristic behaviour by Mrs Sprackett.

'But Mr Stripp's married! Surely she knows that?' said Rosalind.

'Perhaps not. We'll get to the bottom of it after Christmas but at this moment we've got a house full of guests expecting Christmas lunch. I think we should get Mrs Sprackett up to her room out of harm's way so that she can sleep it off. I'm sure the girls can manage.'

'Yes, you're right,' agreed Rosalind. 'I'll take over the supervision of the kitchen. By the looks of things everything's more or less ready. I can flit to and fro as necessary.'

They got Mrs Sprackett to her feet between them and spirited her upstairs with as little fuss as possible. The cyclone had more or less blown itself out by this time and she offered no resistance as they got her on to her bed and covered her over as best they could. As far as George was aware the assembled throng was blissfully unaware of the dramatic scenes being played out just a few feet away from them. Rosalind shepherded the girls back into the kitchen calming them with soothing words in which way she had the most uncanny knack.

The expression, 'out of the frying pan into the fire' came to mind when George later recalled the next in the sequence of events which was making this Christmas a somewhat eventful one. After ensuring that Rosalind and the girls were safely ensconced back in the kitchen he made his way back to the drawing room. Things had moved on apace since his unscheduled departure half an hour earlier. The spree of imbibing that had been so heartily under way at his exit was still in full flow evidenced by the volume of conversation which, at its lowest, resembled a fairly rowdy football crowd and, at its zenith, attained heights probably only so far encountered by witnesses of the dreadful action of Madame Guillotine during the reign of terror, such were the screams and shrieks from all quarters, not least Nellie Stripp who had found the reserve port and was making very short work of it. Humpidge and the Aged P were still engaged in an earnest but stentorian conversation; Lady Disdain was roaring with laughter at something Caroline had related to her; a pack of cards had been produced from somewhere and Morgana and Guinevere were evidently teaching Vicky, Alex and Celandine how to play something probably illegal, an empty bottle of Italian vermouth standing in the middle of the table telling its own story; Stripp was regaling Eugene with some long complicated story or joke which necessitated the flailing of arms and pulling of grotesque faces which by turns caused Eugene to frown, flinch or laugh. George beamed around the room like some life-saving lighthouse, making sure, as far as he was able, that everyone had seen him and that from his expression they could deduce that all was well and that lunch was pretty much on the horizon. He was just on his way back to the kitchen to ascertain the state of play there when he met Rosalind coming the other way. 'Everything's under control, George,' she said reassuringly. 'I've calmed the girls down and they're managing splendidly. The turkey's done and so is the beef and ham. They're all ready to carve. I think we should get everyone seated.'

'Well done, old girl,' he said with some relief. 'I'll do my best to usher them in but I tell you it's pretty wild in there. Perhaps they'll calm down a bit when they've got some grub inside them.'

It took about fifteen minutes to get everybody seated in a position convenient to each individual. Humpidge and the Aged P were inseparable and had to be placed together; Nellie Stripp had taken a shine to Eugene and there was a bit of a merry-go-round while she, Celandine and Eugene circled each other, Eugene eventually sandwiched between them; Lady Disdain and Caroline were still deep in conversation and sat down together simultaneously, still carrying on their discussion; Vicky, Alex, Morgana and Guinevere at first assembled themselves in a row, decided this was not conducive to plotting and rearranged themselves several times eventually deciding on a *vis-à-vis* configuration which involved everyone else 'moving up one', an exercise which caused great consternation especially to Nellie Stripp who was alarmed at the prospect of being parted from Eugene as she was already situated at the end of the table. George and Rosalind secured a convenient station nearest the kitchen so that he was on hand to carve the joints etc. and Rosalind was in a position to 'flit' as necessary. Before he could get down to the serious business of carving, however, he was kept busy replenishing glasses, the capacity for alcohol consumption apparently no less diminished by the extended pre-lunch interlude in the drawing room. Several bottles of red and white were uncorked and emptied at an alarming rate, so much so that he was in real fear of running low before the Christmas season was over.

'Beggin' your pardon, mum,' said Polly to Rosalind coming into the kitchen in a state of agitation, 'but the turkey an' the joints is all ready to be carved them 'avin' been restin' a good while now like you said as we 'ad to let 'em an' Dolly don't think as 'ow we oughter let 'em stand much longer on account of 'em gettin' cold but that Maggie says we oughter bring the soup in now because that's goin' to get cold too if we don't get a move on not that we're tryin' to rush things as you might say but Mrs Sprackett'd 'ave our 'ides if we let things get cold.'

'That's all right, Polly, you're all doing very well,' reassured Rosalind in her usual calm manner, 'Bring the soup in first and keep the joints covered until we've finished. They'll keep warm for a good while yet.'

'Very good, mum, I've skimmed the soup like as 'ow Mrs Sprackett taught us, an' I don't think there's no fat left on the top but I'm ever so sorry if there is an' I 'opes as 'ow you won't 'old it against us if there is, mum, me 'avin' skimmed it most particlar and let it settle and there ain't no skin formed on it so I s'pose it's not too bad considerin' wot we've been through this mornin' with Mrs Sprackett bein' taken bad an' all.'

'Polly, just bring it through, please. I looked at it just now and it's quite acceptable.'

This was going to be the longest Christmas lunch he had ever experienced, thought George.

At length a full complement of steaming soup bowls adorned the dining table, each accompanied by a bread roll. So far so good. Nellie Stripp appeared tickled. 'Ooh! What beautiful soup! I never saw such soup! It gladdens my 'eart to see it a'steamin' there. What flavour is it, if I might make so bold as to ask?'

'I believe it's onion,' said Eugene, helpfully.

'Ooh! I do believe you're right!' enthused Nellie Stripp, picking up her pudding spoon and sampling the soup noisily. 'Ooh! Beautiful soup. Ain't you clever? Not out've a packet neither I shouldn't think!'

This exhibition was observed with a mixture of surprise, horror and amusement. George endeavoured to distract attention away from these somewhat unusual proceedings by attempting to attract Humpidge's attention in an effort to get him to say grace. This was a little more difficult than he had anticipated as he seemed to be preoccupied with his soup, examining it closely and pointing out something to the Aged P who also shared an apparently keen interest, looking from his bowl to hers as if in comparison. Eventually George got the idea across and Humpidge rose somewhat unsteadily to his feet.

He cleared his throat. 'Dearly beloved …' he began. 'No … Man that is born of a woman … No, that's not it. Who giveth this …? Blast! Ah! *Benedictus, Benedicat per Jesum Christum Dominum Nostrum. Quid enim sumus nos Dominus vere gratia accipere. Amen.*'

A chorus of 'Amen' from around the table amid some puzzled looks, the *omnium gatherum* apparently, like George, having little Latin and less Greek. Having got there eventually he breathed a sigh of relief, as did George, resumed his seat heavily and, having satisfied himself of the wholesomeness of the soup, began.

We have, in an earlier part of this chronicle, described in some detail the pitfalls and difficulties encountered when carving roast poultry. These difficulties are magnified manifold the larger the item to be dissected. Thus, when presented with a twenty eight pound turkey, not to mention a sideshow of beef and ham, each of which are a fair old weight in their own right, you might be forgiven for feeling somewhat apprehensive. The soup having been polished off with corporate relish, the big guns were brought in to much evident and audible satisfaction. Having retrieved the carving knife which had lately been the fearsome object waved with such menace by their indisposed cook, George set about putting an even keener edge on it, mindful of the fact that it was about to commence the heaviest duty it was ever going to encounter during the year. There was also a second point to this exercise in that he wanted to prepare himself mentally for the challenge of expertly carving and serving exactly the type of cut requested, previous experience having taught him that this was liable to be definite, precise and accurate, white meat being deemed completely unacceptable when brown meat had been ordered. Consequently he took his time over stropping the knife, all the time smiling at the assembly in the hope that he would convey the certain impression that he knew what he was doing.

While he was doing this, Polly, Dolly, Aggie and Maggie had changed up into top gear and were gliding around expertly with tureens and bowls full of potatoes, roast and boiled; Brussels sprouts (avoiding Mrs Stripp), carrots, parsnips and peas; cabbage (not to be placed near Mrs Stripp), several gravy boats each giving off an appetising aroma (whether Bisto be involved or not); bread sauce, white sauce, stuffing balls (extra to that already encased within the turkey), cranberry sauce, small sausages enwrapped with bacon, horseradish sauce of an incendiary variety (as George was to find out later), freshly made mustard (Colman's being definitely involved), pickled gherkins and a home-made piccalilli which Mrs Spracket had been nurturing all year.

Somehow or other this whole *mélange* was distributed without incident, a sort of production line being set up to charge plates with the meat or poultry of choice and description as ordered. The chattering, whilst still considerable, had subdued noticeably as the repast was consumed. Appetites apparently hardly dented, the plates were in due course cleared away and two monstrous Christmas puddings brought in accompanied by jugs of steaming custard and brandy butter. In case all this should prove inadequate, a mountain of mince pies appeared to the evident satisfaction of Celandine who was very partial to mixed fruit in any guise. 'Dinner plates' had not contracted one iota since the appearance of the 'beautiful soup'. Of course it fell to George to ignite the puddings and soon, the curtains having been drawn to heighten the effect, they were both flaming beautifully, the brandy burning blue and crackling in a suitably festive manner. The first pudding was demolished at an alarming rate, the greater portion of it being divided more or less equally between the plotting quartet. A squabble broke out between Morgana and Guinevere, the former delighting in finding two sixpences in her bowl while the latter searched in vain for even one. The argument was settled when Vicky interceded and diplomatically suggested they have one each.

Somehow, space had been found on the dining table for a bumper crop of Tom Smith's Christmas 'Crackers'. The crockery having been cleared away there began a series of tugs o' war around the table as these novelties were wrestled with causing not a little consternation when Mrs Stripp nearly fell off her chair as she tugged on a cracker with Eugene clinging to the other end. Of course crackers usually contain a puzzle, a hat and a riddle or joke and these were no exception. No doubt the general state of inebriation served to heighten the amusement with which the contents of the crackers were met, a sample of the jokes read out and the hilarity they elicited is given hereafter:-

From Alex:- 'Professor (to medical student): "Will you please name the bones of the skull?" Student (perplexed) 'I've got them all in my head, professor, but I can't think of the names at the moment".

Much hilarity.

From Caroline:- ' "Don't you think," said the old friend of the family, "that you ought to keep a watch on your son?" 'Impossible!' cried the young man's father; 'it wouldn't be long before he exchanged it for a pawn ticket!' '

Endless shrieks.

From Vicky, looking at George the while:- 'Father, meditating on Time's changes: "Ah, yes, the fashions of this world pass away." Daughter: 'Indeed they do, papa. I shall want a new hat next week!"

A cacophony of hoots.

And so on it went. Each joke sending a shockwave of mirth through the house. George hoped Mrs McGillycuddy wasn't listening. When the last cracker had been pulled and the supply of jokes exhausted (their standard didn't improve, we might hasten to add, lest the reader feel short-changed at not being apprised of the whole show) Stripp decided that it was time they had a song. Unsteadily getting to his feet he cleared his throat, 'Ladies and Genlemen an' my dear wife wot is here in the company here assembled on this Chrismis Day, it gladdens my 'eart ta give you, "The 'ouses in Between".'

A prolonged clearing of the throat, then:-

'If you saw my little backyard
'Wot a pretty spot' you'd cry,
It's a picture on a sunny summer day.
Wiv the turnip tops an' cabbages
Wot people doesn't buy,
I makes it on a Sunday look all gay.

The neighbours finks I grows 'em
And you'd fancy you're in Kent
Or at Epsom if you gazed into the mews.
It's a wonder as the landlord
Doesn't want to raise the rent,
Because we've got such nobby distant views—

Oh, it really is a wery pretty gardin,
And Croydon to the southward could be seen,
If you 'ad a rope an' pulley
You'd enjoy the breeze more fully,
If it wasn't for the 'ouses in between ...'

George believed that there were more verses to this song, however it was somewhat abruptly truncated at this point when Stripp turned a rather peculiar colour and sat back down in his seat heavily muttering something about needing to enjoy the breeze more fully at which point this impromptu recital came to a premature, and not unwelcome, by the looks on the faces of the some of the gathering, end. The exception, unsurprisingly, was Mrs Stripp who thought the performance wonderful and said as much to Eugene who, for the sake of good relations, agreed that if the Swedish Nightingale herself had offered a performance in the room at that moment it would have been as a hoarse foghorn in comparison.

It was by now, well past four and a mass exodus began. Society's gale gradually blew itself out as effusively as it had blown in, with much hugging and embracing in the best English and continental fashion, and off to the four corners of south London leaving a strangely quiet house. Lady Disdain had one of her 'heads' and retired to her room, the girls had disappeared and Rosalind was in the kitchen making sure that the crew that had managed so valiantly without their captain was being looked after and had plenty to eat and drink. Any thought of Christmas tea was put on hold as George was sure none of them could have eaten another thing. He retired to the music room and must have fallen asleep because when he awoke it was past six.

Thus ended Christmas Day, AD 1911.

CHAPTER TWENTY-THREE ~

~ Ember Days

—⸎⸎—

Tuesday 26th December 1911

Boxing Day dawned bright and clear. There was an air of calm about the house which was almost palpable after the mayhem of the day before. Much as he enjoyed Christmas dinner George looked forward to Boxing Day lunch almost as much. It was a more relaxed, less fraught affair and far easier on the digestive system which needed a little time to recover from receiving so much rich food in so short a space of time. Of course nothing went to plan *chez* Chesshyre. He was looking forward to a leisurely breakfast when he was passed on the landing by Mrs Sprackett wearing a hat and coat and carrying a suitcase. 'Good morning Mrs Sprackett,' he said in as friendly a voice as he could muster at that time of the day and trying to ignore this obvious flight of shame, 'I hope you're feeling better to-day.' No reply except a shake of the head and a handkerchief held to the nose. He tried again. 'I'm glad to see you up and about again. Are you going far? When will you be back?' At this she hesitated for a moment just as Rosalind appeared. With George behind and Rosalind in front there was nowhere to go except the bathroom which was unfortunately occupied by either Vicky or Alex (depending on who got there first) in the middle of one of their marathon bathing sessions which, judging by the quantity of water being run, was not likely to cease at any time soon.

'Mrs Sprackett? Are you leaving us?' said Rosalind, surprised. She looked up momentarily.

'Oh, mum. Oh, Sir. It's a terrible thing I've done. I shall 'ave t' go. Oh, the shame! The shame!' With this a mournful wail ensued which caused a momentary cessation of ablutions in the bathroom. ''ow can I ever show my face again in this 'ouse, mum?

It's a wonder as 'ow you didn't call the p'lice with me a-rampagin' around the kitchen like a wild animal. Like a wild animal, mum! An' those poor girls a-frightened out of their skins and what with a 'ouseful of guests an' Christmas dinner a-roastin' an' a-cookin'. I must go an' save you the trouble of sackin' me, mum. I shall go to my sister's in Broadstairs if she'll take me in an' it 'asn't been reported in the papers as 'ow I was on the ram-page on Christmas Day. Oh, the shame! The shame!'

'Mrs Sprackett,' said Rosalind. 'How long have you been with us?'

'Eighteen years come April, mum.'

'And you're going to be with us for another eighteen years at least. I won't hear of you leaving. Who will fry Mr Chesshyre's breakfast kippers? No-one can fry them like you, Mrs Sprackett.'

'Oh, I should never look at a kipper again, mum! Every time I should look at one I should see the master's face!'

'Mrs Sprackett, you've had a nasty shock and things have got on top of you a little, that's all. If you still want to go to your sister's in Broadstairs then perhaps it would be a good idea for you to have a little holiday. But we want you back, Mrs Sprackett. You really are practically part of the family. We really couldn't do without you, you know. Why don't you wait while Mr Chesshyre calls a taxi? You'll feel much better once you've had a few days away to rest and recover.'

'Oh, mum! I don't deserve it, mum! But you an' the master 'ave always been so kind to me. I shouldn't wonder if I'd a ended up in the workus after goin' on the ram-page. I shouldn't blame you if you'd a called the p'lice an' 'ad me harrested.'

George excused himself from this woeful scene and telephoned Alf who said he'd be with them in ten minutes. They could whisk Mrs Sprackett away before anyone else got wind of things and by the time she returned everything would have blown over. In the meantime George would take the opportunity to speak to Stripp to find out his side of the story. Alf was as good as his word and they bundled Mrs Sprackett unseen into the back of his cab with instructions to Alf to see her safely onto the Broadstairs train at Victoria.

This early morning melodrama concluded, George made his way to the dining room hoping to commence a leisurely, belated breakfast. He left Rosalind to explain Mrs Sprackett's absence to the rest of the household in her usual diplomatic way. He should have made a hash of it and would have inevitably been faced with a barrage of questions. He was still feeling the effects of the previous day's intake so was quite happy with a bowl of 'Force' and a slice of toast and marmalade. No-one else seemed to be about. Aggie and Maggie had stopped overnight, sharing with Polly and Dolly, but had departed very early. He should have to speak to Caroline to make sure that they were all right and had suffered no ill effects from the previous day's shenanigans.

George supposed he had to admit to having mixed feelings where Christmas was concerned. Normally there was a lot of rush and hustle and bustle in the run up to it. Of course in previous years he had always been away at the office and somewhat insulated from all the goings on and preparations at home. The Exchange had seemed to be almost a kind of oasis of calm amid the frantic round of shopping and social visits. Christmas Day and Boxing Day were over as soon as they arrived and then it was back to the office to begin another year of getting and spending in which way we lay waste our powers. This year, of course, had been rather different. He'd not been in to the office since his heart attack and hence had been in the middle of things in the run up to Christmas and its aftermath. No escape back the day after Boxing Day. They were approaching the year's end and he should finally have to make a decision as to whether he'd give up his part-nership for good and retire. It was a time for reflection, a time for looking forward, a time for regret for the things we have not done and a time for regret for the things we have done. This year had certainly been one full of events. They'd moved house during one of the hottest summers he could ever remember. What days those were! He looked back at them now with some fondness. Despite the fearsome heat and the trials of travelling on the slow train to and from suburbia along with countless thousands of others, he always came back to a welcoming home; to his adored wife, Rosalind and his adorable but infuriating daughters, Vicky and

Alex. No matter what he did they were unfailing in their love for him and, of course, the converse was true. It didn't matter that nothing much happened, it mattered that they were always there and that he knew that they were. Of course, eventually the girls would marry, He was sure of it, and when they did they would leave and start lives and families of their own. He hoped they would be happy and that they would live long, peaceful and fulfilled lives. The times change so fast, the fashions of the world pass away and there are always new hats to be coveted.

***

And so they found themselves on the threshold of the year 1912. The new diaries sleeping, as yet blank, awaiting events, good and bad, victories and defeats; successes and failures; winners and losers; those yet to be born; those yet to die. All over Britain a new start, fresh hopes, ambitions and goals; the old year dead and gone forever, consigned to the annals of history to be pored over and analysed in years to come. In a hundred years time who would remember the Chesshyres? What would become of No 3 The Limes, Scattersdale Avenue Streatham, London SW? Who would grow old with it as the house grew old? Would it falter and decay as we all do in time? Would it be swept away by *modern* progress?

The clock in the hall is chiming midnight. 1911 is no more. Welcome to 1912! We all raise a glass for the sake of *auld lang syne!*

And so, from all of them; a harassed George Chesshyre, Rosalind, Vicky, Alex, Clementine, Celandine, Polly, Dolly, and Mrs Sprackett, (*in absentia* and 'indisposed'), Tarporley & the Kittens and everyone else who has figured in this chronicle:

A Happy and Prosperous New Year to you all – whoever you may be – wherever you are: town, country or on a 'Slow Train to Suburbia!'

Goodbye!

~ The End ~

www.ingramcontent.com/pod-product-compliance
Lightning Source LLC
Chambersburg PA
CBHW021234250626
47155CB00008B/3012